BIG CITY BLUE

New York was a big town.

It was big enough to be home to a street bum like Ricky Miracle and a media baron like Ivor Thorpe. A saintly Mother Superior like Sister Michael and a porn film stud like Rodney Lancaster. A glamorous TV newsperson like Connie Talbot and a Mafia kingpin like Carlo Madalena.

It was big enough to harbor every brand of sin, crime, and corruption know to man and woman either out in the open or festering below the surface.

But as far as a man in blue like Vince Crowley was concerned, New York wasn't big enough to hide a killer. . . .

DEATH SPIRAL

PRAISE FOR *STREET DANCE* BY BILL KELLY AND DOLPH LE MOULT

"The real thing . . . grim, jagged, honest."
—Jerry Oster, authour of *California Dead* and *Sweet Justice*

"A good, solid procedural sparked by its evocation of the city."—*Publishers Weekly*

DEATH
SPIRAL

Bill Kelly, NYPD
Dolph Le Moult

AN ONYX BOOK

NEW AMERICAN LIBRARY

A DIVISION OF PENGUIN BOOKS USA INC.

PUBLISHER'S NOTE

This book is a work of fiction. Names, characters, places, and incidents
either are the product of the author's imagination or are used fictitiously,
and any resemblance to actual persons, living or dead, events, or locales
is entirely coincidental.

Copyright © 1989 by Bill Kelly and Dolph Le Moult

ONYX TRADEMARK REG. U.S. PAT. OFF. AND FOREIGN COUNTRIES
REGISTERED TRADEMARK—MARCA REGISTRADA
HECHO EN DRESDEN, TN. USA

SIGNET, SIGNET CLASSIC, MENTOR, ONYX, PLUME, MERIDIAN
and NAL BOOKS are published by New American Library, a division of
Penguin Books Inc., 1633 Broadway, New York, New York 10019

First Printing, July, 1989

1 2 3 4 5 6 7 8 9

PRINTED IN THE UNITED STATES OF AMERICA

Every cop knows in his heart of hearts that the job is at the very core a game. Kids don't play cops and robbers for nothing. They understand in the purest sense that the chase is what makes the game fun, and winning in the end is the payoff. All the posturing and preening, the swagger and the glitz; uniforms and sidearms and two-fisted, virile camaraderie are nothing if they cannot win. Winning gives them meaning, it gives them substance and validity. To win means to be a successful hunter . . . to feel a quickening heartbeat as the quarry becomes revealed . . . the pulsating rush of adrenaline as he dances in your gunsights . . . the thrill of final capture.

Nobody would even play the game if they couldn't catch the bad guys.

1

RICKY MIRACLE HAD NEVER MISSED A MEAL. LOOKING back over the past couple of years, he had to admit that some of them had been less than banquets—catch-as-catch-can, you might say—but that was only natural for someone who lived the way he did, picking up a piece of sandwich here, a partially eaten apple or banana there, chicken legs and wings that were hardly bitten into from the dumpster behind Kentucky Fried, a half-filled cup of boiling hot coffee he could glom from the Puerto Rican busboy out back of the diner—all good stuff, once you got over being squeamish about eating other people's leftovers.

The trick, he knew, was having a system, knowing the neighborhood. Knowing the right place to be at the right time of day or night was important. Sanitation men had schedules just like everybody else, and keeping one step in front of them was what made the difference if you wanted to get a shot at the decent stuff before it got carted off to the incinerators or the landfills or sat around long enough to get wormy and rancid. Almost seven years of living on the streets had taught Ricky that there was food and there was garbage, and knowing one from the other was what separated the men from the boys.

Not that Ricky thought he was anything special. He knew you didn't have to be a rocket scientist to make it out on the streets. Grit, determination, and imagination was all it took, plus a little common sense, but that seemed in short supply lately. Every day, more and more greenhorns were dropping like flies because they couldn't tell the difference between what would kill them and what would make them strong. Anybody with half a brain should have been able to figure out that meat that smelled like fish was a bad gamble. Even fish that smelled

7

like fish was better left alone. "The nose knows" was a good motto to live by on the streets.

A few basic rules was all: The less it smells, the better. No smell at all was best. All kinds of fruit were okay, even bruised or discolored, but vegetables could be chancy, especially if they were prepared with cheese or cream. Anything in its original form was better than anything chopped up. In restaurants, the odds were better than even that the meat in stew and hash was rotten before it was cooked, and it didn't take an Einstein to figure out that anything in heavy sauce was probably crawling underneath. Chinese food was a sure ticket to the shits.

Food in dumpsters was generally better than food in garbage cans, but if garbage cans were all there was, rubberized plastic was better than aluminum, except in the dead of winter. Anything in a closed container was out of the question. Nobody threw away Tupperware unless it held something too gross to let loose, and sealed plastic bags sometimes had cat shit poured right in with the chow. Cold weather was better than warm, for reasons too obvious to mention. Crows and starlings pecking around the bins was a good sign, but packs of hungry dogs were next to useless. Anything not immediately recognizable, anything that moved, or anything from a Jamaican restaurant was sure death.

All in all, a street-savvy guy could do all right for himself if he minded his own business, learned not to rely on anybody but himself, and used the brains God gave him. It wasn't the easiest life in the world, but for the most part it was passably comfortable, it was unhurried, and it was free. Nobody was on his back to do this or that, be here or there, and he didn't have to suck up to anybody. He wasn't pressed to do what he didn't want to do, and he wasn't about to be fired if he didn't do it. It was a sure bet that nobody was going to throw any benefits for Ricky Miracle if things didn't work out. He was strictly on his own and that was fine with him.

Except those times when he hit a seam in the system. He'd find himself sitting in a spot that wasn't particularly comfortable, and his experience told him that he just had to sit there until one thing ground itself out and something else came along to take its place. Times like that were usually cold and he was usually hungry and wanting a pop of Ripple or Boone's Farm to get things back on an even keel. Now was one of those times.

He squatted next to a still smoldering oil drum; its residue of coals and ashes sent a lazy billow of smoke skyward, popping now and then, propelling orange sparks like nervous fireflies into the dark morning air. The soft glow of the fire silhouetted the shapes of evergreens around him: Scotch pine and blue spruce and Douglas fir set trunk to trunk against the frozen earth: a mobile forest he could hide inside, stacked and trussed and trimmed, waiting for early holiday shoppers to take them home and gussy them up for Christmas.

"XMAS TREES & WREATHS" read the hand-lettered streamer above Ricky that jerked convulsively in the freezing December wind. ". . . FORMERLY ACROSS THE STREET." The empty lot that had been the site of the holiday enterprise in years past was paved over and turned into additional parking space for the Gold Star Diner: all but empty at this godawful hour. Black Formica tables and countertops gleamed inside, prepared for the morning rush that arrived with the first tentative shafts of sunlight. A skeleton crew of waitresses with sore feet and sour dispositions splashed hot coffee in the general direction of ceramic mugs, plopped orders of runny scrambled eggs and cold rye toast before a meager gathering of bleary-eyed night visitors, and prayed for the end of the graveyard shift. Nobody made any money at five in the morning. All you got at five in the morning was bunions and bad attitudes.

Next door to the diner, the neon sign in front of the Shangri-la Motel screamed into the frigid night: "EATS, GAS, TV . . . AIR- ONDITI NING . . . POO IN REAR." The missing letters seemed entirely appropriate to Ricky, considering the fact the Shangri-la was probably the sleaziest motel in the East Bronx. Thousands of hookers and homos, transient Johns and married cheaters, had humped and howled in dark cubicles beneath that sign. They had been grunting and groaning and whipping one another into a frenzy on a cash-only basis since he'd first landed on this street; enduring the grime, the smells of unwashed sheets and bodies to preserve their anonymity; guys with chicks, guys with guys, chicks with chicks—everybody having a go at everybody else, chasing their particular perversions whether they had poo in their rears or not.

The four-way traffic signal at the intersection changed from red to green, and a few desultory vehicles moved up the empty avenue toward him. Delivery trucks mostly: "KLEIN'S STATIONERS," "BLUMBERG FRESH PRODUCE," "MEATS." There was a black, unmarked panel truck that Ricky knew belonged to Karp, the repo man. Where could it be going at this time of the morning? Maybe Karp was repossessing a stereo or TV, maybe a washing machine or a sofa. Ricky knew no item was too large or trivial, no hour too inconvenient for Karp to do his dirty business. He would sell you anything from a lamp to a roomful of furniture that you couldn't afford, no money down, ten bucks a week for the rest of your life, and the first week you missed a payment he was on top of you with the repo truck like flies on fresh shit. It was rumored on the street that he'd sold the same Zenith color TV more than sixty times. The locals told about how he once repossessed a queen-size Sealy mattress right out from under a honeymoon couple—left the poor saps humping on the bare floor, the story went.

Karp was the most hated man in the East Bronx. No doubt about it.

Ricky watched the truck until it disappeared above the rim of the hill beyond him, then hunkered back inside his World War I army greatcoat and concentrated on his condition. He was freezing. The fire in the oil drum was nearly out, and keeping it alive meant getting more fuel. That meant moving around in the bitter wind, breaking small branches off the Christmas trees, and that could be big trouble at this hour of the morning. Shapiro opened up the lot early and the greedy sonofabitch could spot a snapped twig at fifty yards. Give him a reason to think you were fucking around with his merchandise and it would be bye-bye Ricky Miracle. Shapiro was a mean mother. Like most part-time businessmen in the neighborhood, he had friends who would shove an icepick in your ear just to watch your eyeballs rotate.

Across the street, a couple emerged from one of the Shangri-la's units closest to the street. A man and a woman, he guessed. It was hard to tell at this distance and in this light. They paused on the sidewalk in front of the motel, spoke briefly, and parted on foot in separate directions. What was it? Ricky wondered. Adulterous lovers grabbing a few secret hours? An in-and-outer by one of the local working girls and her customer? A one-nighter born in a neighborhood meet-and-greet saloon? Anything could happen at the Shangri-la and it usually did. The cops who weren't grabbing a quickie in there themselves made the place a regular stop when they cruised the area in their squad cars. Bad shit was always going down, and it was even money they could stir up something rotten on a slow night.

Framed against the slowly lightening sky, a sole figure, hunched over, emerged from one of the units in the rear. Ricky squinted against the wind and felt his eyelids moisten, an inadvertent tear streaming down his tightened cheek. He could see the figure stumbling toward him, carrying a shapeless bundle. Halting, reeling like an old drunk, it discarded the bundle in a clump of bushes near the road. He waited until the figure had disappeared around the corner before crossing the street.

The discarded bundle was probably nothing, he reasoned—garbage, more than likely, or leftovers taken from one of the rooms where cooking was technically forbidden— but then you never knew. Maybe it was a drug drop. The Shangri-la was known as a hangout where heroin and coke dealers operated openly, seemingly without fear of arrest. Wouldn't it be a pisser if Ricky Miracle ended up walking with some wise guy's stash? A quarter key of nose candy or smack would be just fine, thank you. He could blow half of it and sell the other half on the street—be on easy street for months, maybe years. After all he'd been through, it was about time his luck took a turn for the better.

He approached the bush cautiously, as if what was inside might suddenly explode or leap out at him like one of the banshees of his nightmares. He raked the avenue with his eyes until he was convinced he was alone, then sat nervously at the curb. Staring across the street at Shapiro's Christmas tree lot, he allowed his right hand to wander into the lower branches of the bush until it made contact with the bundle. It was soft, terrycloth, Ricky guessed—a towel probably, or a bunch of them, and slightly moist to the touch. Without averting his gaze, he pulled the bundle through the balky branches, stuffed it beneath his greatcoat, and headed nonchalantly back across the street.

Hidden safely among the rows of Christmas trees, Ricky removed the bundle from his coat and placed it carefully on the ground. One by one he unfolded the layers of terrycloth until there was nothing left to unfold. He could feel his heart pounding as he fumbled through the shapeless, empty mass. Anger and disappointment rose in his chest as it became more and more apparent that he'd come up blank again. The nubby surface of the towels was wet inside, warm and sticky to his touch, emitting a faint, slightly sweet odor he knew but couldn't place. He lifted both hands until they caught a thin shaft of yellow street light streaming between the trees. The sight caused him to recoil in horror. What he saw on his hands, what dripped down his crusted wrists beneath the frayed cuffs of his greatcoat, was blood.

Panic set in, the desperate, irresistible need to flee. This time he hadn't hit a seam in the system. He'd hit a chasm. He could hear the rasp of his labored breathing as he scooped up the towels and staggered toward the street. His heart beat a thundering tattoo as he stuffed them into the smoking oil drum and ran blindly away—anywhere away from that place. Pregnant beads of moisture swept over his face as he ran, gentling the knife edge of bitter wind. The first snow of the season had begun to fall.

2

LIEUTENANT JOHN GLEASON STARED MOROSELY AT THE
snow falling outside his window and groaned to himself.
Another snow, another season, another winter he would
have to spend in the bowels of the Bronx as the Commanding Officer of the 37th Precinct. It was a job he'd
desperately wanted only nine and a half months ago, and
one he would commit murder to get out of today. Thinking about it, he realized his sense of time had become
distorted. Each day of the past nine and a half months
had been a century, each month a lifetime of anger and
frustration, of suspicion and self-doubt—of nagging, un-
fulfilled promise.

He eyed the UF-57 application on his desk, the standard departmental form requesting transfer. It was his
tenth formal request for transfer since he'd been there,
and he had little doubt it would result in his tenth rejection. He'd made too many enemies getting the assignment in the first place—leapfrogging the Bronx Chief of
Detectives and weaseling a transfer from his old office at
One Police Plaza in Manhattan. You just didn't do a
thing like that and expect to make friends in the police
department. There were procedures to follow, protocol
to observe, and most of all, a pecking order in the departmental hierarchy that was as close to holy writ as
cops ever came. Bucking the chain of command was a
one-way ticket to career oblivion, he understood now.
He had no more friends to weasel, no more markers to
call in.

Of course, other officers with ambition cut corners all
the time in their drive to the top of the hierarchy. They
wheedled and connived and cashed in on personal associ-
ations crawling up the ladder, but they were mostly men
of personal charm and magnetism. Gleason knew that he
possessed neither of these qualities. He knew what the

others had whispered about him in the cloistered corridors of One Police Plaza, where he had spent the first nine years of his career—*"The guy's got all the charisma of a tumor."* Now the same guys who had sniggered behind his back at headquarters were part of the conspiracy to keep him forever languishing in the limbo of The Bronx. Nobody, but nobody was going to bat for John Gleason. Not this time.

He lifted the UF-57 and scanned the familiar questions. REASON(S) FOR TRANSFER REQUEST: How many reasons could he put down? There wasn't enough space provided on the sheet. Even if he listed them all, they could never reflect the depths of his unhappiness. He could never convey on paper what it felt like to be treated with contempt by the officers under his command. He knew that the lot of them—detectives Vince Crowley and Tommy Ippollito, Walt Cuzak, Pete Yorio, Steve Appelbaum and Snuffy Quade, Hector Vargas, who they called "Street Crime," even Leila Turner, the newest addition and first female detective ever assigned to the 37th—believed him to be unfit for command. He knew they bit their tongues to keep from laughing, winked at one another when he passed them in the squad room, groaned and rolled their eyes when he was out of sight and earshot.

IF CONDITION REQUIRING TRANSFER IS MEDICAL, PLEASE LIST INDIVIDUAL CONDITION(S) AND TREATMENT BEING RECEIVED: What could he put down? He had been to the department surgeon a dozen times and always received a clean bill of health. The closest the doctor had come to an unfavorable diagnosis was too tell him that he had to learn to take things as they came, to roll with the punches and try not to take everything so personally unless he wanted to end up with an ulcer. He was working on one, Gleason knew. He could feel his stomach knot every time he walked into the station house.

"Incipient ulcer" he scribbled in the space allotted. Why not? If trying to command a ragtag, rebellious bunch like the 37th Detective Squad wasn't enough to fuck up your stomach, if knowing your career was halfway down the toilet at age thirty-nine wasn't sitting on the knife edge of intestinal disaster, he didn't know what was. "There is no treatment for this condition other than an immediate change of venue," he penciled in and began to feel better. Maybe this time . . .

Outside, Detective Third Grade Tommy Ippollito watched the falling snow from the only window in the Homicide Room. "Looks like we might have a white Christmas," he said to nobody in particular. "Too bad we won't be able to see it." He rubbed a film of grime from the crusted pane of glass with his finger and squinted through it. "Who the hell's responsible for cleaning windows around this place anyhow?"

Nobody answered.

"It's not like the city couldn't afford some three-fifty-an-hour hump to wash windows in municipal structures," Tommy went on. "Half the workers in The Bronx are walking around unemployed, for chrissakes."

Snuffy Quade looked up from the earlybird movie on the television set, where he was adjusting the color knob to restore a green Cornell Wilde to robust health. "Why should the lazy bastards wash windows for three-fifty an hour when they can lay around all day on welfare, smoking dope and sucking moonshine?"

"Minimum wage is three sixty-five," Hector Vargas added sleepily.

"Whatever . . ." Tommy returned to the window. "It's a goddamn shame the way they neglect vital services when it comes to cops."

"An outrage indeed," announced the current occupant of the holding pen, a Jamaican Rastafarian in his early thirties who had been busted earlier in the night for possession of a controlled substance. "What a pity that those benighted Philistines who run things downtown have allowed this temple to deteriorate. Are they so blind they fail to see the architectural and historic value of a monument such as this?"

Tommy eyed him querulously. "Are you trying to be wise? You're trying to be wise, aren't you?"

The Jamaican bowed his head. "Forgive me. I forgot myself. Being in a cell like this tends to dull one's senses after a while. I'll do my best to stay in my place from now on. If you provide me with a harmonica, I could even play old Negro spirituals for you."

"What do I do with this humphead, partner?" Tommy asked Vince Crowley, sitting across the room. "Do I teach him a little respect or what?"

Vince looked over at the prisoner. "You know 'Go Down Moses'?"

The Jamaican grinned broadly.

"I mean it," Tommy moaned.

"So get him a harmonica." Vince returned to the pile of unattended paperwork on his desk. He was six days behind on his DD-5 forms, and Gleason was busting his balls about it. The CO might not have learned anything about nuts-and-bolts police work in the time he'd been there, but he sure as hell had learned about forms. It was his background, Vince knew. The dumb shit had spent his entire career working in headquarters at One Police Plaza, dreaming up syrupy press releases for the downtown brass. He'd made the mistake of weaseling a line command, thinking it would be a shortcut to his captain's bars, but found out in a hurry that he was in way over his head. So he immersed himself in paperwork. If he couldn't tell his ass from his elbow out on the streets, he was a regular I.B.M. with a sheet of paper and a ballpoint pen. To him, keeping up with paperwork was the highest form of valor in the police department.

"What'd we do last Tuesday?" Vince asked Tommy.

"Nothing," Tommy replied.

"You sure?"

"Check your book. We drove around. Had some burritos for lunch at the Mexican place and they gave you gas. You farted all afternoon in the car—made me wanta puke."

Vince inspected his notebook and found that Tommy was right. "For this they pay us a salary?" he joked.

"Hey, man, for this we get diddly-squat," Snuffy Quade protested. "We're out there on the front lines every day, risking our asses just to keep the lid from blowing off. We deserve a little soft duty from time to time, doncha think?" He pointed to the yellowing Seth-Thomas on the wall. "How many civilians do you know who are still out there working at this hour of the morning?"

Vince eyed the clock: 5:42 A.M. If weird hours were all that measured your worth to society, cops would be the highest paid guys in America. They'd all been on the job since midnight and still had almost two and a half hours to go. Two and a half hours of boredom, which was what an awful lot of police work was really about, no matter what they said on television or in the movies. Two and a half hours of grinding, tedious paperwork, which you also never saw on the crime shows; chipped metal desks piled high with debris, patched vinyl swivel chairs with wheels that sounded like wounded cats, aged metal typewriters echoing like an artillery barrage off the hollow concrete walls, coughing and sputtering when the keys stuck, which was all the time . . . signs and postings on the crumbling cork bulletin board that never got removed; yawning and scratching, bad breath and stale cigarette smoke, really, really dumb conversations . . . trying not to get on each others' nerves.

The night shift at the three-seven was just about as unglamorous as police work ever got, especially in the winter when street punks huddled in their burrows rather than braving the frigid weather to commit crimes. Almost every type of felony was way down in the cold winter months. Eight out of ten calls were for 1026—domestic disputes in progress—and even though they could be dangerous calls, for the most part they simply kept things from getting too dull for everyone involved. Small-time criminals got just as bored with inactivity as the cops, Vince guessed, so they drank whiskey, smoked reefer, and beat up their old ladies just to break the monotony.

Summer was what it was really all about. Vince knew that his enthusiasms swelled and ebbed with the seasons. He endured the cold months, tried to lose himself in the tedium of precinct routine until the spring. Then the world would pulse once more with the outlaw rhythm of the street felon. Everyone had a hustle—pimps and prostitutes, muggers and moonshiners, numbers runners, racketeers, boosters, and junkies. All of them were in tune with the metabolism of the street, conspiring on corners and in alleyways against the system and against each other to get a piece of the action. Vince liked being a cop then. They all did.

His partner, Tommy Ippollito, was more clinical about it, though. A detective at the 37th for just three years, Tommy was one of the new breed of cops, guys who saw the job as a science rather than a vocation. In Vince's day, becoming a cop had been a safe, secure job where young men without a lot of education or connections could buy a piece of a decent life for themselves and their families. Now cops were criminologists, legal scholars. They earned degrees qualifying them to do what old-timers had been doing by the seat of their pants for years. Tommy hit the books and earned the credits, but he only became a cop when he was out in the trenches listening to Vince. Nobody learned the job from books. You had to be there.

Snuffy Quade, Steve Appelbaum, Pete Yorio, Walt Cuzak—the list of old-timers like himself was shrinking at the 37th every day, Vince thought, and Pete would be retiring at the end of the month. Pretty soon they'd all be gone and the precinct would be turned over to the new breed. Guys with earrings and shoulder-length hair today would be setting the example for tomorrow's rookies. A whole new police department was in the making, and most of the veterans he knew weren't sure they wanted to be a part of it. Tommy would be okay because he understood it took more than letters after your name to be a good cop. For the most part he listened and kept his mouth shut, and every day they climbed into the squad car together Tommy showed more promise than the day before. Sometimes he was more like a younger brother than a partner . . . maybe even a wayward son.

The telephone rang and Street Crime answered it. "Duffy on the line," he yelled across the room at Vince. "He wants to talk to you."

Vince lifted the receiver. "Yeah, Duffy, what's up?"

"I'm over at the Shangri-la," the veteran beat patrolman answered. "I think you better get over here quick. We got a real bad one on our hands. I'm in room 23 now and I got a DOA—blood all over the fuckin' place."

"Anybody outside of you been in there?" Vince asked.

"I don't think so, except whoever did it."

"One body?"

"Female."

Vince slid his notebook into his jacket pocket and signaled Tommy. "I'm on my way, Duffy. Wait a couple of minutes before you put it on the air, okay? I don't want any assholes messing things up before I get there."

Duffy laughed. "I'll post my partner Willy at the door. He never saw a murder before and he's scared so shitless he looks like a walking corpse himself. He'll spook away anybody who comes around."

"Thanks, Duffy." Vince slammed down the receiver and headed for the squad-room door with Tommy.

"What's up, gentlemen?" Gleason blocked their way.

"Got a DOA at the Shangri-la Motel," Vince answered. "A real messy one, from what they tell me. You wanta be in on it?"

Gleason thought about his incipient ulcer. "Better not. My stomach's been acting up again today, and I got a lot of unfinished paperwork to get out. Just keep me informed."

"Yes sir, Lieutenant." Vince left the Homicide Room with Tommy at his heels. Things were beginning to look up. Duffy's call had been like an answered prayer, lifting him out of his dark mood and making him remember why it was he'd taken the job in the first place. It was good to be a cop again.

The rich bass strains of "Go Down Moses" coming from the holding pen trailed him down the stairs.

3

NYPD FORM UF-61
INITIAL REPORT OF CRIME   DECEMBER 14, 1988
HOMICIDE/STABBING.   COMPLAINT # 4548
LISA THORPE W/F   VISIT TO CRIME SCENE
                                             Det. V. Crowley

1. At 0545 hours this date, notified by 37 patrolman Seamus Duffy, shield #872, of a DOA at the Shangri-la Motel, Baychester Ave. and Boston Rd. (Sector Dog).

2. At 0613 hours, accompanied by Det. Ippollito of 37 PDU, arrived at above location and observed a human body on floor of unit 23 of the motel, partially covered by a blanket.

3. Ptl. Duffy stated that he and his partner, Ptl. W. Gant, responded to a report by Guido Sannasarto, night clerk at the motel, and upon reaching place of occurrence were directed by same to the body . . .

The room was a sea of splattered blood: puddles and splashes and bold, daring swirls covering the walls and floor. Carefully recording each element of the grisly scene in his trained investigator's mind, Vince stood in the open doorway of unit 23 and viewed the area in a slow, piercing arc. A dark gray wool and leather stadium coat hung neatly in a closet to the immediate right of the door; a dresser set against the right-hand wall, covered with shattered glass and gore; an overturned table lamp; a television set; more shattered glass strewn across the blood-splattered linoleum floor, a leather purse, seemingly undisturbed, placed on top of a nightstand near the bed; a pile of women's clothes stacked neatly on a shelf beneath the nightstand; two high-heeled shoes placed next to each other on the floor at the side of the bed; the bed itself—soiled, crumpled sheets pushed to the bottom of the exposed mattress, its lumpy surface stained deep red; underneath, the twisted, shoeless foot of a human body protruding from the edges of a blanket soaked in blood.

Vince knew the tableau would be recorded again and again by every sophisticated electronic device known to the department in the hours to come, but he also knew that none of them would be able to match the immediacy of his first impressions. At best, they would provide a dry, two-dimensional testament to the visual evidence of the crime, but they could never capture the jarring, static reality of murder. They could never register the eerie silence, the overhanging aura of finality, the lingering sense of fear and desperation, the sweet-sick smell of blood.

"You check the body?" he asked Duffy.

"What for?"

"You know, to see if she was still alive."

Duffy shrugged. "You gotta be kidding, Vince. There's a hundred gallons of blood in there."

"Looks like whoever did it tried to wipe up the evidence," Tommy noted, eyeing the smears of rapidly drying blood on the floor and walls.

Vince nodded. "Okay, Duffy, call 911 but keep the bastards out until I'm finished in there. That means *everybody*." He turned to Tommy. "Now listen up, partner, what we got here is a pure crime scene. That means nobody's disturbed any of the evidence, and you don't hardly see that anymore. Pay attention, 'cause you'll probably never see it again."

They walked cautiously into the room, Tommy following with a Polaroid camera he'd brought from the car. "I want pictures of everything," Vince told him. "Start in the right-hand corner there and sweep around the room until you get to the body. Everything's important, so overlap. Try to get close-ups of some of that broken glass on the floor." He opened his notebook and began recording his impressions.

"The room is small, approx. 10 × 12 feet. Furniture consists of one dresser, two vinyl-covered chairs,

two small night tables and a bed—double sized.
Sheets and blankets have been pulled away and lie
at foot of bed. Body on floor to right of bed, covered with a blanket. Chair to right of bed is overturned. Broken glass and blood everywhere.

He stepped past Tommy, squinting through the camera, snapping pictures, walked to the body on the floor,
and lifted a corner of the blanket, revealing the victim's
head and a portion of her torso. He could see that she
was young, even through the smudged film of partially
congealed blood covering her face. Beneath the film and
random clots he could see that her throat had been cut.
An uneven flow of purplish liquid still seeped from the
side of her neck, the final, weakened trickle of what had
probably been a pumping torrent just a short time ago,
judging from the pools of smeared, viscid body fluids on
the floor. Those exposed portions of her face were drained
white, like the faces of Japanese geishas Vince remembered seeing in a travelogue on TV. Her hair was long
and straight—light brown from what he could tell beneath the dark coagulation. Medium height and well
built. Her small, blood-spattered breasts peaked to firm,
unerected nipples. He committed the images to memory,
replaced the blanket, and stepped back, shuddering involuntarily. These things never got any easier.

"Somebody's here," Duffy shouted into the room.
"Looks like the EMS wagon."

"Nobody's allowed in until she's pronounced." Vince
walked to the nightstand on the far side of the bed,
where a large leather pocketbook stood closed and un-
molested. He unzipped it, removed the wallet and change
purse, and began checking the ID inside. There was a
New York State driver's license made out to a Lisa
Thorpe; address, 311 Palmer Road, Bronxville. The birth-
date read 01/03/65—less than a month from her twenty-
fourth birthday. There was a color photograph on the
license—a young girl with flowing brown hair, smiling
faintly at the camera, her pale blue eyes dancing. It
seemed to match, so did the age.

The rest of the cards and papers in the wallet confirmed the ID—a Mastercard drawn on the Bronxville
Savings and Loan Association; charge cards from Macy's,

Lord & Taylor, and Bloomingdale's; an AT&T credit card; a membership in the YMCA; an employee's parking pass for Mercy Hospital in The Bronx. All were made out to Lisa Thorpe, 311 Palmer Road, Bronxville, N.Y. Among the jumble of items in the pocketbook were a pair of designer sunglasses, a checkbook and address book, a hairbrush, a plastic-wrapped sanitary napkin, a small package of Kleenex, an unopened pack of sugarless gum, a lipstick, a pastel-colored felt-tip pen—a set of keys.

"Take these to the parking lot and see if they fit any of the cars out there." Vince tossed the keys to Tommy.

"M.E.'s here," Duffy said from the doorway. "Will wonders never cease." It was almost gospel at crime scenes that the medical examiner was the last one to arrive, leaving everyone else standing around with their thumbs up their asses waiting their turns to get at the evidence.

Shem Weisen pushed past Duffy and strode into the room. He looked hostile and grim: the call had kept him from getting to bed for the first time in the past thirty-six hours. His eyes resembled runny fried eggs. "Whatta we got here?" he snarled.

"White female, twenty-three years old," Vince answered. "Looks like she bled to death."

"When did you get a degree in forensic medicine, Crowley?" Weisen snapped, kneeling on the blood-drenched linoleum and removing the blanket from Lisa Thorpe's corpse.

"You tell me," Vince shot back. "I see a throat cut open, I see blood all over the fucking place, I see a stiff who looks like she's been diddling with Dracula. What the hell am I supposed to think?"

"Don't think." Weisen began examining the torso, working his way slowly up the dead girl's body toward the neck. "No obvious bruises or contusions," he said, almost to himself. "No atrophic signs, no rigor or jaundice. No significant pooling of blood in the extremities." He looked up at Vince and grinned. "It's my bet that this one hasn't been dead for more than an hour."

"There something good about that?" Vince asked.

"By me there is." Weisen returned to his probing of the body. "By me, a fresh corpse is like a breath of spring air. You got any idea how many rotten ones I gotta root around in every day?"

"Don't tell me." Vince grimaced. "That's a helluva lot of blood for someone who's been dead only an hour."

Weisen shrugged. "Human body's only got between five and six quarts, depending on size. Whoever did this hacked her open like they were tapping a keg of beer. My guess is she's got less than a quart left in her."

Tommy entered the room. "The keys fit a brown BMW in the parking lot," he said breathlessly. "Registration in the glove compartment's made out to an Ivor Thorpe."

Vince nodded. "Okay, let's initiate a search of the immediate area and see what else we can come up with." He turned to the M.E. "Any signs of sexual assault?"

"Not so far . . ." Weisen answered from the floor. "A little blood but nothing that looks like it shouldn't be there. I'll need to take a vaginal smear to tell for sure."

The outside hall was beginning to fill up. Emergency Services and Crime Scene personnel in the blocked doorway were straining to get a better look at what was happening inside. A unit from the district attorney's office had assembled a video hookup. White-clad EMS workers waited somberly in the dim light of the hallway to verify the death pronouncement. All the mechanisms were in place, and only their allegiance to sworn procedure kept them from being implemented.

"Let 'em rip." Shem Weisen stood and wiped his hands with a paper towel. "I'm finished here."

"What's your diagnosis?" Vince asked.

"Bled to death," Weisen said simply. "Just like you said."

Vince suppressed a smile. "Any idea about the murder weapon?"

Weisen looked around the room. "You didn't find anything?"

"Not yet. It coulda been a piece of that broken glass," Vince said.

"Maybe," Weisen agreed. "But maybe not. The primary wound is jagged enough, but there's a secondary entrance wound to the pharynx, just above the hyoid bone that had to be caused by something pointed."

"In human language?"

Weisen shook his head. "She was stabbed in the throat by a pointed instrument."

"Like?"

"Like something pointed, for chrissakes." Weisen closed his medical bag and headed for the door. "I'll know more after I've had a chance to examine the body more thoroughly."

"When'll that be?"

"After I've had some sleep." He pushed his way through the horde of police personnel who had begun filing into the room from the outside hallway.

Vince returned the items to the pocketbook and began sifting through the pile of clothing beneath the night-stand. There was nothing unusual: a woolen skirt and sweater, a blouse of indeterminate color, a bra and pair of pantyhose, some white cotton panties. He returned everything to its original state and directed his attention to the CSU detectives, who were busy checking the room for fingerprints and cataloging bits of evidence. "I want every piece of that broken glass dusted," he instructed them. "We could be looking at our murder weapon here."

"What about this?" One of the detectives held up a comb he'd retrieved from behind a tipped chair.

"What's it look like?" Vince asked.

The detective shrugged. "Some kinda comb with a pointy end. Looks like there's blood on it."

"There's blood on everything. Bag it and mark it." Vince walked out into the hall, where Duffy and his partner Willy were waiting for further instructions. "Where's that scumbag Guido?" he asked.

"Back in his office being sick," Duffy replied.

Vince walked down the hall to the office and opened the door. "Duffy tells me you found the body," he said to the night manager. "Wanna tell me all about it?" He closed the door behind him.

Guido Sannasarto shrugged. "What's to tell? I'm walking down the hall and I see the door to unit 23 is open. I check it out, see a police car parked across the street at the diner, and run over there to tell them."

"To tell them what?"

"What I seen," Guido said.

"What was that?" Vince persisted.

"You know . . . what was in there."

"What was that, Guido?"

"Blood, a whole lot of blood . . . you know."

Vince moved closer to him. "And that was the first

time you knew about any trouble in that room, when you saw the blood, right?"

"Right."

"You didn't hear anybody yelling in there. Didn't hear any furniture being knocked over?"

"Nothing. Who the fuck knows?" Guido threw up his hands. "I hear shit like that all the time in this place. Whattaya want from me anyhow?"

There was a disturbance in the hallway. Vince opened the door and walked outside where Tommy was examining a partially burned bundle of bloodstained terrycloth towels. "What's all this?" he asked.

"They found these in an oil drum across the street," Tommy replied.

Vince looked through the towels. "Looks like our killer musta panicked. Tried to wipe up all the blood, then get rid of these by burning them. Doesn't make a whole lot of sense, does it?"

"Who said killers were smart?" Tommy commented.

"Some of them are—" Vince saw Gleason approaching them from the motel entrance. "Oh, oh, partner, here comes trouble."

"Crowley, Ippollito." Gleason nodded curtly.

"Stomach better, Lieutenant?" Vince asked.

Gleason hesitated. "I thought I'd better come down here and check things out."

"Yes sir. Well, things are moving right along," Vince said.

"What's it look like in there?"

"A lotta blood, sir."

"Human blood?"

Vince shot a sidelong glance at Tommy. What the hell did he think they were doing in there, koshering chickens? "Uh, there's a dead woman in there, Lieutenant. We think the blood mighta come from her."

Gleason nodded gravely. "Bad business. Have all the proper notifications been made?"

"Yes sir."

"Any problems?"

"None I can think of, sir." Vince knew that Gleason felt he had to ask these dumb questions. As senior officer at the scene, he was technically supposed to take charge of the investigation, even though everyone knew he had neither the qualifications nor desire to do so. All John

Gleason wanted was to be reassured that his men weren't about to embarrass him. He wanted to know that somebody else had everything under control, and he was free to pursue his transfer with renewed vigor and determination.

From here on in, it was Vince Crowley's case.

4

A CORPSE IS A CORPSE, AS THEY SAY AT THE THREE-SEVEN, but some are more meaningful than others. Not even the most sanguine members of the precinct believed all homicides were treated on an evenhanded basis. The reality of class structure prevailed, even to the savaged remains of murder victims in their midst. Stiffs with connections demanded more justice than the carcasses of no-name slobs. There was nothing uncharitable or malicious in that. It was the way the system worked for everybody. Cops too.

Lisa Thorpe had connections. Vince had barely finished his primary investigation at the crime scene when hordes of newspaper and television reporters began to descend on the Shangri-la Motel. Somehow, without benefit of official notification, word had spread through the grapevine of the journalistic community that something newsworthy had taken place in a seedy, twenty-five-dollar-a-night room in the East Bronx.

"Keep all these people behind the barricades!" Vince barked at the thin file of uniformed officers lining the sidewalk outside the Shangri-la. "Anybody tries to come in here gets spread and read."

"Am I missing something, or does this look like more than your typical Saturday night bloodbath?" Tommy asked, making his way through the shouting mob toward the motel office.

Vince shrugged. "It looks like they know a lot more than we do. What'd you come up with across the street?"

Tommy leafed through his notebook. "Nobody at the diner saw or heard anything, *surprise, surprise*. I got Forensics dusting everything they can find in the Christmas tree lot. The owner showed up a couple of minutes ago, guy named Shapiro. He's screaming about his constitutional rights, says we're schlepping all over his merchandise."

"What about garbage collection?" Vince asked.

"The route belongs to B&B Refuse. Trucks went through here about 0500 hours. I sent a patrol car out to their office a few minutes ago."

Vince and Tommy watched as Lisa Thorpe's body was removed from the motel room by uniformed officers and carried to the coroner's van in a black vinyl bag. CSU detectives sealed the door to unit 23 with yellow plastic tape, posted a warning: "CRIME SCENE. NO ADMITTANCE BY UNAUTHORIZED PERSONNEL," and carried their collected evidence to waiting cars in metal attaché cases. Shem Weisen was the last to leave, surprised at the gathering of news personnel on the sidewalk.

"What's all this?" he asked Vince in a tired monotone.

"Beats me," Vince answered. "Maybe the victim was a celebrity or something."

Weisen shook his head and made his way toward the van.

"Can you tell us how she was killed?" someone shrieked at the coroner as he passed. "Was it murder or suicide?"

Weisen climbed wordlessly into the van and shut the door.

"How about it?" They continued the barrage of questions as Vince and Tommy elbowed through toward their waiting car. "Can't you at least tell us whether she was stabbed or shot?"

"There will be no formal statements to the news media on this matter until the family of the dead girl has been notified." Lieutenant John Gleason was standing above the crowd on the hood of a patrol car.

"I thought the dumb bastard went back to the station house," Tommy whispered to Vince as the mob surged forward through the twisted umbilicals of wire powering their poised, hand-held video units. "Amazing the way he just happens to show up when the cameras are rolling, huh?"

"It is true the murdered girl is Lisa Thorpe, the daughter of Ivor Thorpe, the publisher?" An insistent voice rose above the crowd.

Gleason paled. "I can't comment on that right now. I'll be able to tell you more once we've reached the family."

"The family of Ivor Thorpe, is that right?" the questioner persisted.

"Who the hell is Ivor Thorpe?" Vince whispered to Tommy.

"Beats me," Tommy whispered back. "But he must have some clout someplace to get them as excited as this."

Vince shook his head as they climbed into the unmarked patrol car and pulled slowly away from the curb. "Can you tell me how they manage to find out about this stuff so fast? The body's not even cold yet and they got her made "

Tommy shrugged. "It's their business."

"It's supposed to be *our* business." Vince glared at him. "How come these ghouls get all the inside dope while we're sitting here with our fingers up our ying-yangs?"

"Careful how you speak about the members of the fourth estate. Your girlfriend might be in that crowd," Tommy reminded him.

Vince shot a glance at the receding throng of reporters. "I don't think so. Connie's supposed to be filling in at anchor this week."

"Filling in at anchor," Tommy intoned with mock reverence. "Jeez! You're beginning to sound like *Broadcast News.* I don't know why a guy whose main squeeze is an anchorwoman even bothers with lowlifes like us cops."

Vince rolled his eyes. "Just drive, shitbag. I'll tell you when it's your turn to talk."

They arrived at the precinct and found Walt Cuzak alone in the homicide room, nibbling on something that resembled a lumpy snowball. "What's that shit?" Vince asked him.

"Rice ball, you oughta try one. It's a lot better for you than the garbage you eat," Cuzak said, offering an uneaten one to Vince.

"Uh-uh, I'm trying to taper off . . ." Vince grinned at Tommy.

"Okay, you schmucks. Laugh all you want. You won't be laughing so loud when you're all bent over and crippled up, and I'm still in the robust bloom of youth, for chrissakes," Cuzak protested.

"Rice does that for you?" Tommy asked with a straight face. "I thought rice constipated you. Eat enough of that stuff and you'll forget what a good dump feels like. If you ask me, it's about the unhealthiest thing you can eat. Gets you all bloated and tubby."

"There you go, acting like you know everything again." Cuzak scowled. "If you knew anything at all, you'd know that the Viet Congs ate a shitload of rice and it seems to me they did pretty good. I mean, you didn't see no tubbos humping down the Ho Chi Minh trail, did you?"

"Sonsabitches were about three feet tall," Tommy said. "That's what eating rice did for them."

"Your partner's a big fucking know-it-all," Cuzak huffed. "If either one of you knew anything, you'd know that the shit you put into your body is responsible for everything that happens to you—"

Detective Leila Turner entered the room. "Hey, you guys are celebrities. It's all over the TV downstairs."

Vince looked at Tommy. "They already got her I.D.'d, right?"

Turner sat at her desk. "Daughter of that Thorpe guy. The one who puts out all those smut magazines."

"You know, eating those fuckin' burritos is like pumping chicken fat into your veins with a hypodermic needle," Walt Cuzak broke in. "Your body can take that crap for just so long and then it's 'adios amigo.' " He offered a rice ball to Leila Turner, who looked at it like it was a cockroach.

"He publishes other things besides sleaze," Cuzak said. "Isn't he the publisher of *Newsworld* too?"

"Thorpe publishes *Newsworld* as well as *Sports America* and about a half dozen other magazines." Lieutenant John Gleason was standing in the doorway. "He just happens to be one of the wealthiest men in America."

"And his daughter picks our precinct to get herself clipped in," Tommy said. "We oughta consider ourselves honored."

Gleason gave him a withering stare. "If that's your idea of humor, I'm not amused. Now, if you can all pull yourselves away from this scintillating banter for a few minutes, I'd like to see everybody inside, on the double." He wheeled and entered his office.

Vince, Tommy, Walt Cuzak, and Leila Turner followed, closing the door behind them and taking up strategic positions around the room, each unconsciously calculating the greatest distance between themselves and their agitated commander. There was an awkward silence as Gleason stood behind his desk, eyes closed almost prayerfully, summoning his resources and resolve like a weightlifter pumping himself up for an assault on the record. "As you all know by now, an important homicide has taken place," he began slowly. "One that will put every one of us in the spotlight for as long as it remains unsolved."

Gleason paused, checked his hastily scribbled notes, and took a sip from a mug of cold coffee on his desk. "The murdered girl is the daughter of Ivor Thorpe, one of the most powerful and influential men in this city. Mr. Thorpe, as is common knowledge, is the owner of a number of widely read publications. He is frequently quoted. He is a confidant and consultant to some of the highest-ranking politicos in this state, and most important, he is a major opinion-maker. That means he is in a position to influence the reputation of this precinct in a lot of important ways."

Vince shot a furtive glance at Walt Cuzak, who was staring fixedly at a point just beyond Lieutenant Gleason's left shoulder. Walt had begun to meditate, Vince knew, a skill he'd acquired over the years during his endless search for physical, mental, and spiritual health. For the most part, Vince considered it a crock, but he had to admit it was a good way of escaping Gleason's self-serving harangues. As for Tommy, his defense mechanisms were less sophisticated. He shifted uncomfortably from foot to foot, his eyeballs firmly riveted to the ceiling, trying to absorb a few key words here and there in case he was called upon for comment. Leila Turner seemed alert. She was new enough at the three-seven to naively believe the CO knew what he was talking about.

Gleason had begun to pace, the fingers of his right hand drumming a steady tattoo on his thigh. "It should come as no surprise to me that the only substantive information we have so far has come from members of the news media. It shouldn't surprise me, but it does. I find myself constantly amazed that this so-called cadre of trained investigators is regularly upstaged by members of the press." He turned and glared at them. "For the record, the press came up with the link between the murdered girl and Ivor Thorpe before this department had reported a crime ever took place. While we were in possession of the victim's identification papers, clearly stating her background and affiliations, it was a ragtag group of reporters who put the pieces together—"

"Begging the lieutenant's pardon, but we identified Thorpe from the registration of the car she was driving," Vince broke in. "We figured from the name that he was a relative—a husband or something—but this all just happened. Our next step would've been to contact him."

"And the name Ivor Thorpe meant nothing special to you?" Gleason asked incredulously.

Vince shrugged. "I guess I've probably heard of him, but there was no reason to suspect this was the same guy."

Gleason stiffened. "Am I to assume that the detectives in this squad are unable to grasp even the most fundamental elements of deductive reasoning? Are we incapable of conducting an investigation without everything being spelled out for us in black and white? Maybe we should require murder victims to carry a card identifying their killers from now on. That'd relieve us of having to use our goddamn brains at all!" The veins in his neck and forehead were bulging, his face had turned a harsh, mottled crimson. "Not that it makes any difference at this point, but you may just be interested in knowing that the aforementioned Ivor Thorpe was informed of his daughter's murder by the press. How the hell would *you* like to be told your daughter had been butchered by a reporter?"

"She was killed by a reporter?" Leila Turner asked innocently. Vince wanted to kiss her.

Gleason was trembling with anger. He hated Turner; hated her because she was a smart-ass, hated her because she was a woman, hated her because she was black. Most of all, John Gleason hated Detective Third Grade Leila Turner because she invaded his thoughts at inopportune moments with obsessions that at once embarrassed him and filled him with guilt. He saw her at night, or when he was most intimately alone; stretched before him like a prisoner on a medieval torture rack. Her jaw, her even, white teeth were set in a posture of exquisite pain. Her almond eyes penetrated him, her deep, throaty voice beckoned him. He could see himself poised hungrily above her. He could feel her nipples harden on his tongue as he kissed her caramel breasts. Even now, in the midst of unrelenting anger, he could feel himself becoming aroused.

"I'll let that remark pass"—Gleason could hear the

tremor in his voice—"and get right to the point. The point is that, from here on in, I am going to be personally responsible for every aspect of this investigation. Nothing, absolutely nothing, will take place without my explicit approval. There will be no leads explored, no investigative procedures implemented, no suspects interrogated or arrests made without my prior knowledge. And above all, nobody is to talk to any member of the press, or anyone else for that matter, about any aspect of this case. As of now, I'm issuing a strict gag order to every member of this precinct. If any statement is to be made to the reporters, I'll be the one making it. Is that clear?" His gaze raked the room.

"Does this mean you'll be the investigator of record?" Vince asked evenly.

Gleason hesitated. "It means that I want clearance on this case and I want it pronto," he said finally. "I don't want this command embarrassed or humiliated or torn to pieces by the press, and the only way I can be sure that doesn't happen is to keep a lid on everybody until this is all over." He eyed Vince over the rim of his spectacles. "I want crackerjack police work on this one, Crowley. I won't settle for anything less. Everything by the book and everything funneled up the chain of command. You got any problem with that?"

"None that I can think of, Lieutenant."

"Anybody else got a problem with anything I've said here?"

There was no response.

"In that case, let's get out there and do the job the city pays us to do, okay?"

A shuffling of feet, a clearing of throats, a mumbled chorus of assent.

"You're all dismissed." Gleason stood behind the desk, shaking inside as they exited the room. The thought of actually taking responsibility for any homicide investigation, let alone one of such importance, filled him with terror. What was worse, he knew that everybody under his command was aware of that, and there was nothing he could do to change it.

Visions of a naked, writhing Leila Turner crept beneath the fear and anger.

5

POLICE DEPARTMENT OF THE CITY OF NEW YORK
INCIDENT REPORT NARRATIVE SUPPLEMENT

RE: Investigation.   Shangri-la Motel.

      Homicide/Stabbing.
      Lisa Thorpe W/F   Complaint# 4548
      Investigating officer: V. Crowley

The following items were found in brown BMW sedan (N.Y. plate # CN5738, vehicle I.D. # 6330827-48355017-7, registered to Ivor Thorpe, 573 Central Park W., New York, N.Y.).

1. One Sony Walkman portable cassette system w/headphones.
2. One canvas gym bag (red) containing 1 ea.: Gym shorts, T-shirt, brassiere, head & wrist bands, sanitary napkin.
3. Plastic shopping bag (Bloomingdale's emblem) containing blouse (white & yellow patterned) and store receipt in the amount of $27.49.
4. Ornamented metal cross (silver color) and neck chain.
5. $1.85 in U.S. currency (silver).

Aforementioned items vouchered and placed with 37 PDU property clerk 12/14/87.

Ivor Thorpe stood limply in the steel-vaulted catacomb of the medical examiner's building, surrounded by the sour-sweet smells of alcohol, chlorine, and putrefaction. His tall, athletic frame seemed suddenly fragile, the manicured symmetry of his custom-made clothing sagging.

His trim, prematurely white hair seemed to unravel by itself as an impassive Asian intern pulled the metal drawer containing his daughter's sheet-covered body from a cubicle in the wall. Vince could see teardrops beginning to form in the corners of Thorpe's unblinking gray eyes, riveted on the shapeless form in front of him as he struggled to maintain composure. The intern double-checked the toe tag to verify identity, then lifted a corner of the bloodstained sheet, revealing her face. Thorpe stiffened, shuddered involuntarily, then simply nodded. The identification of the remains of Lisa Thorpe was complete.

A male companion steadied him as he began the journey back through the labyrinth of corridors toward the elevator. Following, Vince could see Thorpe's shoulders heaving imperceptibly beneath his tailored suit jacket, the exaggerated restraint of a proud man struggling to contain his grief. It was the first time Vince had seen Thorpe and what he saw was impressive. Even at a distance, the famous publisher looked like a straight-on, no-bullshit kind of guy, the kind who would have made a good cop of he hadn't chosen to become rich and celebrated.

Thorpe and his entourage rode the elevator to the street while Vince and Tommy took the stairs. Like the motel and station house before, the lobby of the medical examiner's building was crammed with insistent reporters, barely restrained behind hastily erected plastic barricades by a cordon of uniformed patrolmen. Vince led the way to the sidewalk, followed by a ring of bodyguards shielding Thorpe from the mob's shouted questions. Outside, politicians and police brass in dress-uniform regalia elbowed one another to get close to the publisher, and preened like mating waterfowl for a few seconds in front of the relentlessly trailing TV cameras. It was a photo opportunity not to be missed.

An impeccably attired chauffeur held the door to a waiting limousine as Thorpe scrambled inside. The reporters surged forward, disregarding the file of police bodyguards, grasping for a parting statement or a picture of unguarded grief as the car prepared to leave. In the melee Vince found himself pinned between the encircling mob and the door of the limousine as it pulled slowly from the curb. He stumbled, unable to free himself from the automobile and the surging crowd.

"Come on in before you get yourself killed." Ivor Thorpe pushed the rear door open as the car came to a halt, allowing Vince to slide safely inside.

Vince sank gratefully into the plush leather upholstery as the car sped away. "Thanks, but I think I was supposed to be protecting you, not the other way around."

Thorpe smiled. "Glad I could help. Sometimes these people get carried away." The accent was vaguely British, but less formal and intimidating than Vince usually found British accents. Thorpe shielded his eyes from the afternoon sun streaming through the car window and looked at Vince. "You're Detective Crowley, aren't you?"

Vince was astonished by the question.

"You shouldn't be surprised," Thorpe went on. "It's my business to know things. I understand you'll be heading up the investigation into my daughter's murder."

Vince hedged. "Well, a lot of people will be involved—"

"I'm not interested in those self-serving imposters back there," Thorpe said, interrupting him. "Anyone who knows anything about the way this city works, knows that the sharks show up at a feeding frenzy. The police department's no different. Men's careers are on the line. Everybody wants to be on the six o'clock news. I've been involved with cops and politicians long enough to know that once you work your way down through the layers of posturers and publicity-seekers, there's always some obscure professional who knows what he's talking about calling the shots at the bottom end. When I first heard about this, I told my people that was the man I wanted to deal with, and they came up with your name. The fact that you were almost impaled on the door handle of my car was just a fortunate twist of fate."

Vince felt suddenly uncomfortable in the padded luxury of the limousine. "I'm sorry about your daughter, sir . . ." he said awkwardly. "You can just let me out anywhere near here, and I'll make my way back to the precinct."

"Not at all." Thorpe tapped on the glass panel separating the front and rear sections of the limousine and instructed the chauffeur to head for The Bronx. "I'm glad we have this time to talk. I'd very much like to go over your plan of action for the investigation and to offer my help wherever it can be of the greatest use."

Vince felt his stomach beginning to knot. Number one on his list of personal convictions was the certainty that civilians had no business messing around in homicide investigations. "I was going to ask you some questions about your daughter . . . I just thought it'd be better to wait a couple of days until you were able to take care of . . . personal matters."

"I appreciate your thoughtfulness," Thorpe said. "But I didn't get to where I am by putting things off. Granted, my first reaction as a father tells me to go away and hide someplace and nurse my grief, but every moment my daughter's killer is allowed to remain on the streets, the dimmer our prospects of catching him become. I certainly don't want to invade your area of expertise, but it seems to me that time works on the side of the fugitive, wouldn't you agree?"

Vince wasn't about to agree or disagree. His every instinct told him that what Thorpe wanted most in the world was to invade his area of expertise. All that could possibly spell was trouble.

"I can understand that you may resent my intrusion into your investigation," Thorpe went on, without waiting for an answer, "but that doesn't alter the fact that I am already involved. You see, Lisa was my whole life. She meant everything to me. Whoever was responsible for this took from me the one thing I valued most on this earth, and I assure you, I will use every means available to see to it that he is caught and punished for this monstrous crime."

Vince nodded uneasily. "I get your point, Mr. Thorpe, and I know what you must be going through. All I can tell you is that finding your daughter's killer is our number one priority. Everything that can be done, will be done. You have my promise on that."

Thorpe leaned back in the leather car seat and stared out the window. "I'm sure you are a man of your word, Detective Crowley, and I'm sure you are very good at what you do. I have no doubt whatsoever that your investigation will be as professional and complete as these things ever are, but as you may have guessed by now, sitting back and waiting for things to happen isn't the way I'm used to operating. I got to where I am because I was too ornery or hardheaded or just plain dumb to admit that there was anything too big for me to handle. The word 'powerless' was never a part of my vocabulary, and I am not going to start using it now. I'd be a fool not to use the resources at my disposal to bring my daughter's murderer to justice and, to be perfectly honest, you and your superiors would be just as foolish not to accept them."

Vince leaned forward and tapped the glass partition. "Once you get across the Triborough Bridge, head north on the Deegan Expressway," he instructed the driver.

"I can see that you're not a man who commits himself easily," Thorpe observed. "I like that. Intelligent men always hold something back. They know better than to use up everything they've got in the very beginning. It leaves them naked and unguarded over the long haul."

"I'd really like to discuss it with you further, but I'm under orders not to speak to anyone about this case," Vince said, grateful to John Gleason for the first time in his life. "I'll contact you in a day or two and take your statement. Until then, please accept my sympathies on the death of your daughter."

Back at the station house, Walt Cuzak and Leila Turner were sprawled in front of the television set in the homicide room. "How'd it go down at the morgue?" Walt asked sleepily.

"You know how these things are." Vince went to his desk and sifted through his phone messages. "Who took this call from Connie Talbot?" he asked them.

Silence. They were engrossed in a nature program on PBS, something about lizards on the Galapagos Islands. "Did Miss Talbot want me to return her call?" Vince shouted over the sound of the set.

"She wants to talk to you," Leila Turner replied disinterestedly, her eyes glued to the picture of an iguana being worried half to death by a playful seal. "That's just awful," she moaned as the seal dragged the tormented iguana from the rocks and into the water for the umpteenth time. "That's the cruelest thing I ever saw."

"Did she say whether she was at home or at work?"

"I really gotta go with the mammal here," Walt Cuzak said, ignoring the question. "You gotta stick with your own species, know what I mean?"

Vince took a chance and dialed Connie at the TV station.

"You guys up at the Thirty-Seventh are really in the spotlight with this Lisa Thorpe murder," she said when she came on the line. "I saw the footage of you getting into Ivor Thorpe's car. Mind telling me how you rate that kind of treatment?"

"Jealous?"

"Are you kidding? Any newsperson with half a brain would give their right arm to get a few minutes alone with the great man. How's he taking it?"

"About like you'd expect," Vince said. "We still on for tonight?"

"I'd expect Ivor Thorpe to be massing his troops for an assault right now," Connie went on. "He doesn't seem the type for passive grief."

"You're right about that," Vince said. "You didn't answer my question. Do we have a date tonight or don't we?"

"A date . . ." Her voice trailed off. "What were we supposed to be doing?"

"I dunno. Hanging out, I guess. You know. Dinner, some conversation . . . maybe some light shmoozing afterward if we're both up to it."

The clamor of voices and heavy footsteps on the outside stairwell distracted him. "Gotta go. Love you. I'll pick you up around seven." He hung up the phone as Tommy, Snuffy Quade, and Lieutenant Gleason entered the squad room.

"I want to see you, Crowley," Gleason snarled, entering his office.

"What's up?" Vince asked Tommy.

Tommy shrugged.

"Now!" Gleason's voice boomed.

Vince walked inside and stood in front of Gleason's desk. "Lieutenant?"

Gleason took a deep breath and exhaled it slowly. He was highly pissed off about something. "Do you want to tell me just what the hell you were doing back there at the M.E.'s office?"

"Beg pardon, sir?"

"Just what the hell were you doing, getting into Thorpe's car like you were one of the family, for chrissakes?"

"Oh, that. He wanted to talk to me."

Gleason glowered at him. "Ivor Thorpe wanted to talk to *you*?"

"Yes, sir."

"You're telling me that Ivor Thorpe, one of the biggest of the big shots in this entire country, had nothing better to do than strike up a conversation with some baggy-pants street cop from The Bronx?" Gleason howled.

"I wouldn't know about that, Lieutenant," Vince replied evenly. "All I know is he practically pulled me into his car."

Gleason paled. "Now, you listen up and listen hard, Detective. From here on in, you will have no contact whatsoever with Ivor Thorpe. Got that?"

"Is that supposed to mean that I'm restricted from questioning him or obtaining a statement from him during the course of my investigation, sir?"

"It *means* that if there is any grandstanding to be done on this case, it will not be done by you."

Vince nodded. "I'll take that to mean that all further grandstanding is to be done by the lieutenant. Will that be all, sir?"

Gleason felt his stomach turning. His incipient ulcer was acting up again. "I'll tell you when we're finished here," he sputtered.

"Yes sir."

"I want a report about everything you and Thorpe discussed on my desk first thing tomorrow morning."

"Yes, sir."

"And any further contact with him will be directed through me."

"Yes sir."

An excruciating silence followed. There were salient points John Gleason wanted to make, but he couldn't think of them. He needed time to regain control of the situation, but things were moving too fast, and fast footwork was not his strong suit . . .

"Do I have the lieutenant's permission to leave now?"

Gleason knew that his fitness for command would be measured by his actions during the coming days and weeks. He would be judged by his ability to withstand the press and glare of publicity with poise and control . . .

"If there are no further orders, I'd like to get back to my paperwork, Lieutenant."

Finding an appropriate way to dismiss Crowley was only the first step . . .

6

CONNIE TALBOT STRETCHED LUXURIANTLY IN THE OVER-sized tub. Steam vapor penetrated her nostrils, pressing out the hard edges of the day, soothing her tired muscles, caressing the stiff spots that seemed to multiply with every year on the job. How many hours had she spent standing on cold, drizzly sidewalks waiting for an interview, or cramped in the rear of vans speeding from one end of the city to another, hunkered among the snarl of cables and technical equipment that would bring another newsworthy event to the viewers of the six o'clock nightly news? If only those who saw her as a glamorous television personality could see her now.

For Connie, the glamour had worn off a long time ago, along with the guilt that had come with sudden success. She no longer felt like she was stealing the network's money every time her paycheck arrived in the mail, even though it was light-years beyond any salary she might have dreamed about as a young girl in Wearisome Bluff, Texas. The money had given her comfort and respectability, but it had never brought the exhilaration she once imagined it would. It had never provided the self-assurance or peace of mind. As for the glamour, it had eroded into leg cramps and indigestion with every cold cheeseburger eaten on the run, cynicism and frustration over every tenement fire that could have been avoided, over the torn bodies of beaten and neglected children, the hypocrisy of uncaring politicians.

She scanned the outlines of her naked body beneath the steaming surface of the water. Not bad for a thirty-seven-year-old, she thought, Her weight hadn't changed much since high school, but the proportions were subtly different. Where once the trim, hard outlines of her hips and abdomen rose in firm, defiant undulations, it now erupted in billows of soft, malleable flesh that refused to

harden despite her faithful morning routine of high-impact
aerobics performed to a VCR exercise tape. Breasts that
once peaked resolutely to erect nipples that strained the
fabric of T-shirts and skimpy cotton blouses were now
draped ingloriously across her chest, nipples pointing to
either side like splayed sentries guarding her flanks. Still
the package held together, she thought, with a lot of
stubborn self-denial, an absolute wizard of a clothes designer, and a little help from modern cosmetology. Dressed
up and feeling sassy, Connie Talbot was still a looker in
anybody's league.

A class broad, Vince Crowley's friends would say, and
Vince Crowley's friends called a spade a spade. Maybe
that was what had drawn her to Crowley in the first
place. His world was too inflexible for artificiality. There
was none of the insincere flattery and empty bombast
that abounded in the broadcast community, none of the
petulance, the bruised egos, or pervading self-importance
of the network stars and executives she had to deal with
every day. They reported the grim reality of the streets
with the urbane detachment of Ivy League upperclassmen
on a field trip to a soup kitchen. Cops lived it and they
loved it and they took it home with them. They were raw
and immediate and, for the most part, they said what was
on their minds. Sometimes it was unnerving but it was
never dishonest. For Connie, that was like a shot of pure
oxygen.

She allowed the water to drain from the tub and stood
in the thick, perfumed atmosphere of the bathroom.
Crowley made her feel good; that much she knew. She
had never allowed herself to become involved with anyone quite like him before. Crowley was intelligent and
uncomplicated, a combination she found irresistible. Most
of the males she had known equated intelligence with
adolescent soul-searching. The ones who weren't looking
for a substitute mom were mucking around for a little
self-esteem. They felt they couldn't really understand a
relationship unless they had enough emotional space to
study it to death. Crowley took things as they came and
he dealt with them.

She toweled off gently, allowing most of the water to
be absorbed by the atmosphere, then rubbed her entire
body with moisturizing cream. It had a heady almond
aroma that penetrated the warm, moist air, evoking mem-

ories of past episodes when the lotion had been used for other, more erotic purposes—hoarse, whispered urgency; tangled nights of overwhelming need; his inexpert fumbling, probing; the brush of teeth against the surface of her aroused nipples; sensuous, slapping sounds of skin and saliva. If Vince Crowley wasn't a sophisticated lover, he was an ardent one, without an overwhelming need to evaluate his performance every step of the way. That was just what she needed at this point in her life. She'd had enough of quirky men who brought their insecurities to bed with them, who rearranged their hair or watched their biceps during the process of their lovemaking. At thirty-seven she understood that sincerity triumphed over sexual artistry every time. Hands down.

There was probably some gray hair somewhere, she thought, standing in front of the full-length mirror on the bathroom door and running a brush through her long, auburn tangles, but she had never really seen it. The color had been maintained almost daily by an army of hairdressers employed by the network, as if the intrusion of a few strands of silver might repel the youth-oriented viewing audience. At times she almost wanted to allow them to show through as a kind of stubborn affirmation that the years had generated some character beneath the custom clothes and cosmetics. She'd wanted to but hadn't. Newswomen who aged on camera were newswomen who became unemployed. Aging anchormen could be considered dignified; aging newswomen were frowzy. It was simply another injustice in an unfair world, one she hadn't developed the bravery to confront. Not yet. Underneath the uncertainty she had a reservoir of unused courage. Maybe Vince's quiet confidence would give her the strength to tap it . . . someday.

The doorbell rang before she was finished dressing. She wrapped herself in a terrycloth robe, walked the length of the duplex apartment to the front door, and unlocked it. Outside, Vince was standing in the hall, carrying a brown paper bag containing what smelled like Chinese take-out.

"You're early, Crowley." She kissed him lightly on the lips.

"I just had to get away from the house." Vince entered the apartment and carried the paper bag into the kitchen.

"Gleason's nuts over this Thorpe homicide, and he's driving everybody crazy."

Connie eyed the food. "I guess this means I shouldn't dress for dinner."

Vince took her hand and squeezed it. "I only have a couple of hours before I'm back on duty. If it's okay with you, I thought maybe we could just sit around in our socks and pig out."

She smiled. "Sounds just fine to me. What do you have there?"

"Good stuff"—Vince began removing cardboard cartons from the bag—"Szechuan cooking, real hot. There's a new place just opened up down the block—Peking Garden, something like that. I got some ribs, some rolled-up beef stuff, and a chicken thing." He opened one of the cartons and offered Connie a lump of reddish meat.

She chewed it uncertainly. "This the beef stuff or the chicken thing?"

"Who knows? It's good, right?"

"I mean, do I pour white wine or red?" she joked, setting the kitchen table.

"Got any scotch around here?"

Connie brought a bottle of Dewar's to the table and poured them both a generous glassful. "You look tired, Crowley."

"I am. How about you?"

She shrugged. "I guess so. Being anchor isn't as physically tiring as being out on the streets, but it's a lot more pressure. Everybody's so damn stress-ridden you can feel the anxiety right down to the mail room. It took me a half hour in a hot tub just to work the tension out of my neck muscles."

"You should've waited for me," Vince said between bites. "It's been awhile since we took a bath together."

"Don't blame me," Connie protested. "I've been here."

"I know . . ." Vince finished the last morsel on his plate and poured another drink. "What can I say?"

"It's what I have to expect if I'm nuts over a cop, right?" She finished the thought for him.

"I don't suppose you'd be up for another bath?" Vince asked innocently.

"Tell me about Lisa Thorpe," she asked, ignoring his question. "Any leads so far?"

Vince shrugged. "Not much to tell. You probably know more about it than I do at this point."

"I'll know more by the time I get to the station tomorrow morning," she conceded. "You can be sure they're researching every millisecond of her life right now for tomorrow's coverage. Important people like her don't get killed every day, you know."

"We could just stretch out in that big tub of yours and tickle each other with our toes, you know what I mean?"

"Besides. This is the kind of story that can make somebody's career. Just getting close to somebody like Ivor Thorpe is almost a guarantee of instant notoriety."

". . . Soap each other up in all the right places, if you catch my drift."

She stared across the table disapprovingly. "If you weren't such a pervert, you'd be able to see that my station is doing your job for you while we're sitting here, Crowley. By tomorrow morning you'll probably know more about Lisa Thorpe and her father than you ever wanted to know."

"I could shampoo your hair. Do your back with that big horsehair brush you have hanging in there—get at all the spots you couldn't reach yourself."

Connie began clearing the table. "You don't want to discuss Lisa Thorpe, right?"

"It's not necessarily that." Vince leaned back in the wooden chair and ran his open palms down the length of his chest into his lap. "I just think we ought to get this bath business cleared up first, you know?"

"Gleason's got you all under a gag order, right?" She began stacking the plates in the dishwasher.

"I could smear you all over with that white lotion after we dry off."

Connie paused. "Tickle each other where?"

"Huh?"

"You said we could tickle each other with our toes. Just where did you have in mind?"

He grinned.

"I'm already clean," she said halfheartedly.

"What I got in mind is real dirty."

"Give me three minutes to clean up in there and run the water." Connie hurried up the stairs and disappeared into the bedroom.

Shielded by the gush of running water, she went to the

john, straightened up the jumble of towels and underclothes left from her previous bath, and sprayed her body in all the right places with an atomizer of Opium perfume. As tired as she was, the thought of Crowley's comfortable, unhurried fingers spreading lubricant into every submissive crevasse of her anatomy caused her to tremble, a reaction she knew he had already anticipated. That was okay too, she thought as she stepped out into the hallway overlooking the living room. The fact that Crowley was sure of himself was only one of the reasons she was as attracted to him as she was.

The fact that he was sleeping soundly on the sofa below only made her smile.

7

NYPD FORM DD-5
COMPLAINT FOLLOW-UP

HOMICIDE/STABBING
LISA M. THORPE W/F 23

DECEMBER 15, 1988
COMPLAINT # 4548
Det. V. Crowley

1. At approx. 0830 hours on December 15, pursuant to the above investigation, the undersigned, accompanied by Det. Ippollito, 37 PDU, visited the apartment of the deceased at 311 Palmer Road, Bronxville, N.Y.

2. We were met by the superintendent of the building, George Wiggand, who provided access to the premises and agreed to be interviewed re the deceased.

3. Interviewee stated that the deceased was a model tenant with few visitors. He could recall no unfavorable or troublesome incidents during the two years deceased was a tenant in the building.

4. Inspection of the premises disclosed no further clues, and premises were sealed preliminary to forensic examination.

5. Before leaving, we interviewed Robt. Elmer, doorman at 311 Palmer Road, who stated that the deceased had not been visited by anyone during the period immediately prior to her murder; that she left her apartment unaccompanied on the morning of December 13 at approx 0600

hours to attend work at Mercy Hospital, Bronx, N.Y., and that she had not returned to the premises.

INVESTIGATION CONTINUES. CASE ACTIVE.

Eighteen hours on, four off, and he was finishing up another eight-hour tour. With the exception of the short nap he'd taken at Connie's, Vince had been on the job for more than two days straight. He looked at Tommy behind the wheel of the unmarked patrol car as he eased into the parking lot at 311 Palmer Road. "How you holding up, partner?"

"I guess I'll make it," Tommy replied, steering the car into a parking spot marked TENANTS ONLY. "It's just too bad that when an important person gets iced, important cops aren't willing to do the dog work." He placed a POLICE OFFICER ON DUTY sign above the dashboard and unhitched his seat belt.

"Hey, we're important," Vince protested. "We're just not celebrated."

"We ain't shit," Tommy muttered. "The important cops are down at headquarters drinking coffee and telling war stories right now. You don't see no gold braid in this goddamn parking lot, do you?"

Vince let it pass. Tommy was beat, just letting off steam. "We'll chalk out after this, get ourselves some Zs. Besides, look at all the O.T. we're raking in." He looked at his wristwatch. "I don't know about you, partner, but I went off the clock fifteen minutes ago."

"I don't even keep track anymore," Tommy said disgustedly. "Money don't get you recognition, it don't get you respect; know what I mean? Even if we nail the scumbag that did this thing, somebody else is gonna get the credit, you know that, Vince. What are we busting our balls for, you wanta tell me that?"

"We'd been on thirty-six hours straight when Billy got it," Vince said. "Two hours' sleep in the back of the van, then four hours at the wheel. Four hours on, two hours off. We were all so fucking groggy we hardly knew our own names. Maybe Billy could've seen the bastards coming if he wasn't so wiped out. Maybe he would've been more cautious."

Tommy nodded respectfully. He'd heard the story a couple of dozen times. Vince's first partner, Billy Whalen, had been blown away by a shotgun blast in his chest while he was taking a leak outside a surveillance van. He knew it was a story that Vince had to tell, a memory he had to keep alive, however painful. Tommy had been around long enough to understand that for a cop, losing a partner was like losing a part of himself. He'd heard stories of amputees who felt pain in their severed arms and legs long after they were gone. The stimulus was brought on by an unrelenting memory and an unwillingness to admit the loss. He suspected that was what it was like to lose a partner.

Vince slid out of the passenger seat and led Tommy into the lobby of the luxurious condominium. He identified himself to the brown-uniformed doorman who confronted them as they entered. "I'm Detective Crowley, Thirty-Seventh Precinct, Homicide. This's Detective Ippollito. We'd like to see Lisa Thorpe's apartment."

The doorman scrutinized his shield and ID card carefully. "I'm sorry, but there have been others," he apologized. "Newspeople and curiosity-seekers. Mr. Thorpe left strict orders that nobody was to be admitted."

"Thorpe? You've spoken with him?"

"Mr. Thorpe was here last night, also this morning. He left here just a little while ago."

Vince shot an angry glance at Tommy. One of the first things he had done was issue an order that the apartment was to be sealed off to everyone but the police. "Who the hell let him in?" he demanded. "Did he take anything with him when he left?"

The doorman blanched. "I'm afraid you'll have to speak with the superintendent." He lifted the receiver from a wall phone and punched in the appropriate number.

The superintendent arrived almost immediately. "Can I help you gentlemen?"

Vince took an instant dislike to him. He felt a super should look like a super, not like a floorwalker at Macy's. "We're here to go through Lisa Thorpe's apartment." He flashed his badge. "But your first line of defense here tells me you let the murdered girl's father inside after the place had been sealed by the police. Is that right?"

The superintendent removed a folded piece of note-paper from his jacket pocket and handed it to Vince. "Mr. Thorpe was authorized by your own department. I verified this by telephone."

Vince scanned the sheet and handed it to Tommy. It was a permission order for Thorpe to enter the premises and it was signed by CO John Gleason. "You spoke to the lieutenant on the phone?" he asked incredulously.

"He told me to afford Mr. Thorpe the run of the place for as long as he wanted." The super replied smugly.

"This piece of paper is history, got it?" Vince growled. "From here on in, nobody's allowed in that apartment without my specific permission." He stuffed the authorization into his pocket and accompanied Tommy and the startled super to the elevator.

Upstairs, the empty apartment still bore traces of the murdered girl's presence. The remainder of a sandwich on the table in front of the TV in the living room, a ceramic mug still half filled with cold coffee, an ashtray overflowing with lipstick-smeared cigarette butts, a paperback novel opened upside-down on the cushion of the couch—the miscellaneous debris of some-one who planned to clean up soon, someone who hadn't planned on bleeding to death in a fleabag motel in The Bronx.

In the bedroom, the bed was still unmade, and a flannel nightgown was flung carelessly across the pillows; her faint, musky body aromas still clung to the sheets. Vince walked to the nightstand and depressed the Replay button on the telephone answering machine. "This thing's blank—you know anything about that?" he asked the superintendent, standing in the doorway.

"Mr. Thorpe played back the messages that were on there," he answered nervously. "Maybe he erased them by mistake."

Vince lifted the plastic cover and looked inside the mechanism. "Nothing's been erased. The tape's been removed from this mother."

The superintendent shrugged. "Your lieutenant said to show him every courtesy."

"Jeezus!" Vince looked at Tommy and shook his head. "What else did *Mr. Thorpe* fuck up while he was in here?"

The super shuffled uneasily. "Look, I don't want any trouble from the police. If your people didn't want him in here, they shouldn't have issued the authorization."

"Did he take anything with him when he left?" Vince persisted.

"There was an envelope—some letters, I think."

"Where did he get the letters?"

The super pointed to one of the drawers in the dresser. "He removed some pictures from the wall, that was about it."

"Okay. You can leave us alone, but stick around downstairs until we leave. I may have some more questions to ask you." He dismissed the superintendent and began sifting through the assorted papers in the drawer.

"Do you believe the balls on that guy?" Tommy moaned when the super was gone. "How the hell can he just walk into a crime scene and take what he wants, just tell me that, willya?"

"Guys like Thorpe are used to getting their own way," Vince replied. "They open their mouths, and worms like Gleason start shitting in their drawers. You and me are never gonna know what it's like to have that kind of power, bro. Not in our lifetimes."

"Well, it stinks if you ask me."

"Looks like our victim was the sentimental sort . . ." Vince said, observing the miscellany of cards, letters, and photographs preserved in cardboard boxes or wrapped neatly with ribbon and rubber bands. "She must've kept just about every piece of correspondence she ever got."

"What about the ones Thorpe took with him?" Tommy asked, scooping everything into a brown paper bag he'd taken from the kitchen. "Maybe there was something incriminating in that stuff. He could've destroyed valuable information when he opened that machine, for chrissakes."

"Could've. Not much we can do about it now," Vince said. "Let's contact the phone company as soon as we get back to the house, though. At least we'll be able to get a record of all her outgoing calls for the past month or so."

Vince closed the drawer and sifted perfunctorily through the others. There was nothing out of the ordinary: underwear, socks, hosiery, some inexpensive-looking jewelry. He walked to the bathroom and emptied the medicine cabinet of pills and medicines. They could prove helpful if it turned out she was addicted to something. Even if she wasn't, the prescriptions would give him a line on the doctors she was seeing. Psychiatrists and therapists could prescribe pills, too. They might be able to shed some light on her mental condition prior to her death.

There was a framed photograph on the bathroom wall. It was a posed shot of Lisa dressed in a simple blue frock standing with a group of black-habited nuns. A small wooden cross hung from her neck.

"Here's one Thorpe didn't get," he said to Tommy. "Whatta you make of it?"

Tommy shrugged. "Some kind of graduation picture maybe. She probably went to some Catholic college or something like that."

"Okay, let's just make a quick search of everything and seal this place for good," Vince instructed Tommy. "Make a note to contact Motor Vehicles, Bronx and Westchester; have them run a computer check on Lisa Thorpe—any outstanding tickets, you know the routine. Bus schedules and cab companies. I wanta know who was on the road in the vicinity of the Shangri-la when she was killed. And we interview Duffy and his partner again. Also the night shift at the diner and that scumbag night manager, Guido. Got all that?"

"I thought we were gonna get some sleep," Tommy groaned.

"There'll be plenty of time for sleep. In the meantime, I want you to call Forensics when we get back to the house and get them up here to dust this whole place for prints. Who knows, maybe we'll get lucky."

Tommy arched an eyebrow. "Yeah, and maybe my old lady will hit .400 for the Yankees this year, too."

8

CITY OF NEW YORK
OFFICE OF THE MEDICAL EXAMINER

AUTOPSY REPORT # 251-46281   DECEMBER 17, 1988
LISA M. THORPE W/F

S. Weisen M.D., P.D. Supervising.

The body is that of a white female, 23 years.
Ht. 5′4 ½″. Wt. 49.5 kilos. Hair, brown. Eyes, blue.

Examination of lower torso reveals one surgical scar, approx. 6.2 cm on the central abdominal region approx 9 cm below the navel. There are no other apparent scars or lesions on the body other than those inflicted at the time of death.

Internal examination of the lower abdomen indicates that a tubal ligation had been performed on the victim during the past twelve months.

Analysis of circular puncture wound to the trachea (approx. .36 cm in diameter) indicates that it was inflicted by a dull, pointed instrument, penetrating the outer skin layer but causing only surface hemorrhage to the tracheal wall and surrounding tissues.

Analysis of the fatal wound to the neck indicates that the victim was slashed with a sharp, jagged object (probably glass) and that the object penetrated and severed the right internal carotid artery, causing massive loss of blood and resulting in death
. . .

Detective Sergeant Dominick "Dog" Scarfatti scanned

the M.E.'s report on Vince Crowley's desk after he had dialed his bookie and placed a sizeable bet on the fourth race at Flamingo. "What say, Crowley?" He grinned as Vince entered the squad room at the three-seven. "Long time, no see, bro—"

"Get your fat ass off my chair, Scarfatti!" Vince growled. "What brings scum like you up here to God's country anyway?"

Scarfatti stretched back in the chair, crossed his legs on Vince's desk, and smiled broadly. "Hey, is that any way to treat an old buddy, Crowley? I thought you'd be glad to see me, especially since we're gonna be *campañeros* on this Thorpe homicide."

"What the hell is that supposed to mean?"

Scarfatti stretched and stood slowly. "Just that the victim's old man placed a couple of strategic calls to all the right people, and the word came down to the Chief of D. that this here was more than just your everyday, run-of-the-mill killing, so he sends us up here to see that everything's done by the numbers."

"The Chief of D. sent you?" Vince was flabbergasted. "Stop jerking me off, Dog. This day's been bad enough as is."

"Nobody's jerking nobody off." Scarfatti allowed Vince to squeeze past him in the narrow corridor between desks and sit in his chair. "I'm Major Case now. Didn't nobody tell you?"

Vince felt the muscles of his stomach twitch involuntarily. This was a turd he was talking to.

"Me and my partner Sammy Feck here—" Scarfatti indicated an overweight, pockmarked man dressed in a shiny brown suit, leaning against the bars of the holding pen. "The Chief of D. decided this case was too important to be left to a buncha assholes like you guys at the three-seven, so he sent me and Sammy up here to give you a hand. Wasn't that nice of him?" Scarfatti smirked, revealing an uneven row of crusty yellow teeth.

"We'll see about that!" Vince headed for Gleason's office.

"That ain't gonna do you no good," Scarfatti said. "Your CO's down at HQ right now, getting his picture taken with the mayor and commissioner. My guess is, they probably already made the announcement that the Major Case squad is on the job, prepared to bring truth and justice to this major metropolitan area. Sorta warms the cockles of your heart, don't it? Restores your faith in the criminal justice system—"

"You know anything about this?" Vince asked Pete Yorio, who was typing a report at his desk.

Yorio shrugged. "Gleason was gone when they got here."

"Hey, no hard feelings, Crowley." Scarfatti offered his hand. "We're not up here to cause you any trouble, you know that. Just kinda act as a pipeline back to the Chief of D., if you know what I mean; keep him informed about what's going down. Now, how about introducing me to your new partner?"

Vince ignored Scarfatti's extended hand. "Tommy Ippollito, this's just about the worst scumbag in the Detective Division, Dog Scarfatti," he said sullenly. "I don't know his partner over there, but if he's anything like Dominick, you don't want to have anything to do with him."

Scarfatti looked wounded. "Hey, goombah, is that any way to talk about an old friend? You and me been through a lot together. True, we ain't always seen things eye to eye, but we respect each other as men, right?"

Vince shuffled through the papers on his desk. "Just keep your distance, Dog. That's all I want. I don't give a shit what you do around this place as long as you stay out of my way. I got a job to do here and I don't appreciate some spy from headquarters looking over my shoulder while I'm trying to do it."

"No sweat, goombah." Scarfatti threw up his hands in mock innocence and backed away from the desk. "Don't take your partner too serious, Ippollito," he said to Tommy. "He ain't no *paisano* like you and me. These Irish guys're always tight-assed as a drum, know what I mean?"

Tommy eyed Vince questioningly.

"If you're finished, I got work to do here," Vince said to Scarfatti.

"I'm gonna need a desk," Scarfatti said, ignoring him. "As long as I gotta hang around this shit-hole for a while, I might as well make myself comfortable, huh?"

"You see any empty desks around here?" Vince challenged him.

"The old place hasn't changed much," Scarfatti went

on, looking around the homicide room. "A few more *'mulinons'* since I was here—downstairs is crawling with them. And I see you got some broads up here . . . shit!" He shook his head disgustedly. "Just think, if I'd been as dumb as you, I probably woulda still been humping my ass around up here with the rest of you bumpkins."

"You want me to take this asshole out for you, partner?" Tommy asked angrily.

"I wouldn't try anything stupid if I was you, junior," Scarfatti's partner, Sammy Feck, snarled from the other end of the room.

"Leave it be," Vince said wearily. "I'll straighten it all out later with the CO." He looked up from his desk at Scarfatti. "You leave my partner alone, and you leave me alone; got that, scumbag? I don't know you and I don't know your partner, Sammy Cheap-Suit over there unless I get a direct order from my CO, *comprende*? Now, are you gonna get the hell out of my squad room, or do I call downstairs for some officer assistance?"

Scarfatti laughed. "You never change, do you, Crowley? You're gonna stay a hard-nose until the day they plant you." He motioned to his partner and headed for the door. "It's a good thing I got a thick skin or I'd take some of that shit you say personally. As it is, I say 'live and let live,' know what I mean?" He threw an affectionate arm around Feck's beefy shoulders. "Life's too short to hold grudges, right? I mean, what's a cop got but the friendship and goodwill of his fellow officers?" He steered them both out onto the stairwell. "We'll be back when you're in a better frame of mind."

"What's *that* all about?" Tommy asked after they were gone.

"Long story . . ." Vince scanned the M.E.'s report on his desk. "He used to work here eight or nine years ago. Until Internal Affairs nailed him for knocking over local drug dealers. He'd bust a street junkie, get him to identify whoever sold him the stuff, then rip off the dealer, keep the money, and give whatever dope they confiscated back to the junkie, automatically turning him into another reliable snitch. It was a beautiful, circular operation until the IAD shoo-flies put a hole in it for him."

"So what's he doing working for the Chief of D.?" Tommy asked.

"He made a deal with them—agreed to turn over on his fellow officers. They got him to wear a wire inside the house so they could find out if any bad shit was going down at the precinct level. They nailed a couple of guys for gambling, some probies for smoking dope, before they decided it was too much trouble for the results they were getting."

"That really sucks," Tommy said. "How'd you find out about it?"

Vince shrugged. "Dog's one of those guys who can't keep his nose out of anything. Creeps like him just naturally get burned sooner or later. I heard they tried to get him to retire, but he knew where too many of the bodies were buried. So they've been shuttling him around from post to post, all over the city since then. I guess it's natural for a rat like him to be a spy for downtown. Bastard's not fit to be a standup cop."

Rookie Detective Hector Vargas, aka "Street Crime," entered the squadroom and handed Vince a copy of the morning *Daily News*. "Looks like your victim was some kind of superwoman," he observed, pointing to the glaring block letters beneath the masthead:

"FATHER OF MURDERED GIRL SAYS: LISA WAS A SAINT!"

Underneath the headline, a snapshot of a smiling Lisa Thorpe was superimposed on a half-page photograph of her lifeless corpse lying on the blood-soaked floor of the Shangri-la. "How the fuck did they ever get that shot?" Vince howled. "We were there for the whole goddamn time and nobody took any pictures."

"Except the D.A.'s picture unit," Tommy reminded him. "Somebody musta gotten to someone up there."

Vince scanned the article beneath the photo:

The mutilated body of Lisa Thorpe, 23, daughter of Ivor Thorpe, publisher of *Newsworld* and *Sportsweek* magazines, was discovered early yesterday morning in an isolated motel in The Bronx. The victim, a student nurse at Mercy Hospital, located not far from the scene of the murder, had been a world-class figure skater several years prior to her murder, having competed in the world championship pairs competition at Geneva, Switzerland in March of 1986.

The remainder of the article was similar, a ringing

accolade to Lisa Thorpe and her accomplishments in life. It was not much different from the tributes paid to most other murder victims by the press, except that this one merited the first page. "What else you got for me?" Vince asked Street Crime.

"We swept the neighborhood and so far we got no confirmed eyewitness. Nobody saw anything suspicious going down. Everything was pretty much the way it always was the morning of the murder."

"How about that scuzzball Guido Sannasarto? Does he remember checking her into the place? Is her name on the register?"

"Negative on both counts," Street Crime said. "We'll have to hang Guido by his toes for a couple of months if we want to get anything out of him. He's already telling us to talk to his lawyer."

"Okay, so where does all this leave us?"

"Well, there's one curious coincidence . . ." Street Crime checked his notebook. "Out of the seven people we interviewed, four of them report having seen a vagrant in the neighborhood—not necessarily at the time of the murder, but just hanging around over a period of days. They say he slept in the Christmas tree lot across the street from the motel."

"That's where we found those bloodstained towels," Tommy reminded him.

"Got a name?" Vince asked Street Crime.

"Ricardo something or other. He's called Ricky Miracle out on the street."

"You talk to him?"

"Haven't been able to find him yet. I've issued a description to all units in the area, and they're out looking for him. If they don't bring him in today, I'll get out a flyer."

"Good enough." Vince placed the *Daily News* article on top of a pile of unattended paperwork on his desk and handed Tommy his copy of the M.E.'s report. "Take a look at this and tell me if anything strikes you as unusual."

Tommy scanned the report. "I dunno, seems pretty standard to me."

"What about that tubal ligation. You know what that is?"

"Not really," Tommy admitted.

"She had her tubes tied. That means she could never

have kids. You want to tell me why a young girl like her
would want an operation like that?"

Tommy shrugged. "Maybe she didn't want it. Maybe it
was one of those woman's things. Women always got
something bad happening to their bodies."

"Maybe . . ." Vince folded the report and placed it on
top of the pile. "Let's remember to check it out anyway.
And run a computer check on that Ricky Miracle guy.
Find out if we have any paper on him."

They were interrupted by approaching noises on the
stairs outside the squadroom. Gleason entered, accompanied by Dominick Scarfatti and his overweight partner.
They were grinning and telling jokes, like asshole bud-
dies who hadn't seen each other in a month of Sundays.
Vince stiffened and shot Tommy a painful glance, reflect-
ing what he already knew in his heart of hearts. For the
duration of the investigation, he was stuck with the Dog
and Cheap Suit.

9

F OR VINCE, THE FACT THAT THE INVESTIGATION WAS NOW
saddled with a couple of parasites from Major Case was
less disturbing than his growing contempt for the system
that allowed it to happen. Dog and Cheap Suit would be
no more than a minor annoyance, he knew. Gleason had
assured everyone that their duties were to be simply
appraisal and assessment; they had no investigative function other than as a liaison between the precinct and the
Chief of Detectives. Translated, that meant that their
function, if they had a function, would be to hang around
the station house drinking beer and eating pizza, pulling
juvenile pranks, cracking lousy jokes, and generally making a royal pain in the ass of themselves while they were
reporting back to Headquarters. Knowing the kind of
cop Dog had become, that much at least was reassuring
to Vince.

Less reassuring was his awareness that the police department had become a honeycombed network of spies
and informers. Self-seeking little men with no scruples
and great ambitions were exploiting the bond of brotherhood that had once been every cop's solemn watchword.
Everywhere the bond was breaking down. Open commu-
nication between policemen had become a matter of who
could be trusted. Who was on the hook to Internal Affairs? Who was wearing a wire?

Riding an elevator in Mercy Hospital with Tommy at
his side, Vince remembered the fraternal tug he had felt
when he first entered the department. He remembered
Ben Volpe, his "rabbi" when he was a rookie, telling him,
"In a crunch, the only people you can count on are your
fellow officers. When you find a partner you believe in,
you can trust that man with your life." That partner had
been Billy Whalen for most of his career, but Billy was
dead and Tommy was still raw and untested. Tommy was

growing up in a department with different priorities and expectations. He had to deal with politically inspired commissions and civilian-complaint boards and a mystifying set of rules and prohibitions that made it almost impossible for him to do his job the way it was supposed to be done. But Tommy had the right stuff. Maybe with enough prodding and coaching, and a few kicks in the ass when they were needed, he could keep it where it belonged.

The elevator halted at the eighth floor and deposited an assortment of nurses, interns, and visitors. Vince and Tommy followed the hallway to the end and stopped at a closed door marked DIRECTOR OF NURSING. "I'm Detective Crowley and this is Detective Ippollito, Thirty-Seventh Precinct, Homicide." He displayed his shield to the tall, middle-aged woman who answered his knock. "I called earlier about the Lisa Thorpe homicide. I'm supposed to see a Mary Boyle."

"I'm Mary Boyle." She smiled and ushered them into the office.

"I hope we didn't come at a bad time," Vince apologized.

"Not at all." She arranged two straight-backed wooden chairs in front of her desk and motioned for them to sit. "We're all so very upset about this terrible thing that happened to Lisa." She shook her head sadly. "I want to be as much help to you as I possibly can."

"We'd appreciate that, ma'am," Vince said, opening his notebook.

She smiled and her face erupted into a web of tiny creases that said she smiled often. "You can call me Mary if it's more comfortable for you."

"Okay, Mary." Vince liked this woman, from her relaxed slouch to her substantial, unaffected grin, to the pair of tortoise-rimmed eyeglasses nestled in her shaggy, close-cropped graying hair, and her long, slender fingers intertwined on the desk before her. "Basically, what we need is everything you can tell us about the murdered girl. For starters, when did she first start working at this hospital?"

"Lisa had been a student here for just under a year." She removed a manila folder from the top drawer of the desk and handed it to Vince. "When you phoned that you were coming over, I took the liberty of copying her records. All the pertinent information concerning her student nursing at Mercy is here."

"Thanks, this will be a big help." He flipped through the pages in the folder. "Can you tell me whether she was working on the night of the thirteenth or the morning of the fourteenth—the morning she was murdered?"

She scanned an open loose-leaf binder on her desk. "Lisa was working the four to midnight shift on Tuesday, the thirteenth. To the best of my knowledge, she left the hospital on time."

"Did you or anybody else see her that night?" Vince asked.

"I don't recall personally seeing her, but she worked her entire shift, according to our records, so many of the nurses and patients must have seen her and spoken with her in the course of the evening. I could make them available to you, if you think it would help."

"It'd help a lot. If you wouldn't mind, I'd like to question everyone who was on duty with her that night: doctors, nurses, janitorial staff—anyone who might have spoken with her or seen her leave the building. I'd particularly like to talk with any close friends she might have had here at the hospital. Do you think you could make up a list of those individuals for me?"

She nodded. "Certainly. It might take me a few days, though."

"I'll need to talk to them as soon as possible—here or, even better, at the station house. I'd appreciate it if you could arrange to have them call right away and set up an appointment." He handed her one of his cards.

"Do you have any idea who might have done this terrible thing?" she asked, taping the card to the front of the binder.

"That's what we're trying to find out. Do you know whether she was involved romantically? I mean, did she have a boyfriend here at the hospital?"

She shook her head. "None that I was aware of."

"Anyone who didn't like her, somebody who might've been carrying a grudge?"

"I'd have no way of knowing that, but it seems highly unlikely. She was very popular with everyone here."

"Nobody you can think of who might have had a reason to kill her?"

"Of course not." She closed the binder and slid her

glasses down her forehead. "But then, I can't think of a reason for anybody killing anyone else. I didn't know Lisa personally, so I really couldn't say. All I can tell you is that, as her supervisor, I was impressed by her work here at Mercy. All the reports I got were good, and her coworkers seemed genuinely fond of her. I wish I'd had the opportunity of knowing her better, but I've never allowed myself to become too close to any of the students. Personal considerations can often influence judgment." She smiled sadly. "Now I wish I'd been less strident. Lisa Thorpe seems like someone I would have enjoyed knowing."

"I understand." Vince closed his notebook and placed it in his jacket pocket. "Is there anything else you can remember that you feel might be important?"

"If I think of something, you can be sure I'll call the number on this card." She stood and accompanied them to the door. "In the meantime, I'll follow up on the names of everyone who saw Lisa that night. You can expect to hear from them all sometime tomorrow."

"I appreciate your help." Vince offered his hand.

"Anything I can do." Her handshake was firm.

Their next stop was the condominium apartment of Ivor Thorpe, overlooking Central Park in midtown Manhattan. They identified themselves to the guard at the security desk in the lobby, waited until he received affirmation over the telephone, and took the elevator to the penthouse.

"Mr. Thorpe will be with you shortly." An elderly butler greeted them at the door, took their coats, and led them to a spacious room off the main hallway.

"Nice digs," Tommy observed, sitting in one of the white provincial chairs that lined the periphery of the room. "Good to see how the other half lives every now and then."

Vince sat across from Tommy in a matching white love seat and sunk self-consciously into the plush, quilted upholstery. "I don't know how anybody can get comfortable in a place like this," he said in a semi-whisper. "It's more like a museum than a home."

"I couldn't agree more, Detective Crowley." Ivor Thorpe was standing in the doorway. "Sometimes I think decorators feel they're not earning their exorbitant fees unless they make their clients as uncomfortable as possible." He walked across the room and shook both their hands. "If you'll come with me, I think we can find a spot in this mausoleum where we'll all feel more like talking."

Thorpe led them to a smaller room in the rear of the apartment, decorated with homey, comfortable furniture. "This was Lisa's trophy room." He pointed to an abundance of cups and medals carefully displayed on shelves running the length of the wood-paneled room. "Some of these go back to when she was only seven or eight years old." There was a catch in his voice.

"I understand she was a pretty good skater," Vince commented, eyeing the trophies and framed photographs of Lisa Thorpe that filled almost every available square inch of wall space.

"To say Lisa was a pretty good skater is like saying Mikhail Baryshnikov is a pretty good hoofer." Thorpe smiled tolerantly. "No, Lisa was a brilliant skater, a true artist. Had she chosen to pursue it, she might have been the best ever." He went to one of the framed photographs on the wall. "This is Lisa at the Geneva World Championships in 1986. You don't get there by being simply good."

Vince looked at the photograph. "Who's that with her?"

"Her partner," Thorpe replied.

"He have a name?"

"Eric Bruno." Thorpe retrieved several bottles from a portable bar by the room's only window. "Can I fix you gentlemen a drink?"

"Nothing for me," Tommy said.

"Me neither," Vince concurred. "Do you have any idea where this Eric Bruno might be now?"

"Not the slightest, I'm afraid." Thorpe poured himself a short scotch and took a sip. "He and Lisa fell out of touch after the championships. I think she felt it was his fault they didn't take first place."

Vince scribbled the name in his notebook. "I'd like to ask you some questions about your daughter, Mr. Thorpe, if you feel up to answering them."

Thorpe nodded absently. "I've spent most of my time in this room since she's gone . . . not really doing anything, just sitting here, looking at the trophies and the pictures: Lisa as a child, her first competition. She was only seven years old and terribly frightened. I remember how she was sure she would fall and embarrass her mother and myself. I gave her a coin, an English sixpence, and told her it had the magic power to keep her from falling. She won that competition, and after that she took that sixpence into every one she entered. She never lost it. I found it in one of her dressing-table drawers when I went to her apartment yesterday."

"About that, sir—" Vince cleared his throat. "It was a mistake for you to go in there before we had a chance to examine the premises. You might have inadvertently destroyed valuable evidence."

Thorpe stiffened. "I did obtain your commanding officer's permission."

"I understand you did, Mr. Thorpe, but I'm in charge of this investigation. I wish you'd checked with me first."

"I was really very careful about touching things while I was there," Thorpe explained lamely.

"How about those phone tapes, sir? Didn't you think they might have been some help to us?"

"I'm really sorry about that." Thorpe shrugged his shoulders. "Standing there in her empty apartment, I found myself wanting to hear her voice. I can't really explain it. Maybe it was a part of me that wanted to deny she was really gone. At any rate, I tried to play back the message she left on her machine just to hear her one more time, and I'm afraid I made a real bollix of things. The truth is, I've never been very keen about mechanical contraptions, and I must have pushed all the wrong buttons. By the time I was finished, I'd managed to unwind the tape from both spools and leave it lying in a proper mess. I suppose I was embarrassed by the whole thing, so I stuffed them in my pocket, took them home with me, and threw them away."

"You brought them here, sir?" Vince asked. "Is there any chance they might still be around somewhere?"

He shook his head. "I dropped them in the incinerator. I doubt there's anything left of them now."

"About the other things you removed from Lisa's apartment. I understand you left with some photographs."

"They were personal," Thorpe said. "There was nothing about them that could aid you in your investigation."

"Begging your pardon, Mr. Thorpe, but I think you should leave that decision to me—"

"The photographs are of no use to you," Thorpe interrupted. "I hope this is not going to come between our cooperating with one another, but I'm afraid I can't let you see them."

"This is a homicide investigation, Mr. Thorpe," Vince replied evenly. "We're trying to find the person who murdered your daughter. I can get a court order ordering you to give them up."

"I hope it won't come to that," Thorpe responded. "I had hoped you might understand that what I do, I do with my daughter's best interests at heart. Since her mother died almost fifteen years ago, Lisa has been my whole life. I've denied her nothing if I thought it would make her happy, and in return she has given me her absolute love and loyalty. No father could ask for more."

Vince looked nervously at Tommy, then back at Thorpe as he stood transfixed before the array of prized memorials he had erected to his daughter. They were more than mere photographs for Ivor Thorpe, Vince realized, watching the beatific glow that illuminated his face. To Ivor Thorpe, Lisa was still very much alive, here in the shrine he had created for her.

10

T HE DAY TOUR: EIGHT A.M. TO FOUR P.M. GLEASON WAS double-shifting everybody, seven days a week, as long as the Lisa Thorpe killing remained unsolved. It was all bullshit, Vince knew; so did everyone else at the three-seven. Stripped of the ever present TV cameras and hordes of reporters, it was just another homicide. Vince had gained no apparent leads at this point, but there hardly ever were at this stage of a murder investigation. Gleason knew that, so did the reporters, but everybody was feeling pressure from above. The reporters had to ask their questions knowing they would get no answers. The Chiefs had to issue statements to the press and make believe they were on top of the situation. Maintaining a high profile was what it was all about.

Tommy entered the squadroom and chalked in.

"Morning, partner. What's happening?" He pulled a swivel chair up to Vince's desk and began unwrapping a cheese danish he'd brought with him.

"This just came in from BCI." He slid Ricky Miracle's rap sheet across the desk for Tommy to read.

"Not exactly Public Enemy Number One, is he?" Tommy observed, running his forefinger down the sheet. "One-two-three busts for vagrancy . . . one possession of a controlled substance . . . He did some time here, ninety days on a breach of peace back in '86 . . . spent only eight days in the box and was transferred to Bellevue Psychiatric to serve out the remainder—"

"Might be something there," Vince said. "If our guy's a psychotic, the hospital will have records. I got a call into them now. Somebody's supposed to get back to me."

Tommy shook his head. "I dunno. Based on what I see here, this doesn't look like a real violent kind of guy."

"You got anyone better?"

Tommy bit into his danish and washed it down with a swig of hot coffee. "If I had to pick somebody from what we got right now, I'd go with the father."

"Man, that's sick," Leila Turner said. "Fathers don't kill their own daughters."

They both looked at her in amazement. "Where the hell were you posted before they sent you here, Disneyland?" Vince asked.

"You weren't there when we interviewed him," Tommy chimed in. "Outside of having a child fixation, the sonofabitch is going around destroying evidence—"

"You got more shit than a Christmas goose, you know that Ippollito?" Steve Appelbaum observed from the open doorway of the robbery room. "Child fixation? Give me a fuckin' break, willya?"

"Fat lot you'd know about it," Tommy said resentfully. "Your idea of a scientific homicide investigation is to count the victim's fingers and toes so you can tell if it's a humanoid."

"How'd you end up with such a *yutz* for a partner?" Appelbaum asked Vince. "The kid goes to a couple of night-school classes and he thinks he's Isaac Newton. Child fixation . . . shit! Everything's gotta have some deep, hidden meaning for these young punks coming up. Guy gets iced and right away the killer's an anal retentive or some crap like that. When're you schmucks gonna wise up to the fact that people kill other people because they want what the victim's got in his pocket, or they're just plain pissed off at him, or they got nothing better to do that day? There's no big fucking mystery about murder. People been doing murders since time began. When you come right down to it, humans are just basically bloodthirsty, plain and simple."

"That shows how much you know," Tommy huffed. "If you knew anything, you'd know that there are whole societies where murders never happen. Shit, there are societies that won't kill anything because they believe everything on the planet has a soul. The American Indians were like that. Everything was sacred to them—trees, rocks. Hell, they wouldn't cut a blade of grass without asking its permission first."

"Their lawns must've been a mess," Vince commented.

"I don't know why I even bother to try and educate

you ignoramuses." Tommy retreated to his desk and immersed himself in the morning paper.

The telephone on Vince's desk rang and he answered it.

"Vince, it's Jessy."

"Hi. It's good to hear from you." He tried to sound nonchalant, but the sound of her voice jolted him. He hadn't spoken to Jessy since their divorce almost four months ago. "What's up?"

"Not much. I was just wondering whether you planned on coming up to Marion to see the girls over Christmas."

He hadn't thought about it. Seeing his daughters, Katie and Kelly, at Christmas was just something he'd always done, even during the two years he and Jessy had been separated before the divorce. "Sure, what day's Christmas?"

"A week from today, but that's why I'm calling. Dad's taking us all up to Stowe for some skiing and we're leaving Christmas day. If you want to spend any time with the girls, I'd come up a day or two before."

"Uh . . . Christmas Eve, how's that sound?"

"Fine, I guess. You want to stay for dinner?"

"Why not? You know what I like." He could hear the stiffness in his voice. "By the way, what do the girls need?"

"I can't think of a thing."

It was a stupid question. Living in the luxury of their grandfather's Connecticut squirearchy, there was probably very little they did need. "Okay, can you think of anything they might *want*? I can't come up there without bringing them something."

"Just bring yourself. See you Christmas Eve."

Vince had hardly time to realize he had promised to see Connie Christmas Eve when the telephone rang again. It was the dispatcher from 911 Central on the other end. "I have a possible DOA at 3719 East Tremont. Mobile units are already responding."

He listed the time and manner of notification in his notebook and headed for the door. "Grab your coat, partner," he said to Tommy as he passed his desk. "Looks like we got another anal retentive out there running amok."

The drive to 3719 East Tremont Avenue took less than ten minutes. They pulled to the curb behind one of the blue and whites parked haphazardly at the scene, affixed their shields and identification to their jacket lapels, and made their way through a crowd of curious onlookers to the front door. "Isn't this Karp's warehouse?" Tommy asked, leaning backward to read the faded letters on the sign above the entrance. "I wonder if somebody finally gave that cocksucker what he deserves."

They elbowed through the patrolmen, detectives, and CSU personnel who blocked the narrow aisles formed by stacked wooden crates of furniture: refrigerators, air conditioners, television sets—just about everything that could be purchased on time and repossessed. "You smelling what I'm smelling?" Vince asked, quickly covering his nose with a handkerchief to mask the permeating odor of putrefication coming from the rear of the warehouse.

"I read you, partner." Tommy grimaced. "This stiff's been hanging around for a while."

"Whatta you got?" Vince asked Pete Yorio, who was standing outside a clogged crowd of police personnel.

"Somebody nailed Karp." Vince could see him grinning beneath his protective handkerchief. "I'm surprised it took as long as it did."

Vince strained to see through the crowd. "Where did they find the body?"

"Jammed inside a freezer chest," Yorio said through the handkerchief. "Whoever did him musta had trouble getting him in there, so they cut his head off and stuffed it in on top of him."

"Who's first on the scene?" Tommy asked, trying to keep from gagging.

"Two rookies, Thompson and McShane. Walt's in there getting their statements right now."

Vince squeezed through the tightly packed crowd until he reached the spot where M.E. Shem Weisen was bent over the open freezer chest examining Karp's remains. "Jeez." He viewed the huddled, decapitated corpse and shuddered. "Who found the body?" he asked Walt Cuzak, who was standing nearby.

"The stockroom kid at Karp's store—kid named Wally Vincenty. Seems Karp hadn't showed up for a couple of days, so he came around to the warehouse to check things out. I guess he just followed his nose when he got here. Ran out in the street screaming his fucking head off when he found the body. Thompson and McShane were cruising by and almost ran the poor bastard down."

Vince took another tentative glance at the body and spotted Karp's severed head resting in the corner of the freezer chest. "What kind of maniac does something like that?" he wondered aloud.

"I guess somebody who didn't like him a whole helluva lot," Tommy said.

"Shit. That'd include just about everyone in The Bronx. Including most of the members of the three-seven," Walt Cuzak suggested. "Karp wasn't exactly what you'd call an endearing man, if you know what I mean. If it wasn't for the smell around this place, these guys would be dancing in the aisles. Half of them were into him for their life savings."

Vince nodded. "He won't be missed, that's for sure, but it's still an ugly way to go."

They pushed their way back through the mob and emerged onto the sidewalk, where they stood silently for a long time and gulped untainted air, waiting for it to wash the stench of rotting flesh from their nostrils.

Back at the station house, they were greeted by Dog Scarfatti and Cheap Suit, who had managed to squeeze two more metal desks into the already crowded homicide room. "Hey, Crowley, where you guys been?" Scarfatti asked, not bothering to look up from the paperback novel on his lap.

Vince ignored the question and knocked on Gleason's door. "Lieutenant, we gotta talk about those two mutts out there," he said when he was admitted. "It's bad enough that we have to put up with them hanging around, but there's not enough room for us as is. They got the place looking like a Mexican whorehouse—"

Gleason raised a restraining hand. "I know it's an inconvenience, but it's one we're all going to have to put up with until this case is solved. Bitching about it isn't going to help. They're here at the request of the P.C. and here is where they will stay, period. Now, if anybody has any reasonable suggestions as to how we can improve the desk situation out there, I'd be glad to take them under advisement. If not, I hope I've heard the last of this matter."

"Yes, sir . . ." Vince headed for the door.

"By the way, what was that call you just answered?" Gleason asked.

"DOA out on East Tremont. Guy named Karp got himself rubbed out."

Gleason rolled his eyes. "Christ! Just what we need, another murder around here. I need everyone we have on the Thorpe homicide. We have no available manpower to spare for another case."

"Yes sir. You might want to bring that up with Detective Cuzak," Vince said. "He probably thinks this is supposed to be treated like any other homicide."

Gleason stared at Vince glumly. "Who was this Karp guy, anyway?"

"Small-time appliance dealer and shylock," Vince replied. "Nobody important."

Gleason nodded. "Have Cuzak see me when he gets back."

Outside, Vince maneuvered through the jumble of desks, sat heavily in his patched vinyl swivel chair and thumbed through his phone messages: a call from Connie . . . someone named McManus, whom he suspected of being an ex-cop trying to sell him Florida real estate . . . a return call from Bellevue. He lifted the phone and dialed.

"This's Detective Crowley, Thirty-Seventh Precinct, Homicide," he said, identifying himself to the female voice that answered the extention written on the message. "I'm looking for information on a former patient—a transfer from Riker's Island named Ricardo Mirable, aka Ricky Miracle—"

"Yes, Detective. I have his admittance paperwork in front of me. Just what is it you want to know?" she asked.

"Mainly, why he was transferred to a psychiatric facility," Vince said. "He's a suspect in a homicide investigation, and it would be a big help if we knew whether he had any major mental problems."

There was a long silence on the other end. "Well, normally I wouldn't be able to release that information to you without written authorization. Our psych records are kept private to protect our patients' rights—"

"Maybe you didn't understand," Vince broke in. "We're talking about a suspected murderer here. I'm not really interested in protecting his rights at this point."

"Well, this hospital has to be," she said icily. "Now, if

you'll let me finish . . . Mr. Mirable was transferred because he was found to be severely claustrophobic and was unable to complete the duration of his sentence in jail. I can tell you that because we acted in a purely custodial capacity in this case."

"What'd he do, flip out in his cell?"

"I'm afraid you'll have to subpoena his records if you want more than I've already told you."

"What'd you get on him?" Tommy asked when he hung up.

"Not much. He's claustrophobic, probably freaked out being cooped up in a cell, so they let him finish out his sentence in a hospital ward. She couldn't tell me more because she was worried about protecting his rights."

"What about Lisa Thorpe's rights?" Tommy groaned.

Vince shrugged. "What can I tell you? Life is unfair."

"Life is a hand-job," Tommy muttered.

"Maybe so." Vince lifted the receiver and dialed Connie. "Hi babe, what's cooking?"

"I'm updating my calendar," she said breezily. "And I wanted to make sure we were still on for Christmas Eve."

11

POLICE DEPARTMENT

CITY OF NEW YORK

From: Commanding Officer 37th Precinct Detective
Unit
To: Police Jurisdiction Concerned.
Subj: Request for Field Information

1. Attached is a photograph of a suspect in a homicide being investigated by this command.

2. It is requested that any field information possessed by you re the possible location of this individual be forwarded to this command.

3. DESCRIPTION: Male, white, possible Hispanic
descent, 5 ft. 6½ in., 19 yrs., slender build,
hair, dark brown to black. Subject has no per-
manent address and is known to frequent abandoned buildings and parks. Subject has no license
to operate a motor vehicle and would likely travel
on foot.

4. USE CAUTION IN APPREHENDING THIS
INDIVIDUAL.

5. Matter carried under 61# 4548, case #2374. Det.
V. Crowley & T. Ippollito assigned.

7. Please telephone any pertinent information to the 37 P.D.U. at (212) 920-3515, 16, or 17.

Lt. John Gleason
Commanding Officer

Vince studied the alert, handsome face of Ricky Miracle accompanying the flyer. Police photographs were not notoriously flattering, but even in the stiff, unsmiling front and side views of the mug shots, he could see what seemed to be an intelligent bearing, not at all what he was accustomed to seeing in vagrants and street scum.

Kids who lived on the streets as long as Ricky usually fell apart in the gaps. The elasticity of youth was soon gone from their faces, replaced with a kind of lacquered, unblinking numbness. Their eyes stared into the camera lens from hollow sockets made languid and insensitive by alcohol and drugs. They were pinched by sleeping on steam vents and park benches and standing alone on cold, windswept corners panhandling nickels and dimes . . . from selling their shriveled bodies to aging perverts who flogged them and pissed on them and threw them back out into the freezing streets when they'd worn them out. The face that Vince saw in Ricky Miracle's mug shot had none of that world-weary exhaustion.

Vince folded the flyer, placed it in his jacket pocket, and returned to the interview room, where Tommy, Street Crime, and Leila Turner were processing the last of more than twenty hospital employees who had volunteered to come in and be questioned.

"How goes it?" he asked Tommy, who was sorting through his paperwork in the outside hall.

"Just finished up with the last of them," Tommy said. "But I could've quit after the first two or three. Everybody's got the same story. She did her job the night of the murder and left alone at quitting time. Nothing unusual, everything by the book."

"Did you find anyone who might've had a resentment against her?"

"You gotta be kidding." Tommy leafed through the pages. " 'Lisa was the most giving person I ever met' . . . 'She had a kind of inner beauty' . . . 'All the patients and nurses loved Lisa' . . . They're all like that. I mean, this chick had to be unreal. They just don't make people like her anymore."

"Only the good die young," Vince said somberly.

"If it wasn't so goddamn corny, I'd have to agree with you; at least in her case."

"Good thing a slime like Karp gets himself clipped every now and then. Keeps us from getting too soupy and sentimental."

"Speaking of Karp, what's happening with that?" Tommy asked.

"Technically, Pete and Walt are assigned, but Gleason told them to shitcan it, at least until this Thorpe thing is wrapped up."

They maneuvered through the labyrinth of desks in the homicide room. "The phone company came through with a list of all Lisa Thorpe's outgoing calls for the month of December." Vince handed a computer printout to Tommy. "I also asked them to run one on Ivor Thorpe."

"Good idea, but don't be surprised if they refuse to cooperate. The way things are, Thorpe's probably one of their biggest stockholders." Tommy scanned the list. "You see anything interesting here?"

"Not offhand," Vince said. "Get Turner and Street Crime to run them down when they're finished interviewing. You and me are going out to the island."

They checked out a unit and drove across the Triborough Bridge toward Queens. "Funny how that works out," Tommy mused, easing onto the Van Wyck Expressway. "Here we got two murders in the same precinct. One victim is loved by everybody and the other victim is hated by everybody. Kinda makes you wonder, doesn't it?"

"About what?"

"I dunno . . . life, mortality, shit like that. You wonder about what happens now. Do they both get what's coming to them? Take heaven and hell. I mean, does the Thorpe kid take the elevator upstairs while that Karp motherfucker deep-fries in the netherworld?"

"*You* wonder," Vince said. "That stuff just confuses me."

"You know, sometimes I'm not even sure there is a heaven," Tommy went on. "Get this. Suppose all the good and unselfish people go to heaven, right? Wouldn't they spend all their time feeling sorry for the poor bastards in hell, being they're so unselfish and all?"

"You never stop, do you?"

"Hey man, you have to think about this shit." Tommy stopped the car in front of the Bayshore Ice Rink. "There's gotta be more going on than just what we see. The Bronx isn't what it's all about, Vince. New York City isn't the Cosmos, if you catch my drift. What we got here is just the tit of the iceberg."

Vince bit his lip and led them into the ice rink. "We're looking for Herman Feld," he told the attendant at the skate-rental desk.

"Upstairs. First door on your right."

They followed the directions and knocked on the rink supervisor's door. "I'm Detective Crowley, Bronx Homicide Division. This's Detective Ippollito," Vince told the balding, middle-aged man who admitted them. "We'd like to ask you a few questions about Lisa Thorpe."

"I've been expecting you." Herman Feld ushered them into his office. "I'm not sure how I can assist you, but I'll tell you whatever I can."

"You were Lisa Thorpe's skating coach, correct?" Vince asked, his pencil poised above his notebook.

"Oh yes." Feld beamed. "For almost all of her career." He drew back a curtain, revealing a window in the office wall. "Do you see those skaters down there?" He pointed to a group of eight or ten youngsters practicing intricate skating maneuvers on the ice below. "Those are my pupils: young, dedicated, some of them even quite talented. I tell them what I know. They practice. Maybe they enter some local competitions and win an award or two. But they are not champions, none of them. Lisa Thorpe was a champion. The only one I ever trained."

"I see. I take it that you and her got along pretty well, then."

"I loved her," Feld said flatly. "She was an emerging flower who brought beauty into my life every day. Sometimes I would forget I was her coach and just sit watching her go through her routines, hypnotized by the absolute grace and effortlessness of her skating. A teacher is blessed to have just one such pupil in his lifetime, Detective. I never expect to have another like her."

"I understand she had a partner, Eric Bruno. What can you tell me about him?" Vince asked.

Feld shook his head. "Not too much, I'm afraid. You see, I coached Lisa as an individual skater. When she decided to take a partner, they trained under his coach, Egon Bosticz."

"Can you spell that for me?"

"I'm afraid that won't do you much good. Bosticz died several months ago. A pulmonary deficiency, I think, but I'm not really sure. He and I were not what you would call close."

Vince looked puzzled. "Let me get this straight, Mr. Feld. You're telling me that you taught Lisa Thorpe how to become a champion, and then she dumped you for another coach?"

Feld smiled. "Not quite. You see, Lisa was a champion before she ever came to me; with a champion's drive and singleminded dedication. Nobody can create a champion. That, my friend, is a state of mind. All a coach can do is teach technique, and hope. One day it became clear to Lisa that world-class competition in pairs skating was softer than in individual skating, and that she had a much better opportunity of winning a championship in that discipline. So she simply went for it. I wasn't really surprised."

"Not even a little hurt, a little resentful, maybe?" Vince asked skeptically.

"Perhaps at first, but I got over it. You have to understand about champions; they are not like ordinary people, like you and me. Lisa was, above all, competitive. The competition was all that mattered. If winning meant striking a bargain with the devil, she would certainly have done so."

"Doesn't that seem a little cold-blooded?" Vince asked.

"Not if you understand the nature of the champion. Not if you understand that winning is the absolute goal, and any skater who allows friendship or sentiment or life itself to interfere with that goal lacks what it takes to win." He went to his desk and extracted several video-cassettes from the top drawer. "Can I show you gentlemen something?"

Vince looked at Tommy and shrugged. "Why not?"

Feld inserted one of the cassettes into a VCR and

activated the tape. "This is Lisa and her partner at a competition in Paris, just prior to the World Championships in Geneva." He joined Vince and Tommy as the TV screen came alive.

"Notice how she radiates confidence," he said proudly as the two skaters began to glide rhythmically across the shimmering ice. "She is a much stronger skater than he is, but he is able to hide most of his deficiencies behind her brilliance." Feld stood, entranced, as her partner lifted Lisa high over his head. "See the arch of her back, the hand position . . . the graceful line she creates." The screen was alive for him, the competition still taking place.

"Watch the landing," Feld urged them as the partners skated face-to-face for a moment before he lifted and threw her, spinning in the air, to a perfect touch-down. "Lisa rarely missed, and even when she did, she covered so beautifully the judges thought she was innovating." Feld smiled and nodded to himself. "This is called 'mirror skating,' " he explained as the skaters drifted apart to opposite ends of the arena, executing identical movements to the music. They seemed to be voiceless lovers separated by a void. "Notice her face, her eyes," Feld instructed them. "She is losing him now and she feels the deepest torment. Great skating is also great acting, and Lisa was a great actress."

The skaters came together in a final, wrenching reunion. Then she fell away like a limp rag doll: lifeless, clutching his outwardly extended hand. "This is the finale," Feld said reverently. "The Death Spiral." Vince and Tommy watched as her prostrate body arched, the delicate curve of her neck extended backward seemingly beyond its capacity, her long brown hair brushing the spinning surface of the ice. "And so she dies . . ." Feld walked slowly to the VCR and stopped the tape. There were tears in his eyes.

"I don't get it," Tommy said when they were back in the car, heading for The Bronx. "Unless I missed something in there, she fucked him over pretty good. I mean, the guy taught her everything she knew, and she blew him away like a turd. And the poor sap still loves her ass. How do you explain a thing like that? You tell me how she can shit all over somebody and still make them love her? What the hell did this babe have?"

12

"EVERYONE INSIDE, PRONTO!" JOHN GLEASON STOOD in his office doorway and glared into the homicide room. "And bring your files with you. I want to go over every case we're carrying."

"We oughta leave somebody out here to man the phones," Snuffy Quade suggested.

Gleason looked nervously at Leila Turner and felt his upper lip beginning to perspire. "Man the phones," he said abruptly. It was better she stay outside anyway, he thought.

Vince retrieved Lisa Thorpe's file from his bottom drawer, checked to make sure all pertinent data was enclosed, and entered Gleason's office with the others. "Can't we do this without these slugs, sir?" He indicated the Dog and Cheap Suit, who were holding up the back wall.

"Hey, you don't want us, just say the word, Lieutenant," Scarfatti said, making no attempt to sound sincere. "We don't wanna stay where we ain't wanted."

Gleason hesitated. Whatever he did was going right upstairs. "Stay where you are," he said finally. "And the next wiseguy who opens his trap without being asked a direct question goes on report . . . is that clear?" He looked directly at Vince. "Then we can get down to the business at hand." He walked around his desk and sat. "Let's start with you, Crowley. Give me the latest update on the Thorpe homicide."

Vince opened the folder. "There were two wounds on the body," he began. "A nonlethal wound in the throat that Forensics says was caused when she was stabbed with one of those pointy-handled combs women use. The second wound severed her jugular vein, causing her to bleed to death. They can't prove it, but they're pretty

81

sure her neck was sliced open by a piece of glass from a mirror that shattered during the struggle that preceded her death."

"What's that mean, they're not sure?" Gleason demanded.

"Just that. Ninety percent of the glass on the floor was covered with blood, so it was impossible to dust it for prints. They only found four readable prints in the whole room and those were partials. We think one of the fingerprints belonged to the victim, but BCI came up empty on the others—"

"Meaning?" Gleason interrupted.

Vince shrugged. "Meaning we don't know who they belong to."

"Did it occur to you that they might have been left by whoever killed her?"

"Of course it did, but we don't know that for sure."

"You're telling me it's possible the murderer engaged in a wild, frenzied struggle with the deceased and didn't leave any prints?"

Vince searched the room for support. Everyone was looking somewhere else. "What I'm saying is that if any of the prints belong to the murderer, they're not on record at BCI."

"Well, why didn't you say that in the first place?" Gleason asked irritably.

"I guess I just lost my head." He could feel the muscles in his neck beginning to knot.

"Do you think it might be remotely possible that those prints belong to a vagrant named Ricardo Mirable?" Gleason went on.

"Ricardo Mirable?"

"You're surprised I should know about Ricardo Mirable?" Gleason boomed. "Of course, it must come as a shock to you that your commanding officer should know what every goddamn newspaper in this *city* knows!" His voice shook. "It didn't occur to any of you to let me in on the fact that we have a suspect in this case, did it? I have to read it in the fucking *New York Post*!"

Everybody shuffled uneasily.

"Allow me to elucidate for you . . ." Gleason lifted a copy of the paper from his desk and began to read:

" 'The victim, daughter of well-known publisher, Ivor Thorpe, had attended Woodcrest College in Tarrytown, New York, while she was preparing for the world pairs figure skating finals in Geneva, Switzerland. Despite a loss in the championships, she eschewed offers of a professional career to enter the religious order of the Little Sisters of Charity, in Greenwich, Connecticut, where she remained a novice until leaving to become a student nurse at Mercy Hospital.

" 'Police now believe' "—Gleason paused and looked around the room—"'Everybody listen real good to this: 'Police now believe that a homeless man named Ricardo Mirable, known to residents of the area, may somehow be linked to the gruesome slaying, and have initiated a city-wide manhunt.' " He held the paper aloft, revealing the frontal mug shot of Ricky Miracle emblazoned on the first page. "You wanta tell me how this happened?" he shrieked. "You wanta tell me how we can have a fucking city-wide manhunt going on when I don't even know about it? Who the hell is this Ricardo Mirable and why don't we have him in custody?" He let the paper fall limply to the desk.

Silence. "I think it was all in the DD-5s, Lieutenant," Vince said after an awkward pause. "I know *I* listed him as a possible suspect."

Gleason turned ashen. "That's part of the trouble around this place," he hissed through clenched teeth. "Nobody communicates with anybody else. If I want to know anything, I have to go rummaging through a lot of forms, instead of hearing it directly from the men in my command." He stood and walked to the front of the desk. "Well, that's all going to change, starting right now. From here on in, we have daily briefings on everything that's going down. Anybody have any trouble with that?"

Again silence.

"Okay . . ." He was trying to keep from trembling. "What else is current here?"

"I've got the Karp homicide," Walt Cuzak said.

"I told you I don't want to hear about the Karp homicide!"

"It's a current case, sir—"

"It's a shit case!" Gleason bellowed. "Karp was a

piece of shit who lived a shit life and was probably murdered by someone just as shitty as he was. Lisa Thorpe was a fucking *nun*, for chrissakes!"

That much, at least, was news to Vince. Nobody he'd questioned had ever said a word about it, not even her father.

"Okay, from here on in, this whole command is going to be under a lot of pressure to find this Mirable character. What kind of leads do we have?" Gleason asked.

"Not much yet, sir," Vince answered hesitantly. "The flyer just went out this morning."

Gleason took a deep breath and exhaled it loudly. "I want clearance, and I want it quickly. The media's going to be looking for some answers, and I plan to tell them we're thirty seconds away from arresting this scumbag and charging him with murder one. Is that clear?"

"Begging the Lieutenant's pardon, but that might be a mistake at this point," Vince said. "Mirable's wanted for questioning. We really don't have anything on him except that he was seen in the area. I don't see any way we have enough to make a murder charge stick."

"I'll be the judge of that. You just do what you're paid to do and bring the sonofabitch in. No more excuses; I want him in custody now! Any questions?"

Some muffled throat clearing. A jingling of pocket change.

"In that case, you're all dismissed." Gleason turned his back on them until the office was cleared.

"Any phone messages?" Tommy asked Leila Turner.

"Here, sort them out for yourself!" She dumped the messages in a narrow aisle between the clutter of desks and headed for the door. "I'm going for coffee."

"What's eating her?" Snuffy asked, retrieving the scattered slips of paper. "She on the rag or something?"

"She's probably pissed off about being left out of things," Vince said.

"Nobody leaves her out of anything," Walt Cuzak protested. "You know, it's not like we requisitioned a lady cop up here or anything. Somebody's gotta be low man on the totem pole, and the last time I looked she was still the new kid on the block. Rookies answer phones and go for danish. So what else is new?"

"If you ask my opinion, I'll bet her problem is she's never been porked properly," Scarfatti said. "A little dose of sizzling tube steak'd fix her right up, guaranteed."

"You volunteering for that duty, Dog?" Vince asked. "Or are you just shooting your mouth off as usual?"

"I like my meat white," Scarfatti sneered. "How about you, Vargas?" he asked Street Crime. "Why don't you give your black sister a good porking for the sake of the unit?"

"You sleazy, honky bastard!" Street Crime lunged toward Scarfatti, but Vince blocked his way.

"Stay cool, man." Vince eased him into his seat. "He's an ass-wipe, Hector, not worth the aggravation. Save your energy for something that deserves it."

"Lemmee tell you something, slimeball," Vince said to Scarfatti, who had nonchalantly resumed reading his paperback novel. "One of these days, you're gonna be walking past a dark alley, and some dude's gonna pull you in and punch your ticket for good. I'd be willing to put up odds right now that whoever does it will be one of New York's finest." He grabbed his coat and headed for the door. "Anybody wants me, I'm out doing a little Christmas shopping."

Downstairs, he encountered a red-eyed Leila Turner heading back to the squad room. "I thought you were going for coffee," he said.

"What's the use? It'll still be the same when I get back."

"I'm buying," he offered.

She eyed him curiously. "You know, I can't really figure you out, Crowley. You're one of the good old boys up there, that's for sure, but you don't seem as threatened by me as the rest of them. I get the feeling you're more frightened by new ideas than you are by women detectives."

"Coffee?" he said evenly.

She shrugged. "Sure . . . why not?"

Vince drove to the Gold Star Diner and led her to a booth in the rear. "Now, what new ideas am I supposed to be so afraid of?" he asked when they were seated.

"Oh, you know, all you veterans are the same . . ." She scanned the menu. "Everything's okay as long as it's the same way it was when you were back at the academy.

Somebody comes along with a new way of doing things and you let up a howl."

"You mad at all veterans or just the ones at the three-seven?" he asked.

She shrugged. "Hell, I don't know. I guess I'm just mad."

"That they push you around up there?"

"Maybe," she admitted. Vince started to reply, but she held up her hand. "Don't tell me. All rookies get the same treatment. But all rookies aren't women and all rookies aren't black. Maybe that's not what it's all about, but I learned early on to keep my head down on the firing range. It doesn't help much to know they weren't aiming at you when you're lying there with a bullet upside your black head."

He allowed himself a smile. "I won't insult you by telling you it's all in your head, or even that I understand what you're going through. All I can say is you look to me like someone who can take care of herself. You know, we get guys up here who are real dim bulbs, if you know what I mean. They put in the time, grab the pension, and run. You don't seem like that kind of person to me. Now, the way I see it, you can go on being cute and vulnerable, or you can get on with the business of becoming a good detective."

"Filing affidavits?" she interrupted him. "Checking telephone logs, taking messages?"

"That's all part of it. We all had to do it."

Leila nodded. "I guess I just want it all, Crowley. I want to be asked to participate in the big cases. I don't want to learn about homicide investigation by eavesdropping on your conversations."

"So participate," Vince said. "Don't sit around waiting for it to happen. Make it happen. Go to Gleason and tell him you want to be assigned to a case."

"You gotta be kidding." She shook her head. "He'll throw me out of his office."

"You're not gonna know unless you try. Like I said, you look like someone who can take care of herself."

"You're serious, aren't you?"

"Tell him you want the Karp homicide. Cuzak and Yorio are assigned, but they're up to their asses in the

Thorpe case. Tell him you want Karp and tell him you want a young white stud you can boss around for a partner."

She laughed for the first time that afternoon. "I just might do that, Crowley." She flashed a dazzling row of even white teeth. "I just might do that."

13

"CADILLAC" TOURNEAU SPOTTED VINCE AND TOMMY entering the Port-au-Prince restaurant, doused his reefer in the water glass on the table, and shoved the soggy roach in his pants pocket. "Crowley . . ." He rose halfway from the table. "Good to see you, *mon ami.*"

"I'll bet it is, Cadillac." Vince slid into the booth across from him, making room for Tommy on the outside.

"What brings you up to this neighborhood?" the Cadillac man asked casually.

"Just making the rounds. What's that garbage you're eating?"

Cadillac grinned. "*Poulet,* with *pois ac duriz colles.* Best in the city, you know."

"Shit!" Tommy made a face. "They don't serve no 'poo-lay' in this cesspool. That's goat if I ever saw it."

"It's easy to see your partner is a food afficionado," Cadillac said sourly. "Where does he get his expertise, from the Cheeseburger-of-the-Month Club?"

Tommy began to speak, but Vince poked him in the ribs. "So how's business, Cadillac?" he asked.

"*Comme çi, comme ça,*" Cadillac replied. "You really ought to try some of this, Crowley. Expand your gastronomical horizons, as it were."

"You do much business the night of the thirteenth?" Vince asked.

Cadillac shrugged. "Business is off. The onset of winter, you know."

"Yeah, well, that was a mild night. The way I figure it, you musta had close to a dozen whores out on the street that night. That jibe with your figures?"

Cadillac spread his open palms skyward, revealing a profusion of heavy gold rings and chains. "Who keeps figures? All I can say is, business has been bad all over. If things stay the way they are, I may have to abandon the profession altogether. Get into something less speculative."

"Excuse me if I don't break down bawling right here at the table, Cadillac, but you got to understand that us cops don't always relate one hundred percent with the problems of you big businessmen. Now, if we can get back to the night of the thirteenth, would you say you were rotating three or four girls in and out of the Shangri-la Motel that night? Would you agree that's a reasonable figure?"

"Just what is it you're after, Crowley?"

"Don't tell me you haven't heard about the Lisa Thorpe killing. It's been in all the papers."

"So what do I have to do with that?"

"Maybe nothing," Vince allowed. "But it's a pretty good bet that one or more of your girls saw or heard something while all that stuff was going down."

"Not necessarily," Cadillac protested.

"Necessarily," Vince corrected him. "Let's not hump each other around anymore than we have to, okay? We're talking about whores who can hear a police radio from a half a mile away. Don't tell me nobody heard a girl screaming for her life out there."

"Perhaps what you say is true . . ." Cadillac stirred the food in his plate with his fork. "But I wasn't there, so I would have no way of knowing." He took a mouthful.

Vince nodded, leaned back in the booth. "I guess it's time for another hooker sweep," he said to Tommy. "You know, we gotta keep the neighborhood safe from these undesirable elements. Maybe this time we should detain them as material witnesses in a homicide investigation. That should keep them off the streets for two, three days."

"What do you want from me?" Cadillac droned. "I thought you already knew who did it. What about that Ricardo Mirable I read about?"

"Information." Vince leaned across the table and whispered conspiratorially, "What I want is for you and me to come to an understanding. I get the information I'm looking for and you get to stay in business. That fair enough?"

"Why don't you just ask them yourself? You know where they are."

Vince grinned. "They're not as emotionally committed to me as they are to you."

Cadillac pushed his plate away and peeled a fifty-dollar bill from his wallet. "I'll find out what I can." He stood to leave.

"Soon," Vince urged. "Christmas is coming and I need a present I can put on my CO's desk, *comprende vous*?"

"Why don't you ask me about the Karp killing?" Cadillac smiled, flipping the fifty onto the table. "I can give you a couple of hundred guys who could have done that one."

"Tell me something I don't already know." Vince nudged Tommy and squeezed out of the booth. "Relax and finish smoking your joint. We were just leaving."

Back in the car, they headed for the East Bronx and the Homeless Men's Shelter. "Were you serious about giving Gleason a Christmas present?" Tommy asked.

Vince arched an eyebrow. "You're shitting me, right?"

"I dunno. The guy's a stale fart, but he *is* the commander. Maybe a present would mellow him a little bit."

"I got bigger problems than John Gleason," Vince said. "Christmas is in four days and I haven't bought anything for anybody. Katie and Kelly don't need a goddamn thing. Whatever I bring them, they'll tell me how much they love it, then they'll shove it in some drawer after I'm gone and never look at it again."

"Get them a gift certificate," Tommy suggested. "Kids like to pick out their own shit."

"That's not a bad idea. But then I got Connie. She's pissed off at me because I broke our date for Christmas Eve, even though she says she's not. I want to get her something real special."

"Gift certificate's the ticket," Tommy said.

"Weren't you listening, for chrissakes? I said something special. What the hell's special about a gift certificate?"

Tommy shrugged. "There's gift certificates and there's gift certificates, if you know what I'm saying. I didn't mean for you to give her one from Ike's Auto Parts. A nice fur, some jewelry . . ."

"You're talking to a cop, remember?"

"So give her a belt."

"I'm in enough trouble already." Vince laughed.

Tommy double-parked the car in front of the Homeless Men's Shelter on Throgg's Neck Expressway and

followed Vince inside. "Alex Guzman around?" Vince
asked the bored youth who met them at the front desk.

"Over here, Detective Crowley!" Guzman shouted at
them from the stairs where he was repairing a broken
bannister.

"Good to see you again." Vince shook Guzman's hand
and joined him on the staircase. "You remember Detective Ippollito . . ."

"So what can I do for you gentlemen?" Guzman laid
down his tools and sat against the wall.

"It's about Ricardo Mirable, Ricky Miracle they call
him on the street."

"I know Ricky," Guzman said. "And I read you were
looking for him in connection with this Thorpe killing.
All I can say is, you've got the wrong man. Ricky Miracle
is no more capable of killing somebody than I am."

"He's not being accused of anything, Mr. Guzman. We
have information that he was in the area at the time of
the murder, and we'd just like to ask him some questions," Vince explained. "Maybe he saw something that
could be of help to us. Can you tell me if he's staying
here now?"

"I haven't seen him in several weeks."

"Does he ever stay here?" Vince asked.

Guzman nodded. "Sometimes he comes for the mid-
day hot meal, but he never sleeps here unless it's to take
a nap in front of the TV set. Ricky likes the wide open
spaces. I'm afraid our rooms make him feel like a
prisoner."

"You have any idea where he might be now?"

"He could be anywhere." Guzman shrugged. "But I
have a feeling he's probably hiding out right now. Ricky's
not stupid, you know. He can read the papers, too."

"If he's not guilty he has nothing to be afraid of,"
Vince said. "He could turn himself in and clear himself
once and for all. We can't hold an innocent man."

Guzman studied Vince's face. "I'm not sure whether
you really believe that yourself, Detective Crowley, but
you can be sure Ricky Miracle doesn't. Try telling a
homeless person that they'll get justice from the police,
and they'll laugh in your face. All people like Ricky know
about the law is that it makes their lives more miserable
than they already are. With apologies to you and Detective Ippollito, the police treat the homeless like they're

enemies of society. They're pushed and shoved and bullied and ridiculed and made to feel like they're less than human. Asking any street person to turn himself in and seek justice under the law is like inviting a turkey to Thanksgiving dinner."

The attack caught Vince off guard. "I'm not here to defend myself," he said finally. "But I don't think you know me well enough to make that kind of charge. Now either you know where I can find Ricky Miracle or you don't . . . This time without the lecture, if you don't mind."

"I don't know where he is," Guzman said. "I'd tell you if I did. I'm sorry if I got a little heated there. I know you're not the problem. It's just that working like I do, with the poor and disenfranchised of this city, I sometimes become cynical and suspicious. Maybe you do care, and maybe I care, but we're an infinitessimal minority. Most people couldn't care less about the poor and the homeless, and that, sadly, does include most members of your department."

"I can't speak for the rest of the department. All I can tell you is that Ricardo Mirable is wanted for questioning in connection with a homicide, and if you're shielding him in any way, you could be guilty of complicity in a capital crime. I hope that's not the case because I've always respected the work you do here and I'd hate to have to pull you off the streets where you're doing so much good." He handed Guzman one of his cards. "So you'll call if you see him or hear anything about him, okay?"

"Sure I'll call." Guzman stuffed the card in his hip pocket. "But I'm telling you, you have the wrong man. Ricky's got a lot of problems, but violence isn't one of them. If anything, he's a classic passive personality, content to live what you and I would consider an unbearable existence as long as nobody bothers him. All he wants out of life is enough food to keep from starving, enough cheap wine to keep from shaking apart, and a place where he'll be left alone. I've known Ricky Miracle for a lot of years, and I'd be willing to stake a year's salary that he's incapable of committing a violent crime."

Vince smiled. "I don't know what they're paying social workers these days, but if it's anything like what cops get I'd say that's not much of a bet."

"Good point," Guzman conceded. "I'll let you know if I hear anything."

Outside, Tommy made a U-turn in the middle of the block and headed back toward the precinct. "You know, I gotta agree with him about this Ricky Miracle guy. He's definitely a classic passive personality, no doubt about it."

"You know, maybe if I got her a nightgown . . . That's something really personal, something she wouldn't get except from somebody close to her."

"You weren't listening to a thing I said, were you?" Tommy sounded wounded.

"Sure, I was listening. You said Ricky Miracle was a classic passive personality."

"Everything points to it," Tommy went on. "Passives avoid conflict, never initiate it."

"Maybe some underwear . . ."

14

In the bleak midwinter
Frosty wind made moan,
Earth stood hard as iron,
Water like a stone . . .

What started as a few random snowflakes in the City had turned into a full-fledged snowstorm by the time Vince reached the Connecticut line. The residue of fallen slush that had turned brown and sooty in The Bronx remained a blanket of hard-packed white as he drove through the outskirts of Marion. It banked against the bleak, mottled foothills, beside the road, ascending in swirls driven by the wind.

Snow had fallen
snow on snow . . .

He hunched forward instinctively in the front seat of the car, squinting through streaks of ice that resisted the incessant sweep of the windshield wiper. He searched for familiar landmarks through the spindrift of the storm: the sawmill, Main Street, and the windswept village green. An uninhabited gazebo stood forlornly among the circling gusts.

Snow on snow . . .

The words were from a poem he had heard somewhere, by a poet he couldn't remember—Yeats? Frost? Rossetti? It was Rossetti, he decided, surprised at himself for knowing. He was surprised he even remembered the poem. He'd learned it in school, or maybe Billy Whalen had recited it for him years ago, he thought. Perhaps he'd read it on his own. That had been surprising,

94

that he had been interested enough to pick up a book of poems and actually read it. Stranger still, he even enjoyed them. It was a pastime he'd only recently begun experimenting with.

It had begun soon after Billy's death, when he'd been unable to understand the grief he felt. Billy had been his only partner for most of his career, his only real friend and confidant. After Billy was shot, even during the years he had been a vegetable in the hospital, Vince had been able to maintain the fiction that his partner still had a chance. The day Billy died ended the self-deception. Vince wandered around in a daze, unable to silence the echo of Billy quoting poetry to him when they were on duty: Tennyson and Masefield and D. H. Lawrence. The couplets and quatrains reverberated in his subconscious, as they had once done in the cruising squad car, soothing him, cleansing him like the simple prayers he remembered from his childhood.

One day he had found himself in the poetry section of the Public Library, fumbling among the volumes on the shelves. He had selected a few at random, brought them home under the cover of darkness, and read them in secret. Cops didn't read poetry, much less enjoy it. It was like wearing high heels to work.

> *In the bleak midwinter*
> *Long ago . . .*

Maybe it was a way of keeping Billy alive in his mind, he thought as he maneuvered the icy streets toward Dennis Sloan's mansion on the outskirts of town. Maybe he was conning himself into believing he could make himself over into what Billy had always told him he was capable of being. He did know that sometimes the rhythms lingered. Sometimes he found himself absorbed by a rhyme scheme in the middle of utter chaos at the precinct. Why not? If Walt Cuzak could meditate to obliterate John Gleason's self-serving harangues, Vince could lose himself in a secret symmetry of words . . . as long as the secret didn't get out.

> *. . . Snow on snow,*
> *snow on snow . . .*

He turned into the mile-long driveway leading to the house, flanked as far as he could see by rows of naked elms. Now was the moment of truth, he thought as the trees sped by the car window like sentries shivering in the icy wind, the moment he had been dreading since he and Jessy had split four months ago. He hadn't seen the girls since then, had spoken to them only once or twice on the telephone. How would they react to the idea that they were no longer a family? he wondered. Even during the separation, both of them had held onto the belief that it was temporary, an unfortunate mistake they would be able to straighten out sooner or later. Another fiction. Life was loaded with them.

Katie would take it hardest, he guessed. She was younger and more naive. Kelly was twenty, or was it twenty-one? It was hard to keep track. Anyway, she had a life of her own. She would graduate from college next spring, probably marry a Preppie or a Yuppie and settle down to a life of moneyed ease in the heart of the suburbs. She was self-involved enough to let him off the hook, and that was fine with him.

But Katie was still incomplete, still trying to find out where she belonged. She had made a big deal about the divorce because she made a big deal about almost everything. Even here, sheltered in the safe, patrician splendor of Marion, Connecticut, she saw a world that frightened and confused her. Vince wished he'd been able to help her with that, but he had only succeeded in adding to her confusion. She still loved him, he knew, but it was an angry and suspicious kind of love.

"Hurry, up, you're letting the snow in!" Jessy met him at the door and hustled him inside. "God, how did you make it in this weather?"

"No problem. How're you doing?" He removed his coat and handed it to her.

"About as well as can be expected." She stepped out of the shadows and kissed him lightly on the cheek. "How about you?"

"Hanging in there." Even in the flat light of the hallway, Jessy's upturned face radiated the kind of thoroughbred charm that had attracted him to her so many years ago. Comparisons with Connie were inevitable, he realized, following her through the hall toward Dennis Sloan's private study. Where Jessy's beauty was haughty and aristocratic, Connie's was down-to-earth. Jessy's flawless skin, perfectly coiffeured wheat-colored hair, the slender arching curve of her lips, suggested afternoon garden parties and debutante cotillions. She was a never-aging testament to correct genes and breeding.

Connie was younger, with fewer visual assets to begin with, but she had a special kind of physical energy and untutored freshness that set people at ease. There was a lilt to Connie, a buoyant, undisciplined simplicity that felt somehow warmer than Jessy's self-contained grandeur. Still, Jessy was a magnificent woman, Vince thought. He was still astonished that she had ever married him in the first place.

"You could probably use a stiff scotch after that trip," Jessy said, stepping behind the walnut-paneled bar. "Three fingers or four?"

He eyed her uncertainly.

"Don't worry." Jessy spotted his discomfort. "Nothing stronger than Diet Pepsi for me. I'm still sober, still going to AA meetings." She poured a generous portion of scotch into a glass and handed it across the bar. "As a matter of fact, I'm actually getting to enjoy it, sort of. At least the part about waking up without a hangover."

"To sobriety." Vince toasted her and took a sip of the scotch. "Where are the girls?"

She grimaced. "Don't ask, Vince. It's been a positive nightmare."

"Everything okay?"

"Oh yes, everybody's fine," she reassured him. "It's just that this storm has messed everything up. Kelly's snowed in up at school, and Katie phoned from a Howard Johnson's motel in Hartford. Nothing's moving north of here, so she's spending the night there."

Vince shrugged. "So I guess that leaves the three of us, you, me, and your old man—"

"Wrong. Dad wasn't planning to come up until tomorrow morning anyway," she corrected him. "So it's just you and me." She poured herself a Diet Pepsi and walked to a sofa in front of the fireplace. "I hope you're not upset."

"Me, upset?" He reached into his jacket pocket, retrieved the envelope containing the gift certificates for the girls, and handed it to Jessy. "I was going to give them these for Christmas. I figured they'd rather get something for themselves."

"I'm sorry." Jessy put the envelope in her purse. "I know you were looking forward to seeing them."

"Not much any of us can do about the weather." Vince sat next to her on the couch. "So how've you been? You seeing anyone?" he asked awkwardly.

She smiled. "Nobody important. How about you?"

"Not really," he lied. "I guess the job is too hectic for me to start a social life."

"I remember."

"It wasn't all work," Vince protested. "We had some good times."

"I remember them too."

"Parties, boozing . . ."

"And look at where it got me." She laughed.

Vince took another sip of the scotch and stared out the enormous picture window at the icy gusts that pelted the shuddering glass. There had been good times, probably too many of them, he thought. Somewhere inside, he felt a trace of guilt at not having been at Jessy's side when she was going through all of that; a trace of regret that he wasn't with her now that she was better.

"Pardon, ma'am, but might you tell me how many there will be for dinner?" Clarisse, the Sloan's cook stood in the doorway. She recognized Vince and gave him a shy smile.

"Looks like just us." Jessy shrugged. "The storm's strung everyone else out all over the state. Why don't you forget about dinner for tonight? We'll dig something out of the fridge for ourselves."

Clarisse nodded and left. "She always liked you." Jessy said.

"My kind of people." Vince grinned.

There was an awkward moment of quiet. "So how's life today?" Vince asked finally. "Still going to the AA meetings?"

"Sure. It was hard in the beginning, but it grows on you. Every day gets a little easier than the day before."

"So how long's it been?" Vince asked.

"A little over a year. They had a cake for me on my anniversary . . . sang 'Happy Birthday,' the whole bit."

"I'm sorry I didn't remember," he apologized. "Are you happy?"

It was as though she was hearing the question for the first time. "Is anyone?"

Vince looked around the spacious study. "Seems to me you've survived pretty well."

"It's a life," she said wearily.

"Less of a chore than being the wife of a flatfoot?"

"Being married to you was never a chore. Loving you was probably the only real thing I ever did with my life. You gave it all to me right up front. Never tried to hide what you were or sugar-coat the way things were going to be. I was the one with the illusions. I was the one who couldn't take having a husband who shared more with his partner than he did with me." She stirred her Pepsi absently with her finger. "It's my fault, Vince. Not yours. It was never your fault."

He found himself staring into the fireplace, hypnotized by yellow tongues of flame dancing on the crackling logs. "Ever think about getting back together?" he found himself asking.

"I've thought about it, but every time it started to make a little sense you'd pull some dumb street cop routine and snap me back to reality. Then I'd remember the endless nights alone, waiting for the knock on the door from the departmental chaplain, telling me you finally made hero." Her voice trembled. "When my head is right, I never think about Vince Crowley. I never cry about him."

"What's it like now, right this minute?"

A half smile. "What're you driving at?"

"I want to say what's on my mind, but it's not easy."

"Nothing ever is."

Vince swallowed hard. "I'd like to make love to Jessy Crowley . . . at least once more before she becomes Jessy something else . . . or even after, if that's the only way I can have it. There's probably a better way of putting that, but I was never very good with words."

She smiled. "Sure, you were. You just didn't think it was allowed."

Vince leaned forward and kissed her—softly at first, like an unsure schoolboy gauging his limits. "You still use the same lipstick," he whispered. "I've dreamed about that taste."

The transition to the upstairs bedroom was awkward, but neither of them seemed to notice. Vince slid his hand beneath her blouse and pressed her sensitive back, fumbling like an adolescent with her bra strap.

"Let me help you." She undid the clasp from the front.

"When did they start making them that way?"

Jessy pulled him toward her and he smelled her perfume and her sweat. He felt her heaving chest once again and the soft, cooing noises that rose hoarsely in her throat. He remembered the right places to touch, the dimpled texture of her skin trembling beneath him. He wanted to lose himself completely, but something held him back. The sights and sounds and smells of sex came at him like phantoms from the past and he held them off, like a blind man shocked back to sight . . . too stunned at his good fortune to savor every sunset, every precious blade of grass.

"It's been so long . . ." He could feel her tears against his cheek.

In the bleak midwinter
Snow on snow . . .

15

NYPD FORM DD-5   DECEMBER 25, 1988
COMPLAINT FOLLOW-UP   COMPLAINT # 4548

HOMICIDE/STABBING   Det. V. Crowley
LISA THORPE W/F 23

1. At approx. 1047 hours on Dec. 25, the undersigned received information about the possible
   whereabouts of Ricardo Mirable, sought for questioning re above homicide.

2. The undersigned, along with Det. Ippollito, 37
   PDU, went to an address at 720 Throgg's Neck
   Expressway and entered the premises where we
   apprehended the subject.

3. During the trip to the station house, the subject
   became contrite, and made a complete voluntary
   confession to the murder of Lisa Thorpe.

4. Subject later recanted his confession in the presence of a public defender.

INVESTIGATION CONTINUES. CASE ACTIVE. MERRY CHRISTMAS!

Somebody's gotta work Christmas day. Technically it
was Vince's day off, but the drive back from Marion had
convinced him that working was better than sitting around
the house feeling sorry for himself. The humdrum of the
squadroom was preferable to the tumult of his thoughts.
Boredom and cold coffee, aimless conversations and the
ritual of paperwork were what he needed. Dummy work.

Connie was working, too, and that was a good thing. If he saw her today, he would have to disguise his doubts about his own feelings concerning the night with Jessy. What was worse, he knew his face would give away the guilt he felt.

What had in fact happened was no more than an unpredictable roll in the hay. Jessy had made that clear to him before he left. They'd both been carried away by the moment. The storm and the fieldstone fireplace had dimmed their fickle memories, she'd told him, obscured their better judgment. Both of them owed too much to themselves to let that happen again. As usual, she'd lost him somewhere in the translation, but he was too numb and exhausted to figure it out now.

"You were around in 1955. What the hell happened around that time?" Tommy was working on the umpteenth great American novel he'd begun writing since he started working at the three-seven.

Vince stopped trying to fix the stuck key on his typewriter and searched the ceiling. "Not much as I recall . . ."

"A whole year in your life and nothing happened?" Tommy eyed him incredulously.

"You're writing about me?"

"Shit no. You're about the dullest fuck I ever met," Tommy said. "It's the period I'm interested in. I'm looking for sort of a historical twist."

Vince shrugged. "I dunno. You might want to try some other period, then. Nothing happened in 1955. Ike was president and the country was closed for the duration."

"Yeah, that's why nobody's written about it," Tommy said enthusiastically. "The deal is, you've gotta write about something nobody else has ever written about before, something people will look at and say: 'Holy shit! I didn't know that.' "

"That's kinda rough, don't you think?" Vince suggested. "People have been writing for a pretty long time now. There's not much material that hasn't already been covered."

"No, no, no. You don't get it," Tommy protested. "You don't try to find a whole new subject—just part of an old one that other guys have sort of neglected. Look at it this way: Everybody writes about the big stuff, World War Two, Korea, Vietnam. That's fine, but there's a whole lot of history that happened in between that they're ignoring altogether."

"Maybe that's because nothing happened during those times that'd interest anybody."

"Negative, partner." Tommy smiled knowingly. "Lots of interesting stuff went down if you were just sharp enough to catch it."

"And I suppose you were—"

"I would've if I'd been there. It's a writer's business to be observant."

Vince leaned back in his chair. "Well, why don't you educate me a little bit here? Give me a couple of examples of interesting stuff that happened . . . oh, let's see, between World War Two and Korea. Get me excited about that period in history."

Tommy paused. "You know, that's the beauty of writing. Writers got something called 'license,' if you know what I mean. If things don't go down just the way they want, they can change them—sort of enhance them."

"Change history?"

"Well, not really change it. Make it peppier."

"Peppier?"

Tommy threw his hands in the air. "Why do I even try to explain this shit to you? One day—just one fucking day in my entire life, I'd like to have an intelligent conversation with *somebody* in this goddamn precinct—"

The metallic ring of the telephone cut him off. Vince lifted the receiver. "Thirty-seventh precinct, Detective Crowley."

"It's Cadillac, Crowley." The voice on the other end was agitated. "Your vice goons busted three of my girls last night."

Vince knew nothing about it. "So whatta you want from me?"

"You're breaking my balls, you know that . . ."

"Those women were committing a crime, Cadillac!" Vince said. "You know I'm sworn to uphold the law. Protect public morals."

"Don't jerk me off, okay?" Cadillac snarled. "I did some checking on that kid you were interested in. I tell you what I know and you call off the Gestapo, okay?"

Vince grinned across the room at Tommy. "You got my word on that, Cadillac. Honest injun."

"There's a shooting gallery in an abandoned warehouse out on Throgg's Neck Expressway," Cadillac said. "Word I get is he could be out there."

"You got an address for me?"

"No more bogus arrests!" Cadillac demanded.

"Have I ever lied to you before?"

". . . 727."

Vince hung up the phone. "Come on, partner. You and me are gonna get ourselves a suspect."

Tommy looked around the squad room. "Gotta wait for Turner to come back and man the phones."

"Where is she?"

Tommy shrugged. "Probably in the can. You can tell. Every time they walk out with their pocketbook it means they're off to the ladies' room. What the fuck do they do in there anyway? I mean, you can just piss so much—"

"I heard that." Leila Turner entered the room and went to her desk. "I'd tell you if you weren't such a jerk, Ippollito." She smiled at Vince. "You go ahead. I'll handle the phones. We all gotta do it, right?"

"Right." He grabbed his coat and led Tommy down the stairs.

The pavement outside the building at 727 Throgg's Neck Expressway was littered with debris. What remained of a shattered wooden fence that had once surrounded the building was covered with soot and graffiti. Gaping holes revealed a bleak expanse of crumbling brick and broken windows: the all too familiar signature of vandalism and neglect. Tommy pried open the rusted lock on the front gate easily with a nearby piece of two-by-four and followed Vince into the building.

Inside, the main floor was honeycombed with overflowing storage areas: office furniture stacked in heaps, rusting bed springs piled on top of one another, electrical wiring ripped from the walls, air-conditioners torn from their mountings. Everything was covered with a two-inch layer of pigeon and rat and dog shit. Everywhere the pervasive smells of decay.

"What a hellhole," Tommy said, picking his way through the excrement on the floor. "Why don't they just tear these fucking places down?"

"Junkies gotta have some place to live—" A flurry of pigeons screeched from above as Vince moved warily toward a door at the far end of the floor. Abandoning their burrow behind a buckling lintel in the ceiling, swooping past him, brushing his face. The inhuman howl of a cat erupted in the darkness. He remembered hearing stories from Vietnam vets about how they would be lifted from the quiet, seedy seclusion of a whorehouse in downtown Saigon and catapulted by helicopter into a jungle firefight in a matter of minutes. He felt like that now. A minute or two ago he was inhaling Jessy's perfumed body in privileged Marion, Connecticut. Now he was back in the battle zone. Down and dirty, the way cops like him were meant to be.

A hand signal to Tommy and one well-placed kick to the door. "Police. Everybody up!" he yelled at the gathering of pitiful bodies lining the floor of the room inside. "Anybody gets cute, gets their head blown off!" His gun remained undrawn. This was not a threatening bunch.

"Which one of you scumbags is Ricky Miracle?" Tommy asked them as they stumbled groggily to their feet.

Empty stares.

"I'm gonna ask one more time." They searched the blank, uncomprehending faces. "Ricardo Mirable, *comprende*?"

Vince walked past the file of zombies, backing them against the wall, lifting sagging chins, staring into fixed, bloodshot eyeballs. "Who's this look like, partner?" He dragged an unwilling body from the wall and pushed him toward Tommy.

"As I live and breathe . . ." Tommy shoved Ricky Miracle against the wall, patted him down, and put him in cuffs.

"That'll be all, ladies and gentlemen," Vince said, retreating from the room with Ricky in tow. "Thanks for inviting us over."

"Yeah," Tommy added. "Have us back when you've finished redecorating."

Outside, they secured Ricky in the rear seat of the patrol car and headed back to the precinct. "I don't suppose there's anything you want to tell us before we take you in," Vince said to him. "Sorta clear your conscience, if you follow me."

Ricky stared back sullenly from the rear seat. "You arresting me, man?"

"Who said anything about arrest?"

" 'Cause if you're arresting me for something, you gotta read me my rights, man. I know about Miranda."

"Hey, you hear that, partner? We got ourselves a legal scholar here," Vince said to Tommy.

"And I know about the Exclusionary Rule," Ricky went on. "So if you got any questions for me, I want my lawyer present when you ask them."

"Shit. A guy like you must have a whole battery of high-priced lawyers on the payroll," Tommy guffawed. "I dunno, partner. I think this jailhouse Clarence Darrow's got you and me over a barrel."

"Could be." Vince made a show of looking out the front windshield at the hood of the car. "Jeez, partner. I never noticed how filthy this unit had gotten. Let's stop at the carwash and shine 'er up before we bring this sleazebag in."

Tommy looked puzzled.

"You know . . ." Vince urged.

"The *carwash*!" Tommy's eyes lit up. "Shit, yeah. It wouldn't do for a couple of class guys like us to be driving around in a dirty squad car, would it?" He turned into a side street and headed for Tremont Avenue.

Ricky Miracle's eyes grew wide as Tommy drove the car onto the conveyor belt of the carwash. The color drained from his face as they began to move through the tunnel inch by painful inch. A barrage of menacing rubber fingers and circling brushes choked them in from all sides, enveloping them in suds and noise and blackness.

"Nothing like a clean car," Vince said casually. He could see Ricky sitting stiffly in the backseat, his eyes pressed closed, beads of sweat pouring down his forehead. "They even drive better when they're clean."

Ricky remained resolutely silent.

"I'll be a sonofabitch!" Tommy exclaimed as the car emerged into the daylight. "Isn't that a spot they missed on the right fender there?"

"You know, I think it is." Vince looked at the phantom spot. "Better run it through again, partner. No sense doing a half-assed job of it."

Ricky stiffened in the seat. His feet were pressed against the rear floorboard of the car, propelling him backward, as they began their second run through the tunnel. His shoulders and arms had begun to tremble involuntarily.

"You know, these automatic jobbies ain't never gonna replace the old hand-jobs," Tommy observed halfway through. "I wouldn't be surprised if we gotta run this cocksucker through five or six more times before they get it right."

Vince nodded. "Wouldn't surprise me." Ricky was beginning to retch in the backseat. "But you gotta do what you gotta do, know what I mean?"

"One more time . . ." Tommy made a U-turn and headed back for the carwash entrance.

"What the fuck do you guys want?" Ricky Miracle's voice was a pitiful whine.

"We want what you want," Vince said as Tommy pulled onto the conveyor belt once again. "We want the truth. That's what we all want, right?" He winked at Tommy. "And as soon as we get you back to the station house with your lawyer, we'll see what we can do about getting it."

"If these bastards ever get this car cleaned," Tommy added.

"Get me outa here," Ricky moaned. "I'll tell you what you want."

"You gonna make a voluntary confession?" Tommy asked.

Ricky's chest and abdomen were heaving. His breath came in deep, sucking gasps.

"Without prompting or coercion?" Vince added.

"Just get me the fuck out! I'll cop to anything."

16

A light was extinguished in New York City. Once the light burned brightly, illuminating dark recesses of hate and ignorance and misunderstanding. And the light was named Lisa, and all who were privileged to have known her during the short span of her life cannot but feel that she embodied the true essence of the words of the Prophet Isaiah: "The wolf also shall dwell with the lamb, and the leopard shall lie down with the kid; and the calf and the young lion and the fatling together; and a little child shall lead them."

Vince read the Publisher's Letter on the last page of the January issue of *Newsworld* magazine. Ivor Thorpe's final tribute to his daughter was also a ringing denunciation of the system that allowed her murder to happen. Lisa's death was the result of an unwieldy, outdated criminal-justice code, of a hospital-care system that permitted outpatient schizophrenics and psychopaths to wander the streets of New York without supervision; a venal, uncaring police department that allowed places like the Shangri-la Motel to remain a base for drug dealers and prostitutes. It was a city without values, without conscience, without grief . . .

Vince handed the magazine to Tommy. "Heavy stuff, partner. It's getting harder and harder to tell the good guys from the bad guys."

Tommy scanned the article. "Funny, there's nothing in here about how his perfect daughter happened to end up in a scumbucket like the Shangri-la in the first place." He shoved the magazine back across the desk contemptuously. "Guys like Thorpe really frost my ass. There's a hundred murders a year in places like that, and you never hear a peep out of them about how rotten the system is until someone close to them gets nailed, and all of a sudden the cops and the courts are a buncha shitkickers. Society's just fucking great as long as it keeps them fat and happy."

Vince shrugged. "I guess he's gotta complain about somebody."

"Let him complain to me personally," Tommy snorted. "I don't have a million readers to bitch to every time things don't go my way, know what I mean?"

"Maybe he'll let up now that we got a suspect," Dog Scarfatti chimed in. "Sometimes all you gotta do is throw these humps a bone and they shut right up."

"Maybe now that we have a suspect, you and your partner can crawl back into your hole downtown and leave us alone," Vince suggested.

Scarfatti guffawed. "No way that'll happen. Now that we got the little turd, the P.C. wants to make sure you're doing everything you're supposed to be doing to see that he gets convicted, kapish?"

"Ricky Miracle's no more guilty than I am." Vince scowled. "If you had half a brain you'd know that."

"Hey, I didn't collar him, did I?" Scarfatti threw up his hands in a pose of mock innocence. "I didn't run the sonofabitch through a carwash and squeeze a confession out of him, did I? If you didn't think he was guilty, what'd you bother to arrest him for in the first place? Why didn't you just leave the poor bastard out on the streets where he could go on shooting DDT and snorting bus fumes? You wanta tell me that, Crowley?"

Vince took a deep breath. "Go home, Dog. Give us all a break, huh?"

"So don't bust my *cujones*," Scarfatti went on. "That kid is as good a suspect as you're ever gonna get in a case like this. Eyewitnesses put him on the scene. His coat was loaded with dried blood that Serology says matches the murdered girl's blood type. A-B fucking negative, for chrissakes! He even confessed before his P.D. got ahold of him. What the hell more do you want?"

"All circumstantial," Vince said dryly. "And not even very good circumstantial. They won't get him past the grand jury."

"I trust you intend to keep that opinion to yourself," John Gleason said icily from his office door. "Particularly in view of the fact that the Commissioner and the D.A.

just announced that they have a solid case against Ricardo Mirable."

"You gotta be kidding," Vince moaned. "I could expect something like that from the P.C., but I thought Tom Quinlan had more brains than to shoot off his mouth like that."

"He's probably getting squeezed from upstairs just like everybody else," Tommy observed.

Gleason looked nervously at Dog and Cheap Suit. "In my office—both of you."

Vince made his way through the labyrinth of metal desks into Gleason's office and waited while the CO poured a glassful of water and popped a pill.

"I suppose you both think it's real cute to mock your superiors," Gleason began. "You must get a real kick out of trying to make the Commissioner look like a fool in front of the other officers."

"Begging the lieutenant's pardon, but the P.C. doesn't need me for that," Vince broke in.

Gleason gave him a withering stare. "You think that's funny, Crowley?" He turned angrily toward Tommy. "How about you, Ippollito? You think your partner here is a funnyman?"

Deadly silence.

"Because if you do, you can both leave your shields on my desk and get your smart-asses out of here. I will not tolerate disrespect in this command. Is that clear?"

Again, silence.

"Good. Then let's make sure that from here on in, we keep our opinions to ourselves. It's going to be hard enough making a case against this Mirable character without bickering among ourselves."

"Beg pardon, Lieutenant, but isn't it the D.A.'s job to make the case against him?" Tommy asked. "I thought we did our job by making the collar."

"Nobody asked what you thought, Ippollito," Gleason growled. "Granted, this may not be the time to review your job description, but the truth is you are supposed to operate in an investigatory capacity. That means you provide evidence for criminal prosecution. Does that square with the way you see your role here?"

Tommy shifted his weight uneasily.

"This's a weak case, sir," Vince broke in. "I think what Detective Ippollito is trying to say is that it might've been better if they waited until we had better evidence before they made any announcement to the press."

Gleason nodded. "Well, what's done is done. Now it's our job to see to it that the case gets stronger. That means we gotta squeeze this Mirable motherfucker until the evidence against him oozes out of his asshole. We see eye to eye on that?"

Mumbled agreement.

"Good enough." Gleason turned away from them and stared vacantly out his office window. "We're gonna squeeze him and squeeze him and squeeze him until he breaks. We're gonna keep up the pressure until we got him right by the you-know-what. Any questions?" Gleason asked, reinvigorated by his sudden surge of resolve. "Good. Now, I want both of you out at Riker's, pumping this little prick for information. Every minute you're not needed in here, I want you out there leaning on him. I don't care what you have to do—"

"He knows about the Exclusionary Rule," Vince broke in. "Anything we get without his lawyer being present is going right down the toilet."

Gleason stiffened. "Since when did you become a civil libertarian, Crowley?"

"Am I to take that to mean the lieutenant would approve of unconventional procedures?"

"You're to do what I goddamn well tell you to do! Is that so hard for you to understand?"

"No sir. Will that be all?" Vince shot a nervous glance at Tommy.

"Yes." Gleason eyed the bottle of pills on his desk and poured another glass of water with a trembling hand. He could feel the involuntary muscles in his right cheek beginning to twitch. "Unless you have any questions."

"When are we getting rid of those two scumbags from downtown?" Tommy asked.

"When the Commissioner is satisfied that we have the situation in hand," Gleason answered stiffly. "Translated, that means when Ricardo Mirable is brought to trial for the murder of Lisa Thorpe."

Outside, Street Crime pointed to the telephone on Vince's desk as he maneuvered through the narrow aisles. "Call for you on hold—she insisted on waiting till you got back."

Vince lifted the receiver uneasily. "Crowley . . ."

"It's Connie." She sounded tentative.

"Oh, hi, babe. Sorry I haven't gotten back to you, but things have been nuts around here since we collared Ricky Miracle. You know how it is—"

"Is everything okay?"

He felt his stomach fluttering. "Sure, why wouldn't it be?"

"I don't know . . . I'm not sure. I just haven't heard from you in a while . . ."

"Cop stuff, Connie. This case is a killer." He tried to sound convincing. "We're all under a lot of pressure to get this one off the front pages . . . and the six o'clock nightly news."

"Not much chance of that happening, especially now that you've made an arrest. This trial will probably be the news event of the year."

"Don't count on it ever coming to trial." He was instantly sorry he'd said it.

"Really? The word I'm getting is that it's just about an open-and-shut case. You have some new information for me?"

"I'm not supposed to discuss it. Let's just say it's not as open-and-shut as some people are making out."

"Can I quote you?" she asked.

"Not on your life."

Connie paused. "Well, it's good to hear your voice, Vince."

"Yeah. That goes for me too."

"Any idea when we might be able to get together?" Her voice was strained.

"Soon. Let's really do it soon. It's just that I've been so crazy here—"

"You're sure everything's all right, Vince?"

"What could be wrong?"

"I don't know. How was your day in Marion?"

"You know, the usual."

"How were the girls?"

"Katie and Kelly?"

"Your daughters," Connie said.

"Okay, I guess. Why the third degree?"

There was a pause. "Something happened, didn't it?"

He laughed hoarsely. "Sure, something happened. Something always happens when I go up there. I'm sorry we couldn't get together for Christmas, but I was involved in chasing down a murder suspect that day. It kept me kinda busy, if you know what I mean—"

"You slept with Jessy, didn't you?"

His world caved in. The fingers of his hand gripped the telephone receiver until his knuckles began turning white. "Oh jeez, what makes you think a thing like that?"

"I don't know . . . It's just a feeling I have." Her voice was trembling.

"A feeling?"

"Don't ask me to explain it. A woman just knows."

He took a deep breath. "So I'm already guilty, is that it? You're not interested in anything I might have to say about it?"

Silence. "I don't really want to know, but I can't bear not knowing."

"You wouldn't believe me even if I said nothing happened, would you?" Vince asked.

"I don't know, Vince. Go ahead and say it."

"You've got me guilty no matter what I say, babe. That's not fair. Even cops gotta play by the rules."

"I don't know what the rules are here, Vince. I've never read any rulebooks about just how far I'm allowed to go when I find out the one man in the world I thought I could trust has been making love to his ex-wife. If there's some sort of convention that applies here, I'm just not aware of it. All I know is how much it hurts."

"I do love you, Connie, you have to believe that."

She was weeping silently. "I don't know what to believe anymore, Vince."

17

R ICKY FELT THE THUNDER AT THE BASE OF HIS SPINE—A jackhammer series of jolts that penetrated his body like electroshock. He sat on the bare metal webbing of the bed and leaned against the wall. Inhaling the flat smells of whitewashed limestone and stale urine, he felt cold concrete blocks digging into the plane of his shoulders, his elbows, his throbbing head, delineating his frail, bony body against the suffocating press of steel and cement. He waited for the thunder to pass, afraid to breathe, as if each new intake of air would summon another wave of nausea, of empty retching, of ice-cold sweats.

Take-it-to-me . . . *Take-it-to-me* . . . The thunder sounded like a diesel locomotive roaring through the hollow tunnel of his consciousness . . . *Take-it-to-me* . . . When was the last shot—the last pill—the last drink exploding in his chest like an awakening morning glory? He realized it was no longer a train he was hearing but the chattering of his own teeth, resonating through the cell: *Take-it-to-me* . . . *Take-it-to-me* . . .

He was freezing. His legs were drawn up on the bed like bent, spindly twigs, his arms wrapped tightly around him. His entire body was rocking back and forth, eyelids pressed together like an old Jew at prayer. The movement helped some; it seemed to shift his focus from the relentlessly closing walls; funneled slits of pure white light through the dark corridors of his mind . . . images that were gentle, distracting. Memories, perhaps . . . Hopes . . .

The distant point of light was the flame of a kerosine lamp dangling over a crude wooden table . . . white moths and fruit flies excited by the glow circled above him . . . the strains of a melody lingered somewhere in the background; a rich, contralto female voice . . . an unconscious stab of memory from long ago. *"Go down,*

go down Moses. Go down to the land of Pharoah . . ."
There was no face to the soft, crooning voice . . . an
indistinct female torn from the loop of foster homes,
hospitals, and institutions he'd inhabited over the years.
It flickered for a moment with the insects at the lamp,
then disappeared.

Take-it-to-me . . . Take-it-to-me . . .

"Rise and shine, Miracle man." The guard's mocking
voice jarred him out of his reverie. "You got visitors."

Ricky stood uncertainly—his wrists and ankles were
secured with chains and irons—then shuffled the length
of the hall to the insistent prodding of the guard's night-
stick in his kidneys and the baleful, suspicious stares of
his fellow inmates.

"Hello, Ricardo. Good to see you again." Detective
Crowley greeted him in the prison's interrogation room
and signaled for the guard to remove Ricky's manacles.
"You remember my partner, Detective Ippollito, don't
you?"

Ricky nodded sullenly. "Whatta you want, man?"

"Just a couple of questions, Ricardo, unless you insist
on having your P.D. present. In that case we can come
back later."

Ricky thought of returning to the encircling nightmare
of the cell. "Uh-uh. It's okay, man. I got nothing to hide
from you. And I didn't do nothing, just like I told you
before."

Vince watched Ricky carefully. There was none of the
swagger he'd shown the day they pulled him in, none of
the street-cool contempt for authority he'd managed to
convey while he was still high on booze and crack. Two
days in stir without a fix or a pop had knocked all that
out of him. Walls closing in on him like a concrete vise
had made him sweetly reasonable as only the dying can
be.

"Yeah, we know what you told us before, but there's a
lot of stuff that just doesn't add up," Tommy said. "Like
how come you got the victim's blood all over your coat
like that? You didn't mention anything about blood when
we talked to you before."

Ricky shrugged. "I got in a fight. Maybe it was my
blood, maybe it was the guy I hit. How the hell do I
know?"

"Look, Ricky," Vince broke in. "We want to be fair

here, but our hands are tied as long as you keep telling us fairy tales. *We* know you were in that motel room with Lisa Thorpe that night and *you* know you were there, so why not can all the bullshit and tell it like it is. We'll see to it that you cut the best deal possible with the D.A. You got my word on that."

"Hey, man, I'm supposed to believe your word?" Ricky looked astonished.

"I say we dump this asshole back in the box and forget about him," Tommy muttered. "He's just another dumb street punk who don't know what's good for him."

"My partner's got a point," Vince observed. "You're gonna do time for this murder no matter what. We're just here to give you a chance to make it easy on yourself. You want to be a hardcase, go ahead. I got better things to do than hang around here all day." He stood to leave.

"Wait a minute." Ricky gripped the arms of the chair, trying to control his shaking hands. "I can tell you what happened, but it's not gonna be what you want to hear."

"Why don't you let us worry about that?" Vince handed Ricky a lit cigarette. "Just take your time and try to remember everything." He activated a micro-recorder on the desk.

Ricky took a deep drag from the cigarette and allowed the smoke to drift lazily from his nostrils. "It's like this, man," he began. "I was in Shapiro's lot across the street when I seen this person throwing something in the bushes by the sidewalk—"

"Hold on, Ricky," Vince interrupted. "Where was this person when you saw him?"

"In front of the Shangri-la, man, coming from out back of the place, holding something like a package and then dumping it in the bushes."

"Did you get a close look, Ricky? You know what this guy looked like?"

Ricky shook his head. "It was too dark, man. To tell you the truth, I couldn't see if it was even a man or a woman. Whoever it was, come out of the motel, staggering like, and dropped this thing in the bushes . . . then just took off around the corner."

"And all the time, you were in the Christmas-tree lot across the street," Vince prompted.

"Like I said, I was keeping warm by the oil drum."

Vince shot a glance at Tommy. "And what time would you say that was?"

Ricky pondered the question. "I dunno. It was dark. Either of you guys got a Tylenol or something? My head is splitting, man."

"You tell us what we want to know, and I'll see to it you get transferred to a hospital bed—all the medication you need," Vince said.

"You shitting me, man?"

"I do square business. Anybody'll tell you that."

Ricky ground the cigarette out nervously. "Well, that's my story, man. I seen this guy drop a package, and after he left I went over there and hid it under my coat and brought it back to the lot."

"You telling me it was a guy you saw, now? I thought you said it was too dark to tell."

"So kick me off the fuckin' Earth." Ricky rolled his eyes. "Guy, girl, what the fuck difference does it make? It coulda been an ape for all I know. I thought maybe they was making a dope drop, so I took it for myself."

"And . . . ?"

"And it was a buncha towels, all rolled up. I seen they had this blood all over them, so I dropped them in the fire and hightailed it outa there. I got enough trouble in my life without shit like that to worry about, you know what I mean?"

Vince nodded. "Well, it looks like you bought yourself a shitload of trouble anyway, Ricky. If what you're saying is true, you would've been a lot better off reporting it to the police."

"Whatta you think I am, fuckin' nuts, for chrissakes?" Ricky's jaw dropped. "I'm supposed to walk into the bulls, looking like I do, and cop to stealing a bunch of bloody towels? You got any idea what they woulda did to me—a down-and-dirty street slob with a record? They'da took one look and shot me dead on the spot; that's what they woulda did!"

Vince tried to suppress a smile. "So look what running got you."

Tommy slammed his notebook shut in disgust. "You expect us to believe a cock-and-bull story like this? Whatta you take us for, a couple of rubes?"

Ricky shrugged. "I told you the truth. I can't do nothing better than that."

"You want us to believe you got smeared all over with the murdered girl's blood from a couple of towels you picked up? Come on, Ricky. Give us a break here."

"I dunno whose blood it was."

"Type A-B negative," Tommy said. "Same as Lisa Thorpe's, but strangely enough, not the same as yours. You know what I think? I think you walked into her room looking for dope or a piece of pussy, and surprised her. I think she started yelling and you panicked and stuck her in the neck. That's what I think, hotshot. I think you murdered Lisa Thorpe, no ifs ands or buts about it."

"I'm not ready to go that far," Vince broke in. "I don't want to call what you did 'murder.' Not yet anyway. I think maybe you just got scared—pushed her down maybe, or nudged her a little bit. You might've even tried to reason with her, calm her down. You're not a murderer, Ricky. We both know that. You just made a dumb mistake and this broad ended up getting herself killed." He reached across the table and placed a comforting hand on Ricky's shoulder. "That something like the way it went down, son?"

"I was never in the Shangri-la. I never knew no Lisa Thorpe, and I sure as hell never killed her. It happened just the way I told you, I swear to God, man."

Vince looked exasperated. "You gotta help me out here, Ricky. I go back to my CO with a dumb story like this, and he'll have me counting Oldsmobiles on the Verrazzano Narrows Bridge. I gotta feed him something he'll believe. You know what I'm saying?"

"You want me to confess to a murder I didn't do, just to make you look good in front of your boss?"

"I want you to get it off your chest. It'll make you feel better."

"I already feel better. I felt like shit when I came in here, but you guys got me laughing now. You're both so fuckin' unbelievable that I know I gotta have more brains than the two of you put together."

"So you're gonna stick with your story?" Tommy asked.

"Yeah, I'm sticking with it," Ricky said defiantly.

"Well, that's just too fucking bad." Tommy put his notebook in his jacket pocket. "You would've been a helluva lot more comfortable in a nice, roomy hospital, you know?"

"I can't do anything for you if you won't cooperate," Vince added.

Ricky's shoulders sagged, his face a hollow mask of resignation. "Go ahead, man. Do what you want to do." His teeth had begun to chatter again. The locomotive in his head was a fast-forward express. "It don't make no difference what I say to you guys anyway. You got yourself a collar. That's all you care about, right?"

Outside, Tommy shifted the car into reverse and backed out of the parking lot. "So whatta you think?" he asked when they were underway.

"If he's guilty, I'm the tooth fairy."

"It kinda looks that way, doesn't it?"

"He's got no reason to lie to us," Vince went on. "He tells us what we want to hear, and he's guaranteed a warm, safe bed in Bellevue. He pulls our chains and he's back in the box. This kid's not stupid. He knows how the game is played."

"I dunno . . ." Tommy pulled onto the Deegan Expressway. "These street kids got a real independent streak in them. Busting balls is a way of life with them, if you know what I mean. I've seen some of them cut off their nose to spike their face."

"Maybe the kid's just got some character," Vince observed.

Back at the precinct, he called Tom Quinlan. "Do me a favor and have Ricardo Mirable transferred to Bellevue under twenty-four hour guard," he asked when the Bronx D.A. came on the line.

"You gotta be kidding me, Crowley," Quinlan groaned. "This guy is a suspected murderer. He's a fucking dangerous character. Rikers is too good for the son of a bitch."

"He's suffering in that cell, Tom."

"He's a murderer, for chrissakes. People *want* to see murderers suffer."

"Listen to me, Tom. You want a warm body sitting in the courtroom, you better get him outa there on the double. You keep him in that cell and I guarantee he'll find a way to kill himself."

"You telling me he's suicidal?" Quinlan asked skeptically.

"Do you want me to spell it out for you? Get him into a hospital or you'll end up prosecuting a corpse."

Quinlan paused. "You jerking me off, Crowley?"

"What reason would I have?" Vince protested. "I just

don't want out whole case to go down the toilet because somebody in your office was too damn hard-nosed to see the handwriting on the wall. I just left this kid and, believe me, he's right on the edge."

Tommy eyed Vince curiously when he hung up the phone. "You think Miracle is suicidal?"

"He could be." Vince sorted through his phone messages.

"That's not the impression I got."

"Everybody sees things different."

"You know what I think?" Tommy sat across the desk from Vince and leaned forward on his elbows. His voice became conspiratorial. "I think you made all that shit up. That's what I think."

Vince shrugged. "So kick me off the earth . . ."

18

NYPD FORM DD-5
COMPLAINT FOLLOW-UP

HOMICIDE/STABBING   DECEMBER 29, 1988
LISA THORPE W/F 23   COMPLAINT # 4548
                                Det. V. Crowley

1. Pursuant to Grand Jury proceedings re the above homicide, a review was held at the office of the District Attorney, Bronx, N.Y., at approx. 0930, above date.

2. Present at the meeting were: The undersigned, Dets. Ippollito, Appelbaum, Quade & Cuzak, 37 PDU; as well as D.A. Thomas Quinlan, Asst. D.A. Walter Brewer and special investigators Freeman and Wilde, Div. of the District Attorney, Bronx County.

3. After reviewing all pertinent evidence, and discussing same, it was determined that a prima facie case had been established against Ricardo Mirable (aka Ricky Miracle), and that an indictment would be sought before a Bronx County Grand Jury on 31 Dec., 1988.

INVESTIGATION CONTINUES. CASE ACTIVE.

Tom Quinlan paused outside the projection room at Bronx Criminal Court, hooked his Malacca cane over his left forearm, and allowed one of his assistants to open the door. The cane was little more than a prop, an allowance to the doctors who had recently performed

121

heart-bypass surgery on him. He was supposed to be taking things easy these days.

"Hey, Tom, you're looking pretty good for an old guy." Vince stood and greeted him at the door.

"Don't talk to me about old." Quinlan scowled at Vince, indicating the dangling walking stick on his arm. "I'm just about falling apart while we stand here." He shuffled to a chair in front of the TV monitor and sat ponderously. "Anybody tells you getting old is fun, you tell 'em they're fulla shit."

"You guys don't know from getting old," Steve Appelbaum grumbled from across the room. "My teeth are falling outa my head. My back hurts all the time. Nothing works like it's supposed to work anymore."

"Hey, you guys aren't any older than I am," Vince observed.

"And who are you, Tom Cruise?" Appelbaum raised an eyebrow. "Let's face it. Ain't none of us getting any younger. We're all turning into a buncha *alta cockers*.' "

"Speak for yourself," Tommy piped up. "I still got a lot of good years in me."

"Knowing you is the only thing that makes me think being old is a good deal," Appelbaum replied.

Tommy sneered. "Laugh all you want, humpheads. At least I can still get it up for the chicks. That's more than I can say for you limp-dicks."

"Not so fast," Quinlan protested. "Vince here's got a good-looking young girlfriend, and he seems to keep her happy."

"*Had* a girlfriend," Vince corrected him. "She's kinda pissed off at me right now."

"Woman are always pissed off about something," Tommy said. "Watch daytime TV sometime. You know, those talk shows where women show up to bitch and moan about men. By them, every guy they ever met is a real hard-on. It's like they get it off sitting around sharing how miserable they are with one another."

"Connie's got a legitimate bitch," Vince admitted. "I tore her up by doing something really dumb."

"It don't make no difference *what* you do," Tommy went on. "Women just gotta complain. It's in their natures. You'd think it was our fault they got unsightly panty lines and retain water all the time."

"Can we get on with this?" Tom Quinlan asked wearily. "I'd like to sit here all day listening to your philosophies of life, but I got a luncheon with my accountant in a little more than an hour."

"Still socking away those convertible C.D.'s, huh?" Vince grinned and inserted a cassette into the VCR when everybody was seated. "I dunno how you humble civil servants manage to get so rich so quick."

"Careful money management." Quinlan scowled. "Roll that mother."

Tommy dimmed the lights and the screen lit up with the grizzly panorama of the murder scene at the Shangri-la. The room remained silent as the camera's lens probed the partially covered body of Lisa Thorpe, focusing on the wounds to her neck, her blood-spattered face and upper torso, her staring, sightless eyes . . .

"This was almost a half hour after we got there," Vince said as the camera panned around the room, highlighting a seemingly meaningless variety of blood smears and objects. Some of the bits of broken glass strewn across the floor were circled with yellow chalk. "Forensics had started dusting, but nothing was removed from the room yet."

"Whatta you make of those blood smears all over the wall?" Quinlan asked.

"The killer must've panicked," Tommy answered from the back of the room. "Near as we can tell, he tried to mop up all the blood before he left, took most of the towels with him, and dumped them when he got outside."

"In the oil drum across the street," Quinlan said.

"We're not so sure about that anymore." Vince allowed the videotape to run out and signaled Tommy to turn up the lights. "There's a good chance they were dumped in a bush outside the motel before they got to the drum. We clipped some branches with what could be dried blood on them this morning. I'll have a report later today."

"About the room itself . . ." Quinlan pointed to a montage of color photographs lining the wall. "That's a real violent scene there. Not just the blood, but the upturned furniture, the smashed mirror—everything. Would you agree Lisa Thorpe fought like hell before she was killed?"

Vince nodded. "No doubt about that."

"Okay. How do you see it going down?"

Vince walked to the pictures on the wall. "If I had to go with what we got right now, it sets up like this: The victim gets to the Shangri-la at roughly midnight on the fourteenth. There are no records to verify that, but judging from the number of cigarette butts in the ashtray and Lisa Thorpe's established pattern of smoking, we can make an approximation."

"What about the motel's register?"

"Nobody's signed it in weeks. The Shangri-la doesn't stand on formalities."

"Somebody must've checked her into that room," Quinlan persisted.

"Night manager's a halfwit named Guido Sannasarto. Most of the time he can't find his way to the men's room. His uncle's an underboss in the Madalena crime family, so I guess they gave him the job just to keep him out of trouble. We pumped him pretty good and believe me, he wouldn't remember if his old lady checked in that night."

"So all we got are cigarette butts? Couldn't some of them have belonged to the killer?" Quinlan asked.

"Not likely. They all had the victim's lipstick and saliva on them."

Quinlan folded his arms, and leaned back in his chair. "Okay, lay it out for me."

Vince went to a blackboard on the wall and drew a rectangular outline in chalk. "This's the room. The door, the bed, the dresser"—he sketched the objects as he spoke. "The way it looks, Lisa Thorpe spent a lot of time, maybe two or three hours, in the bed before she was killed. Presumably with her attacker."

"How about sex?" Quinlan asked.

"Maybe after we've finished here, Tom."

Quinlan groaned. "Did the victim engage in coitus prior to her death?"

"Lab smears say no. At least there was no residual semen. It's also not likely she was raped since there was no trauma to the vaginal tissues. Our best bet is she and her killer just sat around talking and smoking for a while prior to her death. A fight must've broken out over something. There was a scuffle, maybe some punches thrown, then the killer got a hold of Lisa Thorpe's comb and stuck the pointed end of the handle into her neck"—he punched the end of the chalk into the blackboard emphatically.

"Everything from here on in is strictly guesswork, but good guesswork." He drew a line from the bed to the dresser. "She's wounded but not badly wounded. She's scared. She heads for the door and her attacker chases her. They wrestle, bang into the dresser, and smash the mirror." Vince scribbled a series of angry, jagged lines on the board. "More fighting on the ground. The killer picks up a piece of broken glass from the mirror and slashes Lisa's throat. Now she's fatally wounded, but she's not dead yet. Her killer has to hold her on the floor for a while, maybe as long as two or three minutes, before she passes out from loss of blood. By me, that's intent to cause death, if you catch my drift.

"At this point, things start to get a little weird. Our killer panics, becomes irrational. He drags Lisa Thorpe's body across the room and tries to put it back on the bed, and when that doesn't work he covers her up with a sheet—"

"Symbolically erasing his guilt," Tommy broke in.

"Maybe he was just a neat-freak. Anyway, he goes to the bathroom, takes all the towels, and starts trying to wipe up the blood." Vince discarded the chalk and traced a jumble of smudges and swirls on the drawing with his index finger. "When we got there, the whole room looked like a giant, red finger-painting . . ."

"You got any theories?" Quinlan asked.

"It's a kind of exorcism," Tommy persisted. "This guy couldn't live with what he did, so he tried to make believe it never happened."

"Something I can take to court, please."

Vince shook his head. "Maybe Tommy's right. Who the hell knows what makes these guys tick?"

Quinlan eyed the blackboard thoughtfully. "No readable prints, right?"

"A couple of partials. Nothing we can use."

"No eyewitnesses."

"Nobody saw her enter the motel. Nobody heard anything. Nobody saw her attacker leave, except maybe Ricky Miracle."

Quinlan stiffened. "Ricky Miracle? He's my suspect, for chrissakes!"

Vince began erasing the blackboard. "If Ricky Miracle's all you got, I'd have to say you don't got much."

"You have somebody better?" Quinlan demanded.

"Not yet, but I'm working on it. For now, all I can say is that Ricky Miracle's story is the only thing that makes sense up to this point. If what I've told you so far is the way it really went down, there's no way he could be our murderer. There's no way he could've been in that room with Lisa Thorpe in the first place. They didn't exactly run around in the same social circles, if you know what I mean."

"If you're talking about social status, what the hell was she doing in a fleabag like the Shangri-la in the first place?"

"I dunno," Vince admitted. "There's a lot of things about this case that just don't add up—and Ricky Miracle as the killer heads my list."

Quinlan shrugged. "Well, Ricky Miracle is all I got, and Ricky Miracle is who I'm bringing before the Grand Jury day after tomorrow." He stood to leave.

Vince followed him out into the hall. "What's the big rush, Tom? You got no case against this kid, you know that. Give me a little time and I'll come up with a real suspect for you."

"What's the rush?" Quinlan eyed him incredulously. "The rush is Ivor Thorpe's twenty million readers screaming and clamoring for justice here. It's TV reporters like your girlfriend camping outside my office—outside my house, for chrissakes—demanding answers. They're not interested in whether we got a suspect we can convict here. They're interested in tomorrow's headlines!"

"That what you're interested in, Tom—headlines?"

"Fuck off, Crowley!" Quinlan brushed past him in the hall. "You wanta be a Boy Scout, go ahead. I'm responsible to the people who elected me, and I gotta give them what they want."

"And what they want is blood, right?"

Quinlan halted. "Yeah, maybe that's all they do want, but then, maybe they got a right, know what I mean? They're living in a fucking sewer. Every day they look at the news on TV and they see people just like them getting mugged and raped and blown away for doing nothing more than minding their own business. They don't wanta believe it, but deep down inside they gotta know the bad guys are winning; and you and me and the rest of this circus that makes up the criminal-justice system are too hamstrung or too frightened or just plain too lazy to do anything about it. Sure, they want a little blood every now and then, so they can at least delude themselves into thinking somebody's doing *something*."

"And feeding them a sacrificial lamb like Ricky Miracle is going to change all that?" Vince asked.

"Maybe, maybe not." Quinlan resumed walking. "I don't make moral judgments. I leave that up to guys like you and your dip-shit partner in there. While you're sitting around staring at your navels, I got half the city of New York, from the mayor on down, busting my balls for an indictment. You come up with a better suspect between now and day after tomorrow, give me a call. If not, I go with what I've got."

"About that sex you mentioned before. You know Connie's cut me off the last couple of days . . . "

Quinlan smiled for the first time that day. "See you in court, shithead."

19

ANGELA BRUNO BRUSHED AN ERRANT STRAND OF GRAYING black hair from her forehead before answering the door of her New Rochelle apartment. "Please come in, officers." She smiled nervously and admitted Vince and Tommy. "I hope you'll forgive the mess. I started to pick up when you called but I just fell behind . . . You know how it is."

"Don't go to any trouble on our account, Mrs. Bruno," Vince reassured her, entering the cramped living room cluttered with discarded clothing, magazines, and newspapers, empty trays of food and overflowing ashtrays. "We'll try to get this over with as quickly as possible so you can get on with your day."

"Please, call me Angela." She brushed her face with her fingers, inadvertently trying to smooth the puffiness around her eyes. "Take as long as you need, but you'll have to understand that my son tires easily. He may not be up to answering all of your questions."

"Ma'am?" Vince looked at her questioningly. "If there's a problem we can come back later."

She became flustered. "I'm sorry, I thought you knew. Eric is confined to a wheelchair. He's been very ill for a while now."

"Maybe some other time would be better . . ."

"No, no, if you have to ask him questions, now is as good a time as any. Eric isn't getting any better. His disease is a degenerative one: A.L.S. You probably know it better as 'Lou Gherig's Disease.' "

"I'm sorry. I had no idea . . ." Vince said. "We only have a couple of questions, if you feel he's up to answering them."

"Who's that out there?" The disembodied voice coming from the next room was thick, demanding.

Angela Bruno reddened and hustled them down the

hallway to a bedroom in the rear. "Eric's father hasn't been well lately either . . . Eric? There are some police-men here who would like to ask you some questions." She halted at the open doorway of a darkened bedroom. Eric Bruno sat against the far wall. His body was stiff, ungainly, propped tenuously in the wheelchair like a scarecrow struggling against the wind. His head cocked awkwardly to one side, and a dribble of saliva trickled slowly down his chin onto his stained pajama front. "I doubt you'll be able to understand much of what he says, so if you don't mind, I'll translate for you." She led them into the room.

"Hello, Eric. I'm Detective Crowley and this's Detec-tive Ippollito." Vince tried to sound cheerful, but the catch in his voice gave him away. It was like seeing his ex-partner Billy all over again, wasting away day by day in the squalor of Queens Hospital. "We'd like to ask you a few questions about Lisa Thorpe, if that's okay with you." He looked questioningly at Angela.

"It's all right," she reassured Vince. "He's seen it all on TV. Eric understands everything. He just has diffi-culty communicating."

"In that case, can you tell me just when it was you last saw her?" Vince asked.

A painful series of unintelligible utterances. "He says it was a long time ago," Angela translated. "But I can tell you he hasn't set eyes on her since the World Cham-pionships in 1986. Not one visit, not a postcard—nothing."

Eric's mouth moved, and his furrowed brow empha-sized the importance of his deep, throaty rasps. "He's telling you that Lisa was angry with him," Angela said. "He still accepts responsibility for what happened."

"Would you mind telling me just what that was?" Vince asked her.

Angela's jaw tightened. "They were about halfway through their program and doing very well. There was a lift, a fairly simple one they'd done in practice a hundred times, and Eric dropped her. That's all, he simply dropped her, but it was enough to cost them the championship. We had no way of knowing at the time, but it was just one of the early signs of his disease. His muscle coordina-tion was starting to deteriorate. After that he became more and more clumsy. Simple things, like lifting a glass of milk became hard for him. He was finally diagnosed early last year."

"She blamed him for that?" Vince asked, astonished.

"She didn't know he was ill at first," Angela said, translating Eric's earnest gasps. "She felt he was lazy, that he didn't practice hard enough, or care as much about the championship as she did." She looked up at Vince with tear-stained eyes. "He cared, Detective, we all cared. His father got up at four o'clock every morning for years to drive him out to Long Island for practice. He held down three jobs just to pay for the coaching and rink time. We knew that skating was the most important thing in the world to Eric."

"But you told her about him . . ." Vince said.

Angela shrugged her shoulders. "She knew almost from the beginning."

Eric began to retch and Angela rushed to his side. Retrieving a plastic catheter from a nearby table, she inserted it into an aperature beneath his Adam's apple. "He's lost control of his throat muscles, and his tracheotomy tube sometimes gets clogged with phlegm when he's excited," she explained, threading it into his throat like a plumber trying to clear a stopped-up drain. "He'd suffocate if we didn't aspirate it."

Vince and Tommy stood uncomfortably while she finished the procedure. "I think we'd better leave," Vince said as she replaced the catheter on the table and mopped her forehead with the corner of her apron. "I don't think there's any more Eric can tell us—"

"He could tell you plenty if he wasn't still in love with the little tramp!" The shirtless, unshaven man in the doorway was sweating profusely even in the chill of the inadequately heated apartment.

"Please, Frank, not now." Angela Bruno rushed toward him and tried to prevent him from entering.

"Why not now?" He sneered and brushed her aside. "What do we have to lose now—our self-respect?" He walked unsteadily into the room.

"My husband has been under a strain since Eric became ill," Angela explained, following him closely.

"I've been drunk, goddamit!" he howled. "When are you going to get it into your head that I drink too much?" He glared at her.

Vince stepped between them. "Is there anything I can do, ma'am?" he asked Angela.

Frank Bruno's shoulders sagged at this challenge. He walked to the window and parted the heavy drapes, allowing a shaft of sunlight to penetrate the gloomy interior of the room. "How's it going, champ?" He smiled and ran a beefy hand through Eric's matted hair.

"Everything going to be all right here?" Vince asked.

Frank Bruno turned and faced him with bloodshot eyes. "Sure, we're always okay here." He caressed Eric's face tenderly with his hand. "Aren't we, champ?"

"Perhaps you'd better leave now," Angelica prodded.

"Yeah." Vince motioned to Tommy. "So long, Eric. Good luck to you." They exited the room.

"I'm sorry about Frank," she said at the front door. "He was never able to cope with all this. Eric was everything to him. The skating was something magical. It was going to be the success he'd never had himself."

"It's all right, ma'am—"

"He never forgave Lisa Thorpe for abandoning Eric. He felt she could have at least phoned from time to time, just to see how Eric was doing. She and her father could have made a big difference in our lives."

"If there's anything the department can do," Vince offered lamely.

She laughed bitterly. "Sure. Do you have a half million you want to donate to pay Eric's medical bills? Frank hasn't worked in almost a year."

"I wish there was something—"

"We'll be fine." She placed a reassuring hand on Vince's forearm. "I'm just sorry Eric couldn't provide you with more information. They had a manager, Bobo Kurtz. You might want to talk to him. He has offices in the city—Rockefeller Center, I think."

Vince entered the name in his notebook. "Thank you very much, ma'am. I hope Eric is . . . comfortable." He felt foolish for saying it.

"He will be soon." She smiled wanly and closed the door.

Outside, they drove in silence for a while. "I didn't see any trophies in *there*," Tommy said finally.

"They probably sold them all to pay the kid's medical bills."

"What kind of person would just turn their back on a partner like that?" Tommy wondered aloud.

"Sure as hell not the 'saint' Thorpe's been writing about," Vince suggested.

"Or the 'ray of sunshine' everybody at the hospital's been talking about," Tommy concurred. "Whatta you think we got here, Vince?"

"I dunno." He stared vacantly out the window. "I dunno, partner."

Leila Turner met them at the door of the squad room as they entered. "Those phone checks you wanted are on your desk, and there's something really weird going down."

"What's that?" Vince walked to his desk and picked up the computer print-out.

"Look at the number circled in red. It's the Spring Street Athletic Club. Lisa Thorpe called there three times in November and once in December."

"You've gotta be kidding." Vince scanned the sheet in disbelief. The Spring Street Athletic Club was a Mafia clubhouse in Greenwich Village, the primary hangout of Carlo Madalena, one of the most powerful mob chieftains on the East Coast. "You sure there's no mistake here?"

"No mistake. And one thing more. There are two calls to the same number from Ivor Thorpe's apartment and another two from his office," Turner said.

Vince looked at Tommy. "What the fuck is going on here?"

Tommy shrugged.

"Before you get into that, can you give me a couple of minutes on this Karp case?" Turner asked.

"Oh yeah, congratulations. I hear Gleason turned it over to you." Vince grinned at her.

"Don't mention that man to me." She pretended to shiver. "There's something really queer about that man. I mean it, Vince." Her eyes became wide. "I don't know what he does when he's with you, but he gets this real nutty look on his face when he talks to me in private—like he's having trouble breathing."

"Maybe he's got the hots for you," Tommy suggested.

Turner rolled her eyes. "Can we talk about Karp?" she pleaded with Vince.

"Sure. How's it lay out for you?"

She retrieved a thick ledger from her desk. "I've got more than two hundred names here—people who owed

Karp money for one reason or another. Then there are a couple of hundred more who defaulted on their payments and had their stuff repossessed over the past year. Plus disgruntled employees, dissatisfied customers, and half the rest of the people in The Bronx who knew him and hated him on general principle. I know everyone's a legitimate suspect, but I just don't know where to start."

Vince smiled. "A little overwhelming?"

"A lot overwhelming," she admitted.

"Well, if it was my case, here's how I'd narrow down that list. I'd run the M.O. through the computer and cross-check it with all the available suspects." He shot a sidelong glance at Tommy while Turner committed it to her notebook. "Then I'd take all those names that come up positive for habitually cutting off people's heads and bring them in for questioning."

20

Dear Connie,
    I've got a few minutes between shifts, so I thought
I'd write and try to tell you how awful I feel . . .

Vince read what he had written and winced. It was
starting to sound as stupid as all the other letters he'd
written over the past couple of days.

    What happened between Jessy and me, happened.
I can't change that or make it easier for you to
understand. If it helps to know that not seeing you
hurts a lot, then you must be feeling better. It hurts,
and it hurts more knowing its my own fault. I guess
that's probably the worst kind of pain, the kind that
could have been avoided in the first place.
    I see guys almost every day who get themselves
busted for doing dumb things—not really bad things,
just dumb, thoughtless things that happen to be
against the law, and I can't help but notice how it
tears them up. They're not hardened criminals who
figure jail time is the price of doing business. They're
just everyday Joes who got themselves in over their
heads and can't get out. They think they see a chance
to make an easy score without getting caught, and
right away they forget what they're all about. Then
they wake up criminals and have to face the music.
I'm not saying they shouldn't be responsible. I'm a
cop and I believe people should have to pay for their
mistakes. I guess what I'm saying is that it's harder
for them because they never figured themselves for
criminals in the first place. That must be the way I'm
feeling now, like one of those guys who thought he
was a decent Joe and woke up one morning to find
out he was a crumb . . .

He stared at the page. Everything he'd written sounded self-serving and insincere. Connie would take one look at it and write him off for good—if she hadn't done that already.

> Anyway, I know I deserve what I'm getting, Connie. You gave me more than I had a right to expect, and I blew it all away. I'm sorry. I know that's not a lot to say, but it's the best I can do for now. I love you.
>
> Vince

Tommy entered the squad room and Vince folded the letter self-consciously. "What's up, partner?"

"I ran a check on this Bobo Kurtz character, don't ask me why. I guess I'm just naturally suspicious of guys who call themselves 'Bobo.' Anyhow, it paid off. Turns out he's a convicted grifter . . . got paper going back to the Sixties. He did eighteen months for mail fraud in '72."

"No shit? Now how do you suppose a guy like that gets himself involved with a blue-blood like Lisa Thorpe? I mean, there's lots of managers around, right? So why does she hook up with some sleazebucket like him?"

"A very successful sleazebucket," Tommy corrected him. "This guy represents some of the biggest people in sports."

"How do you figure it?" Vince leafed through the Rolodex on his desk. "Why don't you give Bobo baby a jingle and set up an interview for us? I'm gonna try and make some sense out of those telephone calls Lisa Thorpe and her old man made to the Spring Street A.C." He found the number he was looking for and dialed.

"Delucca Auto Body." Nunzio Delucca answered on the first ring.

"*Paisano*, it's Crowley. How's business?"

Icy silence. "Whadda you want from me, Crowley? I'm very busy here."

"Not too busy to talk to an old *campadre*, are you?"

Nunzio groaned. "Look, I been seeing my P.O. regular. You can check it out—"

"Hey, this's a friendly call," Vince interrupted him. "I need a favor from you, okay?"

"What kind of favor?" Nunzio asked suspiciously.

"I need a meet with the Don as soon as you can set it up."

"Whaddaya need me for? I don't hang around with people like him, you know that, Crowley. It'd be a violation of my parole."

"Don't bust my chops here, Nunzio. I don't have time to dance with you right now. You gonna help me out here, or do I send somebody down there to start checking the vehicle ID numbers on those Mercedes and BMWs that find their way into your joint?"

"I'll see what I can do . . . That all?"

"Love ya, Nunzio." Vince hung up the phone.

"Why the runaround?" Tommy asked from his desk. "Why don't we just go down to the clubhouse and question the old man?"

"Nobody treats Carlo Madalena like that. It'd be a sign of disrespect," Vince explained. "What'd you get on Bobo?"

"I spoke to his secretary. He's in, he's out, she never knows where he is half the time. When he's in, he's out; when he's out, he's in. You know how it is with these big shots."

"Say no more." Vince put Connie's letter in an envelope and addressed it. "Sometimes you just gotta remind these guys that they're really public-spirited citizens underneath all that bullshit." He grabbed his coat and led Tommy out the door.

They drove to Manhattan, parked in a bus zone, and took the elevator to Bobo Kurtz's ninth-floor suite of offices at 40 Rockefeller Plaza.

"I've been expecting you gentlemen." Kurtz met them at the door of his luxuriously appointed office and ushered them inside. "I suppose you want to know about my business relationship with Lisa Thorpe."

"If you don't mind." Vince sized him up quickly; slick, urban, arrogant; unapologetically flamboyant from his deep brown artificial suntan to the proliferation of heavy gold chains suspended beneath his unbuttoned shirt. His gestures were charged with short, sinuous movements, like a mongoose ready to pounce. Head to foot, Bobo Kurtz was a guy on the make. "There are a couple of inconsistencies we're trying to clear up, and we were hoping you might be able to help us out."

"Inconsistencies." Kurtz smiled wryly. "Yes, I'd expect there would be when it came to Lisa. She wasn't what you'd call a predictable person."

"So we're finding out. Can you tell us how you and Lisa first became involved?"

He paused. "I don't think I can really tell you how. It just sort of happened. She contacted me a few months before the Geneva meet, and we began working on plans for her professional contract."

"I didn't know there was a professional contract," Vince said.

"There wasn't. We were just exploring her potential market value if she went on to win the world championship. I don't think I have to tell you that the dollar amounts would have been staggering."

"What about her partner, Eric Bruno?" Tommy asked.

Kurtz nodded somberly. "Too bad about Eric. But to be honest, we weren't even considering him in our plans. Eric was a good technical skater, but he had no real dollar potential. Lisa was always the star."

"About you and Lisa: Would you say your relationship was friendly? Did you have any disagreements?" Vince asked.

He searched the ceiling before he answered. "That's a tough one. I don't think it would have been possible to deal with Lisa without having some disagreements. She knew what she wanted, and she was convinced she knew how to get it. All in all, though, I guess I'd have to categorize our business dealings as cordial . . . most of the time . . ."

"Anything more than cordial?" Vince asked.

Kurtz seemed surprised by the question. "If you mean by that, were we lovers—absolutely not. I don't think Lisa was capable of loving anyone but herself."

"That doesn't quite square with the picture most people are painting," Vince observed.

Kurtz shook his head. "Yeah. I read the papers, watch the TV news—"

"But you saw her differently?"

Kurtz spread his palms on his desk. "Look, Detective. I don't wanta go on record as speaking ill of the dead, but if you want the truth about Lisa Thorpe, you're going to have to get past those syrupy press releases her old man keeps putting out. Lisa was no saint, take my word for it."

"She was practically a nun." Tommy said.

"Where I come from, 'practically' don't buy the groceries," Kurtz replied. "I have my own theory about that."

"Mind letting us in on it?" Vince asked.

Kurtz expelled a long, low breath of air. "Look, detectives, I'm no psychiatrist but I think I've been around long enough to become a pretty good student of human nature. I've been involved in some pretty wild schemes in my time, and I think I can recognize a con when I see one."

"Are you telling us Lisa Thorpe was running some kind of con?" Vince asked disbelievingly.

He shrugged. "I can't think of a better way to put it. After Lisa finished out of the money in the World Championships, her asking price plummeted. I know it doesn't make much sense. She was still just as good a skater as always, but in this business you ride success to the top, not failure. I don't think she was ready for the rejection. It just wasn't part of her blueprint. She stood here in this office and lost it. I mean she screamed at the top of her voice—ranted and raged against everybody she thought was lining up against her, starting with poor Eric Bruno and ending up with me."

"She had a temper," Vince broke in.

"Lisa arranged her life," Kurtz said. "She couldn't stand it if anything went wrong with the arrangement, but she was also very resilient. With Lisa, the only thing that mattered was getting to the top, and if one plan didn't work she picked right up with another one. The day I read about her entering the convent I said to myself: 'Holy shit, she actually went and did it. She found a way to make all this pay off for her.' "

"I'm not sure I follow," Vince broke in. "How could going into a convent pay off for her?"

Kurtz beamed. "Don't you see the beauty of it? 'WORLD FIGURE SKATING STAR GIVES HERSELF TO GOD!' " he said quoting imaginary headlines. "She had all those gullible little folks out there eating out of her hand. All she had to do was stick it out for a couple of months, leave, and make a comeback. The poor slobs would be camping out in the streets to buy tickets to see the *skating nun*."

Vince and Tommy looked at each other. "You know this for a fact or are you just guessing?" Vince asked.

"I don't think anyone knew anything about Lisa Thorpe for a fact," Kurtz replied. "Lisa was different things to different people—whoever or whatever she felt would do her the most good."

"So it's just a guess on your part. A guess from somebody who had every reason to resent her."

"I didn't resent Lisa. If anything, I admired her. You know, I've run a few cons myself—"

"We've seen your rap sheet," Tommy observed.

"If what you're saying actually happened, why didn't she follow through?" Vince asked. "She left the convent, but there's no indication she ever attempted to make a comeback. Did she ever call you about it? Did she contact anybody else?"

"Not that I know of," Kurtz admitted.

"So doesn't that shoot holes in your theory?" Vince persisted.

Kurtz shook his head. "I don't care what she did after she left. Nobody's ever going to convince me Lisa was sincere about becoming a nun. You know the old saying: 'Never try to con a con man.' "

"Did she contact you at all after that?" Vince asked.

"No, and I don't know what she did with her life that last year. I heard stories. Friends told me she hooked up with some bad characters, that she'd just started running wild, but I can't say for sure whether they were true or not. All I know for certain is that she never skated before an audience again."

"Any idea who those bad characters might have been?'

"Best guess? Junkies, Hell's Angels—anybody who might satisfy her sense of the dramatic." He smiled a sad smile. " 'NUN BECOMES VILLAIN.' That could've gotten her adrenaline flowing."

"It could've gotten her killed."

21

District Court of the City of New York
County of The Bronx

BILL OF INDICTMENT

Having heard the testimony given before this court
and deliberated over same; we the members of the
Grand Jury find sufficient cause to indict Ricardo
Mirable, aka Ricky Miracle, known hereafter as the
Defendant, for criminal responsibility in the matter
of the felony homicide of Lisa Thorpe. The Defendant will be delivered to duly appointed custodians
of the court and held over for trial on charges to be
specified by the Bronx County District Attorney;
said trial to be scheduled for the soonest available
date . . .

Ivor Thorpe rose ungracefully behind Tommy's desk
like an unfolding jackknife and stood in the narrow confines of the aisle as Vince entered the squadroom. "Detective Crowley." He offered a lukewarm handshake.

"Mr. Thorpe?" Vince returned the handshake and shot
a nervous glance across the room at Tommy, who was
trying unconvincingly to absorb himself at the teletype
machine. "What brings you up here to The Bronx?"

Thorpe cleared his throat. "I'd like to go over your
case against Mirable, if you can spare a few minutes."

Vince squeezed past him and began sifting through the
phone messages on his desk. "I'd like to help you out,
sir, but I'm really not in a position to discuss it at this
point. Not even with you."

Thorpe remained impassive. "I've taken the liberty of
speaking with your commander, and he's given his assur-
ances that you'll be cooperative."

Vince felt the hairs on the back of his neck stand up. "I'm supposed to cooperate with you?"

"Please, please, let's not get off on the wrong foot here." Thorpe's tone became conciliatory. "I'm not here to cause dissension. After all, we're both on the same side, isn't that so? I just feel that if we're to present a solid case against Mirable we should coordinate our efforts, rather than working at cross-purposes. Surely you can't be against that?"

"I'm conducting an ongoing homicide investigation, sir," Vince responded. "That's what this city pays me for. If you have any information that you feel will be useful to me in that investigation, I'll be glad to take your statement. If not, I'd appreciate it if you'd let me get on with the business of finding your daughter's killer."

Thorpe's jaw tightened. "I was under the impression that her killer was already in custody."

"Ricardo Mirable was indicted by a grand jury. That doesn't make him guilty."

"So your deposition in court would seem to indicate," Thorpe said icily.

"Sir?"

"My information is that you attempted to obstruct his indictment with your testimony, that you tried to inject your personal feelings into a legal proceeding."

"My *testimony*, sir, was supposed to be private." Vince could feel his rage building. "Grand jury proceedings are closed to the public."

Thorpe nodded. "True, but surely this isn't the first time you've heard of that prohibition being broken. You don't impress me as being that naive, Detective Crowley."

There was a call from Connie among the stack of telephone messages. "If you don't mind, sir, I have a lot of work to do here."

Thorpe glared at him. "Am I to take that to mean that you're no longer interested in seeing my daughter's murderer convicted?"

Vince reached for the telephone. "*That*, Mr. Thorpe, is the only thing I am interested in. What I'm not interested in is finding a scapegoat for the press and the politicians. I'm continuing to investigate your daughter's killing, and there are things about it I find troubling . . . evidence that seems at odds with the D.A.'s case against Mirable."

"What sort of evidence?" Thorpe demanded.

"I'm afraid I can't discuss it." Vince looked up at Thorpe, standing awkwardly in the pinched confines of the aisle. "Pardon me for asking this, sir, but are you interested in finding out who killed your daughter or are you looking for a convenient body? There are a lot of people out there who want a warm body they can parade in front of the TV cameras, somebody who looks just guilty enough to satisfy the public's need for blood, but I can't imagine that would satisfy you. I'm trying to get at the truth about your daughter's death, Mr. Thorpe. Isn't that what you want, too?"

"Of course it's what I want," Thorpe replied angrily. "I'm insulted that you even asked the question. What I do not want, and what I will not tolerate, is the obstruction of the case against my daughter's murderer by you or by anyone else with a personal bias. Make no mistake, Detective Crowley. I will stop at nothing to insure his swift prosecution and conviction, with or without your help. Do I make myself clear?"

Vince nodded. "Can I get on with my work now, sir?"

"Do not oppose me, Detective Crowley," Thorpe said through clenched teeth. "I make short work of those who oppose me." He wheeled and left the room.

"What's with that *strunz*?" Tommy asked after Thorpe had gone. "I had him for almost a half hour before you got here, and all he did is try and pump me for information. What's he talking about your grand jury testimony for anyhow? You say something you weren't supposed to?"

Vince shrugged. "Not technically. The foreman asked if the blood on Ricky Miracle's jacket had been positively identified as belonging to Lisa Thorpe, and I answered that it was the same blood type as Lisa Thorpe's, but there was no way of telling how or when it got there."

"So what's wrong with that?"

"Well, then he asked whether there was any other way it could've gotten on the jacket, and I answered that we checked out Miracle's story about finding the bloody towels in the bushes in front of the Shangri-la, and found it to be plausible."

"Holy shit!" Tommy rolled his eyeballs. "Quinlan musta busted a gut."

"Quinlan wasn't there." Vince smiled. "He sent some rookie assistant to present the case—a shitkicker named

Terence Doyle. I squeezed it in before he had a chance to shut me up."

"So how did Thorpe find out about it?"

"Who the hell knows? A guy with his money and clout can get to anybody. Maybe it was the foreman, maybe the court stenographer. There's just no way to tell." He shook his head. "I can tell you one thing, though. If even part of what Bobo Kurtz said about Lisa was right, I can see where she got it from. Being cold-blooded seems to run in the Thorpe genes."

"Sonofabitch don't know when to mind his own business," Tommy said resentfully. "He started on me about why I'm a cop. 'Why are you the way you are?' he asks me. 'You look like you got a good brain,' he says. 'You probably coulda been anything you wanted to be.' "

"Sounds to me like he was trying to reach you," Vince observed.

"So why didn't he just say what's on his mind? Why not say 'Work for me and I'll slip you some long green'?" Tommy protested. "He's making it look like I'm some kinda turd being a cop. I wanted to say, 'Hey, I am what I am, you know what I mean? My people were working stiffs, not millionaires like you. My old man was a longshoreman. He busted his balls every day of his life out on the Red Hook piers before he died. He would've been the proudest man on earth if he'd been there when I was accepted by the department.' "

"Sounds pretty good to me. Why didn't you say it?"

"I dunno. Guys like him make me really nervous," Tommy admitted.

"Don't let ass-wipes like Thorpe intimidate you," Vince said, dialing Connie's number. "You got more character in your little finger than he'll ever have in his life." Connie's secretary answered and put Vince on hold. "You know, the trouble with guys like him is they're so used to getting things their own way, they fall apart when they run into a hitch. They haven't been beat up enough to have developed any toughness."

"Thorpe seems pretty tough to me," Tommy said.

"Thorpe's mean. There's a difference."

"All rich people suck." Dog Scarfatti stood in the doorway of the squadroom. "They got no right to complain about anything."

Vince scowled. "So how come you spend all your time scheming to become one of them?"

Scarfatti shrugged. "That's mathematics. You do what you gotta do, know what I mean?" He popped a pistachio nut in his mouth with red-stained fingers and cracked it lustily. "You know the problem with most people is they get having money and being rich all mixed up. Most of the drug dealers in The Bronx got more money than you and me will ever see, but they don't get asked to no society parties."

"Yeah, you can't turn a silk purse into a cow's ass," Tommy agreed.

"The point is, the drug dealer's a slimeball no matter how much bread he's carrying, and your Wall Street big shot's still a big shot even when he's on the balls of his ass," Scarfatti went on. "You shoulda seen the money we found on some of the scumbags me and Vince here usta bust."

"I didn't know you two worked together," Tommy said.

"I'm trying to forget it." Vince lifted the receiver from his shoulder to his ear and heard the monotonous drone of elevator music. "It was a long time ago. Back in Brooklyn."

"We were working Narcotics," Scarfatti said. "Real sweet duty, until those Knapp cocksuckers came along."

"And nailed your ass to the duty roster," Vince reminded him.

Scarfatti shrugged. "Hey, life's full of ups and downs. You don't see me crying, do you?" He drained the last pistachio nut from the bag and discarded it on Tommy's desk. "Remember Stick-Pin, Crowley?"

Vince nodded uncomfortably.

"Who's Stick-Pin?" Tommy asked.

"A real scumbucket," Scarfatti answered. "He was a big-time heroin dealer back in those days. This guy wore more jewelry than the goddamn Queen of England. Had a rock in his tie that was bigger than the Hope diamond. Vince and me raided his place one afternoon and caught him dead to rights, just after he'd spooned all the smack into balloons. The sonofabitch sees us coming and starts swallowing balloons, two, three at a time, until he's tossed down more than a couple dozen of 'em." He began to grin. "Tell your partner what we did then, Crowley."

"You tell him . . ." Vince punched the buttons on the telephone trying to get a response.

"Vince and me put Stick-Pin in the car and stop at the drug store for a six-pack of Ex-Lax. Then we drive him to the local pool hall, lock ourselves in the crapper, pull down his pants, and start feeding it to him. All of it, enough to clean out a herd of constipated elephants. Fifteen, twenty minutes later Stick-Pin starts moaning and groaning like a grounded flounder, you know what I mean?" Scarfatti made a show of imitating him, holding his abdomen and prancing around the squad room. "All of a sudden the dam breaks and there's shit all over the place . . . and all the evidence we'll ever need to nail the little bastard."

"That's fucking disgusting," Tommy said.

"Hey, you gotta do what you gotta do." Scarfatti shrugged his shoulders. "Me and Vince got a commendation for that bust."

Connie finally answered the phone. "Hi, I got a message you called," Vince said self-consciously.

"I got your letter."

"I guess it sounded pretty dumb."

"Not really. Endearing, maybe, but not dumb."

Vince felt a rush of expectancy. "Does that mean there's still a chance for us?"

"I'm not sure. I only know I'm not ready to close you out of my life . . . not yet."

"You want to have dinner and talk about it? How about tonight?" Vince asked.

"Not tonight. Give me a few more days to sort things out. The end of the week, maybe."

"Friday? Linguini and a bottle of guinea red at Colinini's?"

"Friday, then."

"I missed you New Year's Eve."

"Me too." She hung up.

22

"LET US PROCLAIM THE MYSTERY OF FAITH" VINCE READ the stained-glass panel above the entrance to the chapel of the Little Sisters of Charity as he waited in the vestibule for the end of the afternoon service. "CHRIST IS BORN, CHRIST IS RISEN, CHRIST WILL COME AGAIN." Inside, a scattering of women knelt and recited the Angelus. Their blended prayers rose from the simple wooden pews, swelling inside the small sanctuary: *"The Angel of the Lord declared unto Mary. And she conceived of the Holy Ghost."*

He felt a twinge of guilt. How long had it been since he'd been inside a Catholic church—fifteen, twenty years? The rhythmic chanting catapulted him back to the dusty classroom of his past. Our Lady of Lourdes grammar school in Queens Village, smelling of chalk and wet mittens drying on the radiator. Sister Mary Dominick stalked the narrow aisles, an omnipotent, black-clad specter drumming her wooden ruler into the palm of her hand like a metronome. Her dark eyes swept the ranks of desks, searching for cheats, for the unrighteous and unchaste—for evildoers.

"Behold the handmaiden of the Lord. Be it done unto me according to Thy word."

The tiny chapel was a far cry from the churches of his childhood, Vince thought. It was hardly more elaborate than a waiting room in a country railroad station. There were no poised plaster saints and martyrs flanking the rows of pews. No tiers of candles flickered in remembrance. No white marble altar loomed majestically heavenward to arching beams of a vaulted ceiling. The unadorned chapel reflected the simplicity of the congregation, clothed mostly in austere woolen dresses of pale blue or brown, Their shoulders were covered with homespun sweaters or shawls. Only a half-dozen or so of the older women wore the long black habits and starched wimpoles he remembered nuns used to wear. *"Pray for us, O holy Mother of God. That we may be made worthy of the promises of Christ."*

When the worship ended, the nuns filed silently out of the chapel, lowering their eyes as they passed Vince, as if an inadvertent look might turn to longing. He spotted an erect, no-nonsense woman who carried herself as if she was accustomed to being obeyed, and asked, "Excuse me. Sister Michael?"

"You must be Detective Crowley." She smiled as she approached him. "I didn't expect you until later."

"Last time I came to Connecticut I hit a snowstorm, so I left myself plenty of time."

"That seems prudent at this time of year." She offered her hand. "I got out all of Lisa Thorpe's records when you called. Everything you'll need is in my office."

Vince returned the handshake and followed her up a winding snow-swept pathway to the main house. "I appreciate your going to all this trouble for me, Sister," he said as they entered her ground-floor office. "I'll try to be as brief as possible."

Sister Michael sat at her desk and offered Vince a chair. "I'll be glad to provide any help I can. We were all terribly upset when we heard what had happened." She handed him a thin manila folder. "Feel free to use whatever you can from her records, although I doubt there's anything in there you don't already know."

Vince smiled. "You'd be surprised what we don't know about Lisa Thorpe, starting with why she decided to enter your order in the first place."

Sister Michael hesitated. "Entering a religious life is a very personal choice, Detective Crowley, perhaps the most profound decision a woman can make. I'd like to be able to tell you that everyone comes to us out of a deep and abiding love for God and a commitment to dedicate her life to his service, but there are some who have other reasons, not so clearly defined."

"And Lisa Thorpe's reasons?"

"I can't give you a clear answer about that. She was with us such a very short time."

Vince checked his notebook. "My information is that she was here for almost six months."

"That would be about right, but Lisa was a difficult

person to understand. I was reading her evaluation charts this morning—periodic assessments of her progress given by her superiors on various areas of community life—and I can honestly tell you that she was as much of an enigma to them as she was to me. I don't think anyone here really ever understood her."

"Would you say she had a vocation?" Vince asked.

"That's not a word we throw around as much as we once did," she said. "We prefer to refer to those who choose to follow a religious calling as being 'committed' individuals. We seek young women of high principle who are willing to dedicate their lives to the service of God and their fellow man."

"Would you call Lisa Thorpe, 'committed,' then?" Vince asked.

"She wanted us to believe she was. Possibly she wanted to believe it herself, but I think you'll be able to tell clearly from her records that we had serious doubts about Lisa's spiritual and emotional fitness for a religious life almost from the very beginning. Despite what's been said in the newspapers, Lisa never became a member of this order. She was never allowed to take vows."

"But she was a novice, she wore a habit like the other nuns, isn't that so?" Vince prodded.

"In a sense." A small smile crept over Sister Michael's face. "Depending on what you call a habit. Lisa wore what could be considered street clothes—dresses and high heels—like most of the new girls. About the only thing that identifies them as belonging to a religious order is the cross they wear around their necks."

"Can't tell the players without a scorecard, huh?" Vince cracked.

"You're joking, but that's closer to the truth than you think. Sometimes, it seems they'd rather be teeny-boppers than nuns." Her voice became conspiratorial. "Frankly, it's caused some resentment among the older sisters. I have to walk a tightrope with my own dress just to keep from offending either side of the argument." She indicated the knee-length blue skirt, tailored cotton jacket, and modified veil she wore. "I even alternate pectoral crosses, the more traditional silver one on even days, the modern wooden version on odd. There are times when I feel like Solomon himself."

Vince smiled. "And Lisa Thorpe was one of the mods?"

"For as long as she remained a novice, and that was only a few weeks . . . a month at most."

"But you let her stay here—"

"She was given refuge within this community," Sister Michael explained. "The church has a long-standing tradition of offering sanctuary to those who ask for it."

"Refuge from what?" Vince looked puzzled. "If you don't mind my saying so, Sister, Lisa Thorpe didn't have what you'd call a real tough life before she came to you."

"That's rather a subjective judgment, wouldn't you agree?" she chided. "I don't see how any of us can determine what constitutes hardship for anyone else. In our best judgment Lisa was in a state of emotional distress. We felt that keeping her here until she was strong enough to leave was the Christian thing to do."

"I see . . ." Vince scanned the records in the folder. "Would you say that was a common occurrence. I mean, do you allow many young women to stay here for those same reasons?"

"I wouldn't say many," she hedged.

"Would you say ten percent, twenty?" he persisted.

"Probably not that many . . ."

Vince closed the folder. "Lisa was the first, right?"

Her face flushed. "I'm sorry if I've misled you, Detective Crowley. Lisa Thorpe *was* a special case. Among other things, she had some physical difficulties. She'd undergone surgery and was experiencing some resultant depression."

"Would that surgery have been a tubal ligation?" Vince asked, checking his notebook.

She flinched. "I'd have no way of knowing that."

"Any idea what kind of surgery it was?"

"I understood it an ovarian problem—cysts, something of that sort."

"Did she receive any sort of treatment while she was here?" Vince asked.

"Her physical condition was only of secondary importance to us," Sister Michael explained. "Our primary concern was her mental and spiritual health." She leaned forward and propped her elbows on the desk. "I have to be honest with you, Detective Crowley. I made an exception in Lisa's case because for years her father has been a loyal benefactor to our school. He contributes generously to all of our fund-raising efforts and, even now, has

established a nursing scholarship in his daughter's name."
She smiled embarrassedly. "Being a mother superior isn't
all piety and prayer, you know. I'm afraid we wouldn't
get very far without practical considerations."

"Did you like her?" Vince asked after a pause.

She seemed surprised by the abruptness of the question.
"I don't see what that has to do with anything."

"Did you *like* her?" he repeated.

"She was a strange girl. I don't think I ever got close
enough to her to know how I felt about her."

"How about the other sisters? How did they feel about
her?"

"I sensed some resentment . . ." Sister Michael measured her words. "Some of the sisters may have thought
she was taking advantage of her name and her connections."

"And you, how did you feel?"

"A day came when we all agreed it was time for Lisa
to leave. That seemed to reduce tensions and make my
job a little easier. I was grateful for that." She breathed
deeply. "And very happy."

The drive back to The Bronx was uneventful. Vince
switched on the short-wave radio when he reached the
city line and lost himself in the routine of its reassuring
squawk: "Call the area two . . . Sector Dog . . . Available units to six-ought-three White Plains Road . . . Domestic dispute in progress . . ." The uninspired voice of
the female dispatcher eased in under the sounds of surrounding traffic, soothing and unobtrusive, like a tape
cassette of Brahms or Beethoven might have been to a
civilian driver. The radio was his link to the rhythm of
the street, and the street was his lifeline. For Vince
driving out of the canvas of snow-laden pines and scenic
New England churches into the soot and vulgarity of The
Bronx was like removing a pebble from his shoe. He
breathed easier.

"*Units respond to eight-eleven Morris Park . . . Possible jumper . . . Keep 'em coming.*" The dispatcher's tone
was the same, but Vince immediately sensed the urgency.
Isolating important calls from the unchanging drone of
the radio was an acquired skill. Rookies listened for the
codes and catchwords; veterans picked them up instinctively. He swerved against the flow of traffic, exited the
parkway in the wrong direction from an on ramp, and
carved his way through a snarl of automobiles to the

street, activating the burp of his siren in response to their angry honks and shouts.

A haphazard assortment of blue-and-whites, fire engines, and emergency police vehicles blocked his entrance to the access road leading from Morris Park Avenue to the address given in the call: a deteriorating eight-story apartment building in the middle of the Marcus Garvey projects. From the avenue he could see a cordon of patrolmen restraining the growing crowd of curious onlookers and emergency fire vehicles rushing to position an inflatable impact cushion. The upraised stares of the crowd led his gaze to the sixth floor of the building. A black woman was sitting on an unprotected window ledge holding an infant in her arms.

Street Crime stood among the press of police personnel on the sidewalk beneath the window. "How's it going?" Vince asked, approaching him on foot.

Street Crime shook his head. "I dunno. Your partner's up there with Turner and a couple of uniforms. They're trying to keep her talking until they can find a priest or a member of the family."

Vince made his way to a parked EMS van, where detectives were attempting to install an emergency telephone hook-up with the apartment. "What's happening?"

"Nothing yet."

"That's my partner in there," Vince said.

"He's not in any danger. From what we can tell, it's just her and the baby up there. I dunno whether they got inside the place yet, but somebody's talking to her because she keeps looking back into the apartment. I think they got a bullhorn up there—"

His words were choked off by the horrified screams of the crowd as the woman threw the infant into the air. A jumble of tiny arms and legs plummeted through the open space, dropping like a stone onto the cement walkway below. Before they could react, the woman leaned outward on the ledge and allowed her body to fall forward into the emptiness, tumbling like an inexpert diver attempting a summersault. She plunged to a sickening impact a few feet from the shattered body of her child.

Police and emergency medical technicians rushed forward. Their futile efforts to find some lingering trace of life were obliterated by the crowd rimming the scene of death. Vince stood where he was, shuddering from a sudden gust of freezing wind. He'd seen it all before: the tenaments and projects and alleyways coughing up their indigestible children, the castaways of a society that had no room to absorb them.

He could see Tommy emerging from the doorway of the building, stumbling forward with tears in his eyes. Behind him Leila Turner halted on the front steps and vomited into the leafless bushes at the side.

Sometimes the rhythm of the street was a dirge.

23

TOMMY INHALED THE SMOKE FROM HIS CIGARETTE AND held it in his lungs for what seemed an eternity. Vince watched him out of the corner of his eye, holding his own breath in anticipation. "Blow it out, for chrissakes," he said finally.

Tommy exhaled the diluted column of smoke into the squad car. "You shoulda seen her eyes, Vince. Dead, like there was no life there at all." He drove into the parking lot of Bellevue Hospital. "It was like she was a zombie or something."

"You gotta let it go," Vince said. "I know it's rough, but you can't hang onto shit like that."

"I was in the room, no more than ten or fifteen feet away from her. I said everything they told us to say back at the academy. We'd get her help, things weren't really as bad as they seemed—all that crap," Tommy went on. "And she just looked at me with those blank eyes. 'My baby's got AIDS,' she said. 'You got something to fix that?'

"Her arms and legs were like tree bark." Tommy shuddered. "I mean, there wasn't a vein in them that wasn't collapsed and scabbed over. I swear to God, Vince, I almost think she jumped because she couldn't find another spot on her body to stick a needle."

Vince shrugged. "I know it sounds lousy, but they're both probably better off."

Tommy pulled into a parking space and turned off the ignition. "Maybe if she'd been angry, even despondent, maybe I coulda taken it better. But she just seemed tired, you know what I mean?"

"Yeah. Being a junkie's tough work." Vince exited the car and walked across the parking lot to the hospital entrance. "I've seen a couple like her before, and you're right; there's nothing left in them. It's like the dope snuffed out whatever spark there is." He placed a reassuring hand around Tommy's shoulder. "Let it go, partner. She was dead before you ever got there."

"What about the baby?"

"Like I said, they're probably both better off." He led Tommy to the elevator in the lobby and punched the button for the twelfth floor.

They found Ricky Miracle's room and displayed their shields and ID for the uniformed guard at the door before entering. Inside, Ricky was propped in the hospital bed, watching a television set suspended above him.

"How goes it, Ricky?" Vince asked.

Ricky eyed him nervously, turned off the TV. "I heard the jury railroaded me."

"It was a grand jury hearing, that's all," Vince explained. "A bare-bones presentation of the evidence where nobody's allowed to challenge the testimony."

"What evidence?" Ricky howled. "I didn't do nothing."

Vince nodded. "I want to believe you, Ricky. Are you sure there's nothing you haven't told me?"

Ricky slumped back into the pillows. "Oh man, they're gonna nail my ass."

"Not necessarily," Vince said.

"If the D.A.'s case isn't strong enough he won't take it to trial," Tommy added.

Ricky thought about it. "He'll take it to trial," he said finally. "They're all just looking for somebody to take the fall. Why not me?"

"Think positive," Tommy urged him. "We're uncovering new evidence every day."

"I don't get it. Last week you were ready to strap me in the chair, and all of a sudden you're acting like you're on my side here. What gives with you guys?" Ricky eyed them both suspiciously.

"We're not on anybody's side," Vince corrected him. "All we want is to get at what really happened."

"And what happened is what I already told you," Ricky said glumly. "So that's my story, even if I gotta burn for it."

"You're not gonna burn," Vince reassured him. "But you might be in for a rough time back in stir if you can't convince the D.A.'s people that you're suicidal. We're getting pressure to throw you back inside now that an indictment's been handed up."

"Suicidal?"

"That you're gonna find a way to kill yourself if they send you back to a cell," Tommy explained.

He hesitated. "Why are you guys telling me this?"

"It's not gonna do anybody any good if you freak out," Vince said. "Not even the D.A."

"So you're telling me to fake it?"

"If that's what you gotta do."

Ricky looked puzzled. What was happening here contradicted every rule of survival he had learned out on the streets. Cops were the enemy: brutal and uncaring and, most of all, not to be trusted. He'd hardened himself to believe that all he could expect from them was harassment, abuse. Vince could see that he was incapable of grasping anything beyond that conviction, at least for now.

"We gotta go now." Vince motioned to Tommy and headed for the door. "Keep in mind what we said."

Outside, they bundled their coat collars around their ears in the face of the freezing wind. "Why do you suppose he tried to make us believe he'd have to fake it?" Tommy wondered. "The poor bastard probably would end up taking the gas pipe if they put him back in stir."

"Ricky's a street kid. A street kid who admits any kind of weakness ends up bait for the sharks. He doesn't have much more than guts and bullshit keeping him alive out there." Vince climbed into the passenger seat and settled back as Tommy put the car into reverse.

"What's that shit you got there?" Walt Cuzak asked as they entered the homicide room with a bag of food they'd picked up on the way back.

"Cheeseburgers," Tommy said. "And chili dogs." He opened the bag and sniffed inside. "Pure heaven."

Cuzak made a sour face. "Man, you're killing yourself with that shit. You know how much cholesterol you're putting down every time you eat cheese and animal fat. Kee-rist! Your arteries must look like the FDR Drive at rush hour."

"That just shows how much you know, asshole." Tommy handed a chili dog to Vince and bit lustily into a cheeseburger. "The cheese in this thing isn't even real cheese, man. They used processed shit. Even the meat's artificial."

"Worse still," Cuzak groaned. "It's all plastic, made

outa some kind of petroleum derivative. Your veins are probably loaded with hydrocarbons."

"You know your trouble, Walt? You're so fucking uptight about living a long life that you don't have a life worth living. Who the hell wants to spend the next forty years eating bean curds and dessicated liver, for chrissakes? I'd rather be pushing up fucking daisies, man." Tommy finished the cheeseburger and licked his fingers. "You know, life's a banquet and jerks like you are starving to death."

"Am I interrupting something, gentlemen?" John Gleason stood in the doorway. "Because I wouldn't want to stifle any creative thought."

"Anything I can do for you, Lieutenant?" Vince ignored the sarcasm.

"Into my office, Crowley." Gleason wheeled abruptly.

Vince shrugged and followed him. "Yes sir?" he asked, closing the office door behind him.

Gleason sat down and took a slug of Maalox from an open bottle. "You wanta tell me why you're trying to sabotage the D.A.'s case against Ricardo Mirable?"

"I didn't know I was," Vince replied.

Gleason emitted a stentorian burp. "So why all that bullshit testimony in front of the grand jury?"

"Bullshit?" Vince's jaw tightened. "I answered their questions, and I *assumed* my testimony was confidential."

"Cut the crap. I know you've already been through this with Ivor Thorpe. He had me on the horn for more than an hour this morning." Gleason snarled.

"What's his beef?" Vince protested. "He got his indictment, didn't he?"

"His beef is, he got it with no help from you. Where the hell do you come off spouting your private opinions in a legal proceeding?"

"Where the hell does Thorpe come off bribing a member of a grand jury panel to get inside information?" Vince shot back. "What the fuck is this guy interested in anyway, getting a conviction against Ricky Miracle or finding his daughter's killer?"

Gleason curled his lip. "I don't suppose it's occurred to you that he just might be interested in seeing the legal process implemented, as I am. A grand jury has deliberated and decided that there is enough evidence to warrant bringing Ricardo Mirable to trial for the murder of

Lisa Thorpe. There is nothing ambivalent about that. It is a straightforward representation of the will of the people. Now you will either recognize that will—recognize the fact that your commander, the Chief of Detectives, the Police Commissioner, the Mayor, *and* the murdered girl's father are passionately interested in seeing that the matter be brought to trial and the legal process be carried out—or you will walk out that door and hand in your shield at the desk downstairs.

"If Mirable is innocent he will be acquitted. If he's guilty, he will pay the penalty. That is for a judge and jury to decide, not some over-the-hill street cop with an ax to grind." He sucked the empty air with trembling lips. "I will not see the legal process subverted by you or any other member of this command. Do I make myself clear?"

"The only one who's subverting the legal process is Ivor Thorpe," Vince replied angrily. "And anyone else who looks the other way when he uses his money and muscle to intimidate people and bend the process to fit his own ideas about justice. What the fuck am I supposed to do, just turn my back when everything I turn up tells me that daddy's little angel wasn't such an angel after all? Am I supposed to close my eyes just to protect his sick fantasies about her?"

Vince removed his wallet from his jacket pocket and threw it on Gleason's desk. "You want my shield? Here it is. I don't want anything to do with a department that's more interested in kissing ass than solving crimes. I just hope Ivor Thorpe's got a job for you somewhere out in that publishing empire of his after Ricky Miracle walks and you're standing there with your thumb up your ass looking for a new suspect." He turned to leave.

"You're not dismissed," Gleason growled.

"I just quit, remember?"

Gleason retrieved the wallet and handed it across the desk to Vince. "You quit when I tell you to quit, not before. What the hell kind of an officer walks out in the middle of an important homicide investigation anyway? This department's given you a pretty good living for more than twenty years. Don't you think you have some responsibility here, for chrissakes?"

A faint smile creased Vince's craggy face. "I don't want to seem out of line here, Lieutenant, but weren't you just telling me you wanted to see Ricky Miracle convicted? By me, that means there's no more investigation, so I'm not walking out on anything, except maybe a lot of aggravation.''

Gleason stood glumly behind his desk. "What makes you so sure Mirable's going to walk?"

"Because he's not guilty and there's no evidence against him. He's being tried because Ivor Thorpe wants him to be tried, plain and simple, but he won't be convicted. I'm as sure of that as I've been of anything in my life. I could make a better case against you than I could against Ricky Miracle . . . sir.''

"You got another suspect?"

"Not yet, but I will. It's only a matter of time.''

"Okay, stay with it, and keep me informed." Gleason sat and pretended to busy himself with some paperwork on his desk.

Outside the office, Vince examined his gold shield and wallet. The shield was becoming tarnished and the wallet dog-eared at the edges. He would have to get a new wallet, he thought, something that would withstand the impact of being thrown repeatedly on Gleason's desk.

24

THE TELEPHONE MESSAGE WAS SIMPLE AND DIRECT: "MR. M. will be in the parking lot of the Golden Gate Motel at 3:30 today." Vince glanced at his watch. "I'm going out to Ferry Point Park," he told Tommy. "Mind the store until I get back, okay?"

"What's in Ferry Point Park?"

"I got a 3:30 appointment with Carlo Madalena." Vince put on his overcoat and headed for the door.

"*The* Carlo Madalena?" Tommy looked impressed. "Want some company?"

"Not this time, partner. When the Don sets up a meet he means alone." He descended the stairs, checked out a radio at the desk, and drove toward Queens.

The Golden Gate Motel was a seedy assortment of wooden shacks in the shadow of the Bronx Whitestone Bridge, surrounded by the muddy quagmire of South Jamaica Bay, which seemed perpetually at festering low tide. Vince had been there before, responding to everything from fistfights to murder. The Golden Gate was that kind of place. He pulled the car into the parking lot and sniffed the fetid air drifting up from the ooze of mud and discarded garbage at the water's edge. It was a sure bet that today's customers weren't there for the air or the scenery.

A few unoccupied automobiles dotted the otherwise empty lot. Overhead, a canopy of gulls filled the sky, searching for mussels and fiddler crabs that somehow managed to survive in the effluent of the water. An oversized trash dumpster stood sentry at the motel's entrance, and a snarl of angry crows disputed the choice parts of a disembowled rat in its shadow.

The chill mist rising from the bay settled on his windshield and froze, blocking his vision. Vince activated the car's defroster and punched the buttons on the FM radio until he found a station to his liking . . . melodies and orchestrations that soothed; understandable words and phrases he could drift along with . . . even hazard a couple of ragged chords in the uncritical solitude of the automobile.

"Chances are . . ." Johnny Mathis's silken tones filled the car, and Vince found himself humming along. It was a golden oldie, he knew. All the songs he liked were golden oldies, just like the rest of his life. Somewhere along the way he'd settled in a groove and stayed there. He liked music that reassured him instead of jarring him. He chose clothes and mannerisms that were comfortable rather than challenging. Even Connie had told him he was moldering in the past, that he'd better get hip or hep or down, or whatever it was people got. ". . . *just because, my composure sort of slips, the moment that your lips meet mine mine . . .*" Fuck 'em all. He leaned back in the vinyl upholstery and closed his eyes contentedly.

Carlo Madalena's sleek gray Cadillac limousine pulled alongside the squad car at four o'clock. Vince stepped out into the freezing drizzle and nodded perfunctorily to the chauffeur, a burly, uncommunicative man who held the door as Vince climbed into the rear seat.

"Mr. M." Vince offered his hand to the aging Mafia chieftain as the car door closed behind him.

"Detective Crowley." Carlo Madalena returned the handshake weakly.

The old man's health was obviously failing. Curled in the corner of the rear seat, his blanket covering legs that were drawn up so that his knees reached the sagging flesh of his neck. Madalena bore the unmistakable scars of several heart attacks and a lengthy, well-publicized trial for racketeering that was still in progress. He was thinner and older than the pictures of him in the media, and trembling perceptibly. The leathery, plaster-colored skin of his hands and face was mottled with uneven brown splotches.

"It's good of you to see me, Mr. M. I'm sure you don't remember, but we met a long time ago—at the christening of Vito Prestipino's goddaughter."

The old man nodded. "I remember it well," he replied through the gnarled, unlit stub of a DiNobili cigar. "It's not every day a policeman is invited to one of our celebrations. Vito spoke well of you before he died."

"I guess you could say we respected each other," Vince said. "I was sorry he went out the way he did . . ."

Madalena shrugged. "What's past is past. I was his friend, you were his friend. We have our memories . . ." His eyes closed beneath the brim of his battered felt hat, as if he were dozing. As his jaw slackened, the butt of the cigar seemed on the verge of dropping into his lap. He seemed more like an aging pensioner than a powerful mob figure, Vince thought, one of the tired army of Boccie players he saw daily in the city's parks.

"I asked to meet with you because I need information," Vince said. "a homicide investigation I'm working on."

Madalena chuckled. "Since when do the police come to us for information about a crime?"

"I think you can help me here, Mr. M," Vince went on. "It concerns the killing of the Thorpe girl. Daughter of the publisher—"

"That's no concern of ours," Madalena said abruptly.

"But it could be," Vince said. "The investigation has uncovered a series of telephone calls from the murdered girl's apartment to the Spring Street Athletic Club during the month prior to her death . . . also some from her father's business office. I'm certain that you personally would have no knowledge of those calls, but I felt you might be interested in knowing that someone in your organization has involved you in such an ugly matter."

Carlo Madalena paused, chewing energetically on the butt of the DiNobili. "Then, you are not here to seek information, but to give it."

Vince nodded. "In a sense, but I also knew that you'd be displeased with any person in your organization who would be dumb enough to connect you with a messy situation like this. You're a busy man, Mr. M. I understand you have many pressing concerns, and dealing with the murder of someone as socially prominent as Lisa Thorpe shouldn't have to be one of them"

"I can see why my friend Vito liked you." The old man smiled. "You make your point well. More like a Sicilian than an Irishman. And you are right that we do not need this kind of involvement. Certainly you would agree that a few telephone calls could hardly be called a serious matter, but as businessmen, we do not invite the sort of publicity something like that could bring." He gripped his stomach with his open palms. "I got *agida* enough as is."

"Then you understand the need to clear this matter up quickly," Vince said. "If it's possible, I'd appreciate the name of whoever received those telephone calls at Spring Street."

Madalena shifted his bulk in the crowded rear seat in order to face Vince. "You know, of course, that I cannot do that. As much as I disapprove of the excesses of many of the young hotheads in our organization, I could never give someone up to the police for any reason. I'm sure you understand that. This much I can promise you, though. We will deal harshly with whoever is responsible, as is our custom. Beyond that, I can offer you nothing." He twirled the cigar between his lips. "I don't suppose you would have a light on you?"

Vince struck a wooden match and held it under the trembling cigar. "That's good . . ." The old man inhaled deeply and allowed the smoke to drift lazily from his nostrils. He winked slyly in the direction of the chauffeur standing a few feet from the car. "They don't let me light up no more since they found out I got a bum ticker. Treat me like an old woman half the time." He took another drag. "What is this shit, 'smoking is bad for your health' anyway? *A bafangul!*" He spat disdainfully on the floor of the car. "I been smoking ten of these a day since I was six years old, and I got the lungs of a young man." He laughed a fruity laugh.

"No disrespect intended, Mr. M., but without a name I can feed to my superiors, I'll have no choice but to open up my investigation," Vince said. "I gotta go where the evidence leads me."

". . . Cancer, high blood pressure, heart attacks." Madalena held the offending cigar in the air, ignoring Vince's veiled threat. "Next they're gonna be telling us it turns our *cujones* into ricotta, eh?" He snuffed the end in the ashtray, removed the burnt ashes, and began chewing the remainder like a stick of gum. "There. Nothing goes to waste," he said proudly. "I come from a family of twenty-three kids and lemmee tell you, everything got eaten. My old lady would milk a goat until its teats were old like shoe leather, then she roasted the meat, made blood sausage—out of the intestines, boiled the hooves into jelly, and ground the horns into poultices. The skin became shoes, flasks, whatever we needed at the time. By the time she was finished, the only thing left of that goat was ears and asshole.

"Kids today got too much," he went on, almost to himself. "Money, clothes, you name it. They think life owes them a fucking living."

"It's a different world," Vince concurred.

"You better believe it," Madalena said enthusiastically. "They come up wet behind the ears, snot still dripping down their chins, and they expect to move right in and take over. Can you imagine that? These *stunads* never put in a hard day in their lives. Never hoed weeds till their hands bled, never went without eating for more than a coupla hours . . ." His voice trailed off. "Getting old's fucking awful."

"A name," Vince persisted. "I'll make certain that everything's handled discreetly."

"That's a good word, 'discreet.' " The old man nodded. "Youngsters today don't know nothing about discretion. They wanta walk around in eight-hundred-dollar suits, wear expensive jewelry, drive expensive sports cars. It just don't look good, know what I mean?" He eyed Vince speculatively. "You look like somebody who came up the hard way, same as me—same as our friend Vito, God rest his soul. Guys like us grew strong because we had to fight like hell every day just to stay alive—just to gain a little respect. These punks today never developed no strength because everything was handed to them on a silver platter. They come up weak and flabby, and they stay that way."

He stretched his legs under the blanket and leaned back in the seat. "What can I tell you, my friend? I have no tolerance for anyone in my organization who would have anything at all to do with this Lisa Thorpe. She wasn't our kind of people. I would have hoped they might have shown more sense, but sadly, that too is a scarce commodity these days. I believe you are an honorable man and so I will give you this much: I will find out who, if anyone, in my employ was involved in this matter and judge whether your meeting that person would conflict with my business interests."

"I can't ask for more than that," Vince said.

"Good. I have no need to further complicate my affairs at this point in my life," Madalena said. "This trial is killing me, draining the blood from my veins. If helping you can warn me of incompetence in my midst, I will gratefully weed it out."

"Thank you for seeing me, Mr. M.," Vince said. "I hope you're feeling better soon."

"I'll feel better when those fucking doctors stop telling me what I can't do." Madalena swallowed the cigar and grinned. "Good for the digestion," he said, noticing Vince's discomfort. "Didn't your old lady ever tell you that? Cleans you out real good too, gives you the bowels of a teenager. I eat four or five of these every day and shit my brains out. How many seventy-year-olds you know can say that?"

25

THE THICK, RICH SMELLS OF GÀRLIC SIMMERING IN OIL.
An undercurrent of subtler aromas: oregano, thyme, parsley. A press of checkered tablecloths; customers seated back to back amid a bustling cadre of waiters balancing bowls of steaming vermicelli, sour red wine. If space management was an art, Mama Colinini was a virtuoso, Vince thought as he sat in the crowded dining room of the restaurant. What appeared to be a random arrangement of tables crammed together in a tiny space was in fact a triumph of solid geometry. The addition of one more customer, one more serving of Pasta Primavera Colinini, would result in gastronomical gridlock. Mama had done the best with what she had, and that was plenty good enough. Colinini's was far and away the most popular Italian restaurant in lower Manhattan.

Connie was twenty minutes late.

Vince remembered the old days, when Mama Colinini dished out heaping portions of homemade spaghetti in her dinky nine-by-twelve storefront in Brownsville, Brooklyn. He'd been a foot patrolman then, his first post after graduating from the academy. New to him were the blacks, Hispanics, Orientals—a bombardment of cultural diversity that filled him with wonder and fear. He walked his beat carefully, terrified that everything he didn't understand would rise up and hurt him. It was a time when the reassuring smells of steaming calamari and tomato paste drifting out onto Pitkin Avenue offered him refuge from the street.

Mama Colinini had taken Vince under her wing, and tempered his fears with piping-hot servings of carbonara and puttanesca, with sweet, pregnant sausages, tender little neck clams in basil and tarragon and fresh-ground red pepper that made his eyes water. She kept his stomach full, and he returned this kindness by filling the restaurant with his friends and fellow probationaries until Mama Colinini's reputation outgrew the tiny space, and she moved the operation lock, stock, and barrel to downtown Manhattan. Mama's prices grew with her fame, and although cops still came, it was only on special occasions.

Tonight was Vince's opportunity to redeem himself for his dumb one-nighter with Jessy. He'd had a dozen long-stemmed red roses sent to Connie's apartment that afternoon. He'd wanted to bring her a corsage, but the florist had politely told him that sort of thing went out of style twenty years ago. Connie had reminded him more than once that his rules of courtship were mired in another decade. Tommy Ippollito told him it was another century.

"That seat taken?" Connie was standing next to him in the narrow aisle.

"Hi . . ." Vince stood awkwardly and attempted to help her into the chair. "I ordered a drink while I was waiting. You want something?"

"Whatever you're having." She slid the chair to the table. "Sorry I'm late. There was a late-breaking story out in Flushing. A man walked into his boss's office and shot him in the head."

"I sympathize with him. I've felt like doing that myself."

"Well, this poor guy turned the gun on himself when he was finished."

"I'd say that's carrying a grudge too far." Vince hailed the waiter and ordered Connie a rob roy on the rocks. "Were you out there?"

"Uh-uh. Just relaying the live feed from the truck."

Vince looked puzzled.

"Newsroom talk." Connie smiled. "So how've you been?"

He shrugged. "You know, not so hot."

"Thanks for the roses. They must have cost you a fortune."

"Conscience money." Vince grinned sheepishly. "Just another way of saying I'm sorry for what I did."

"Let's put it behind us," Connie suggested.

"No—let me say this. I've thought about it a thousand times, and I won't feel right about things until I get it out." He drained his glass. "The way it is, is that I love you, Connie. And I loved you when I was up in Marion with Jessy. I don't know how you can love somebody and still want to be with someone else. I guess the nuns back at our Lady of Lourdes would've called it 'temptation' —the flesh is weak and all that jazz—but I just can't buy it. That's too easy. I think maybe what I wanted was to believe Jessy didn't really hate me for neglecting her and the girls all those years."

"You were looking for absolution?" A trace of a smile.

"Does that sound dumb?"

Connie stirred her drink absently. "I don't know. A little self-serving, maybe, but who's to say? I wish none of this had ever happened and I know you do, too, but it did, and we can go on endlessly analyzing it or we can get on with our lives. If talking about it makes you feel better, talk to Tommy or the departmental chaplain. I just want to move on to something less painful."

An awkward pause. "You hungry?" Vince asked.

"Um . . ." She peered over his shoulder at the menu on the blackboard. "What's good tonight?"

"Everything."

"Does the fettucini carbonara have bacon or ham?"

"Both, I think." Vince speared a waiter by the arm as he squeezed past carrying a tray of drinks. "So what's it gonna be?"

"The fettucine, I guess."

Vince ordered sweet sausages, veal, and mushrooms over macaroni for himself and dismissed the waiter. "It's been an interesting day. I had a meeting with Carlo Madalena."

"*The* Carlo Madalena?" Connie looked impressed. "And you're still here to talk about it?"

"This is not a menacing guy," Vince said. "He's old and crippled, really kind of pitiful."

"Except when he's ordering his goons to massacre the competition," Connie reminded him.

"We all have our little character defects. Actually, I kinda liked the old guy."

"God!" Connie shuddered. "Sometimes you scare me, Vince. I thought you were supposed to be one of the good guys."

"I am," he protested. "I can feel something for the old man without liking what he does for a living. This is a man who made it to the top of a very tough and demanding profession. Whether you agree with what he does or not, you gotta admit he's something special."

"A thug and a murderer," Connie said sourly. "What business did you have with him anyway? I didn't know you were involved in his racketeering trial."

"I'm not. I just thought he might have some information that could help me on this Lisa Thorpe case."

"Lisa Thorpe?" Connie eyed him quizzically. "You think there's a mob connection?"

Vince shook his head. "Probably not. I just wanted to straighten out a few loose ends."

"What about Ricky Miracle?"

"What about him?"

"I thought he was your suspect"

"Miracle's just a poor, dumb slob who happened to be in the wrong place at the wrong time. He'll be sprung for lack of evidence in a week or two. You can bet the farm on it."

"The D.A.'s saying he has a strong circumstantial case."

Vince scowled. "D.A.s are always saying that. I know Tom Quinlan pretty well and you can take my word for it that he's not gonna embarrass himself in court with what he's got so far. Ricky Miracle will walk before the end of the month."

"Ivor Thorpe's not going to like that."

"Ivor Thorpe doesn't pay my salary."

"So now you're working on a mob connection?" Connie persisted as the waiter deposited their orders unceremoniously on the table. "You think maybe they were trying to get at her father through her?"

"No, I'm not working on a mob connection, and I don't think anything of the kind." Vince scolded her. "Now stop being a reporter and sink your pearly whites into that banquet."

Halfway to Connie's apartment they were grappling like teenagers in the backseat of the cab. Vince paid the driver hurriedly and followed Connie into the lobby, waited nervously by her side for the elevator, and picked up where he had left off as soon as the sculptured brass and mahogany door slid shut.

"Christ. How come we never did this before?" Vince breathed into her perfumed neck as the elevator ascended.

"I don't know . . ." Connie's voice was husky, demanding, rising from her heaving abdomen, the exhilarated swell of her breasts. "But it won't be the last time, if I have anything to say about it." She pulled him backward into the corner of the elevator, and her slender fingers loosened his belt buckle, sliding effortlessly inside, kneading, caressing. Vince found the buttons of her blouse and undid them one by one, struggling to remove it as the upraised arms became caught in the knotted tangle of her sweater. The elevator stopped and they lurched out into the hallway still locked together, stumbling blindly forward like participants in a bizarre three-legged race.

"My God, what if somebody opens their door and sees us?" Connie gasped, gathering up her trailing blouse and sweater and fumbling in her purse for the door key.

"Let 'em look." Vince laughed, aware for the first time that his pants were draped ingloriously about his knees. "It'll liven up this joint." He lifted Connie and carried her into the apartment when the door opened inward. "Now they'll have something to talk about on these long winter nights . . ."

"God, I can't remember ever being this horny," Connie moaned as Vince kicked the door shut behind them with his trailing foot and deposited her gently on the thick pile of the entrance carpet. She touched his sweaty face and shoulders in the darkened room and pulled him down onto the floor beside her. Their partially naked bodies began to move in time to the urgent cadence of their breathing. Vince fumbled with buttons and zippers, with gossamer pieces of underclothing that ripped beneath his impatient fingers until he felt the soft skin of her belly against his hungry lips, inhaled her musky smells of salt and sex, her wanting him . . .

26

Tom Quinlan sorted through the telephone messages on his desk and groaned audibly. Another call from Ivor Thorpe, another withering attack on the office of the District Attorney, the criminal-justice system, and on him personally for having failed to petition the courts in the matter of Ricardo Mirable's trial date: "The right to a speedy trial has apparently become the exclusive privilege of thugs and murderers," the memo said in his secretary's neat handwriting. "Victims enjoy no such right as long as the mechanisms of law enforcement remain in the hands of oafs and incompetents. Call immediately!"

Call immediately: It sounded like a summons. Hardly a day had passed since Mirable's arrest without a telephone call demanding that he do his duty as Ivor Thorpe saw it. Angry calls, abusive calls, calls that astonished him with their venom and ferocity, numbed him with their unyielding regularity. It had crossed his mind to put a stop to it once and for all by slapping Thorpe with a restraining order threatening him with prosecution for interfering in a criminal proceeding, but that was strictly a bluff and Ivor Thorpe wasn't about to fall for a bluff. Besides, a check of Thorpe's lavish campaign contributions disclosed a recent donation to Quinlan's own war chest. In the political arena, there were certain indignities that had to be endured.

"Bring me the Mirable file, and get me Lieutenant Gleason at the thirty-seventh." He punched the intercom button on his desk. "Better yet, make that Detective Crowley. Gleason doesn't know shit from shinola about what's going on up there."

The intercom squawked and Vince came on the line. "Crowley, what the fuck's going on with this Ricardo Mirable investigation?"

"You tell me. Last time I heard, you were going to court with Ricky Miracle," Vince answered.

"Well, maybe we oughta reconsider that," Quinlan hedged as the secretary deposited a manila file folder on his desk. "You guys are sitting on your asses up there. You haven't given me enough to nail the sonofabitch for murder two."

A predictable silence. "You had everything we were ever gonna get on Miracle the day you walked into Bronx Criminal and got an indictment," Vince said coolly. "Don't give me that shit about us not doing our jobs up here, okay?"

"I think we gotta fish or cut bait here, Crowley, know what I mean?"

"If you mean you're letting Miracle walk, sure."

"Walk?" Quinlan rolled his eyes. "Shit! We can't let the sonofabitch just walk outa there, for chrissakes. I'm getting his P.D. up here to plead to a lesser charge."

"Like what?" Vince asked, amused.

Quinlan scanned the list of possible charges. "I got manslaughter one and two here, no way I can make either of them stick . . . I got possession of a controlled substance . . . Possession of drug paraphernalia . . . Loitering for the purpose of taking drugs . . . Vagrancy . . . Unlawful assembly—"

"What about picking his nose?" Vince interrupted. "I think he was going for a greenie when we busted in on him."

"Very fucking funny," Quinlan snarled. "The point is, we make one of these stick, or we end up looking like class A assholes."

"Correction. You end up looking like a class A asshole. I told you all along we had no case against this kid. You want my advice? Cut and run while you still have a chance."

"What about this possession of a controlled substance?" Quinlan asked, ignoring him. "What controlled substance are we talking about here?"

"The kid had a couple of marijuana seeds in the lining of his coat pocket," Vince answered wearily. "You think that's gonna satisfy Ivor Thorpe?"

"Nobody's talking about Ivor Thorpe!" Quinlan snapped. "If Mirable gets prosecuted, it'll be because I think I have a case against him. If not, he walks, plain and simple. What he's not gonna do is sit in some cushy hospital bed at taxpayers' expense while we're making up our minds what to do with him. Starting today, Mirable's back in Riker's, *comprende*?"

"You want a dead defendant, go ahead," Vince suggested. "No way he's gonna make it in a cell. Guaranteed, he'll find a way to kill himself and you'll end up in court with nothing but your lob in your hand."

"You guarantee me that and I'll put the little shit in solitary. I'll even supply the rope for him to hang himself. He croaks and my problem's solved once and for all," Quinlan volleyed

Vince thought about it. "If this was an ordinary homicide I'd agree with you, but the press isn't gonna let this thing drop just because Ricky Miracle takes the gas pipe. They want him—or someone—brought to justice. Rob the public of a juicy murder trial and everybody's gonna be pissed, including Ivor Thorpe. People hate unresolved homicides. Jack Ruby didn't make himself a lot of friends, if you know what I mean."

"They want a conviction, Vince," Quinlan moaned. "Give me somebody I can convict, and Mirable can have the upstairs bedroom in my house, for chrissakes. I'm not out to railroad the kid. At this point I'd be happy if he'd just fucking disappear."

"I can't make him disappear, but I can do the next best thing," Vince said. "You issue a statement saying that new evidence has come to light, that you expect a new arrest to be made shortly, and I'll see to it Miracle's buried away in some drug rehab for as long as it takes to wrap this thing up."

"And how long will that be?"

"Hard to say for sure. All I can tell you is that Lisa Thorpe had a past, and it wasn't the past her old man would want you to believe. This babe made enemies, Tom, lots of them."

"How long?" Quinlan groaned.

"A week, a month, how the hell am I supposed to know? The point is, you've still got Miracle and you've called off the dogs who're screaming about bringing him to trial."

"You shitting me? You really have new evidence or are you just humping me around?" Quinlan asked skeptically.

"What the hell difference does it make? You get some good coverage, the media gets to speculate their asses off about the new evidence, and Miracle's off the hook for a crime he didn't commit in the first place. Everybody's happy."

"*If* there's a new arrest," Quinlan corrected him. "You gotta tell me if you're really onto anything here or if you're just blowing smoke. I'll need to feed them something for right now."

"Things are starting to happen, that's all I can tell you at this point," Vince assured him. "For now, they'll just have to be satisfied with that 'new arrests are expected imminently' crap. You know the routine."

Silence. "It won't work," Quinlan said finally. "Get back to me when you have something real for me to work with."

"So what now?" Vince asked. "You taking Miracle to court with what you got?"

"Shit no. I'm plucky but I'm not stupid. Mirable stays on ice until I got something better. In the meantime I want him out of that $350-a-day hospital suite you got him in. I'm fed up with the press saying we coddle criminals."

"He won't make it back in Riker's—"

"I don't give a good fuck where you put him," Quinlan barked. "Just keep him close enough for me to grab in case I need a warm body."

"Drug rehab okay with you?"

"As long as it's not one of those luxury dry-out spas. The scroungier the better, know what I mean?"

"It'll be a shithole. I promise."

"Don't fuck me on this, Vince,"

"You're interesting but you're not my type." Vince hung up.

"What's that all about?" Dog Scarfatti entered the squad room carrying a bag of Mexican take-out.

"D.A.'s dropping the charges against Ricky Miracle," Vince said casually, leafing through his book of telephone numbers.

Scarfatti perked up. "How come?"

"Beats me . . ." Vince found the number he was looking for and dialed Alex Guzman at the Homeless Men's Shelter.

"He got a new suspect?" Scarfatti persisted.

"Probably. You know he's not gonna tell *me* anything."

"You telling me there's a new suspect and you don't know anything about it?" Scarfatti asked skeptically.

"Hey, what am I, Sherlock Holmes?" A young male voice answered the telephone and put Vince on hold. Dog retreated back into the hallway. Scarfatti would be on the phone to the P.C.'s office in a matter of seconds, Vince guessed, and the P.C.'s office would be calling Tom Quinlan in minutes. The fact that nobody knew what the hell was going on was unimportant. It was a photo opportunity and nobody was about to miss that.

"Men's Shelter." Guzman came on the line.

"Mr. Guzman. Detective Crowley from the Thirty-Seventh Precinct here. My partner and I were in to see you a couple of weeks ago."

"I remember. You were looking for Ricardo Mirable."

"Well, I guess you know we found him . . . and now we're looking for a place to put him."

"I don't get it. I thought he was in jail," Guzman said, puzzled.

"He is, at least technically, but I want to get him into an alcohol and drug rehab—someplace not too posh. You know any place like that?"

"Not too posh?"

"You know, no swimming pool, no volley ball. Shit like that."

There was a pause. "I don't know where you think we're coming from down here, detective, but the people I deal with are homeless. If they saw a volleyball they'd probably try to sell it to buy food or whiskey—"

"I appreciate that," Vince interrupted him. "And I probably could've put it a better way, but right now I'm looking for some nice, quiet, out-of-the-way dry-out farm to hide him in before he gets nailed for a crime he didn't do. I thought maybe you could help."

"Why not just set him free if he's innocent?" Guzman asked.

"It's not that easy," Vince answered. "Besides, I thought you'd be interested in helping Ricky. I mean, he could use a place like that, right?"

"Ricky's been in dozens of rehabs," Guzman said. "Why do you think he's called Ricky Miracle? Every time he shows up at another one, the doctors and nurses tell him it's a miracle he's still alive."

"You saying it'd be a waste of time? Would you rather see him rotting in a cell someplace?" Vince demanded.

"Don't get me wrong. Of course I'll help you," Guzman assured him. "There's a small rehabilitation center not far from here called Liberation House that deals with strictly hardcases, but realistically, I don't have much hope their treatment will work for Ricky. It's almost impossible with kids like him, kids who have spent most of their lives living out on the streets. After a while they revert to being almost feral."

"Call me a cockeyed optimist."

"The world could use more optimists. You bring him to me and I'll see he gets the best treatment available," Guzman said, a trace of enthusiasm returning to his voice. "I guess there's always hope."

Ricky Miracle was less enthusiastic when Vince saw him later that afternoon at the hospital. "Hey man, why can't I just stay here and get straight?" he asked.

"Because the taxpayers get pissed off if they think criminals are living better than they are," Vince told him. "Besides, Liberation House is set up to handle guys just like you. They're specialists."

"I've been there," Ricky said glumly. "They got one TV and it's never working." He eyed the small color set suspended above his bed. A soap opera was in progress. "That place is bogus, man."

"It's that or back to Riker's," Vince said flatly.

"That's not much of a choice," Ricky muttered.

"It's a big choice. It's a chance for you to get your life back together," Vince corrected him. "You're still young, Ricky. You got a good future if you'll just give yourself a shot at it."

Ricky eyed him suspiciously. "Why are you doing this? What difference does it make to you what I do with my life? I'm nobody to you, just some derelict you pulled off the streets and busted on a bum rap."

"It doesn't have to be that way, Ricky," Vince said. "I got a feeling there's somebody more to you than what you're showing me: Maybe somebody special. I just want to see you give yourself a chance to find that somebody. For what it's worth, I'm willing to help."

Ricky's face remained a languid, impenetrable mask, his confusion buried beneath a pose of street-wise con. He shrugged his shoulders in resignation, leaned back into the pillow, and stared blankly at the television screen where his soap opera was being interrupted by an emergency news bulletin:

"We interrupt this program to broadcast a late-breaking news conference being held by the Bronx District Attorney, Thomas Quinlan, and the Chief of Detectives regarding the investigation into the death of Lisa Thorpe, socialite daughter of publisher Ivor Thorpe," the announcer began. "We now transfer you live to The Bronx where the D.A. is about to read a prepared statement."

Vince watched as Quinlan appeared, standing beside the unsmiling Chief of Detectives on the steps of the Criminal Court Building. "Due to an intense interest in the progress of the investigation into the murder of Lisa Thorpe, I am taking this time to announce that a significant breakthrough has taken place in our investigation, and that an arrest of one or more suspects in connection with that crime can be anticipated in the next several days." He raised his eyes from the prepared statement and faced the horde of questioners on the steps below him.

"What about Ricardo Mirable? Are you dropping the charges against him?" someone shouted.

"Mr. Mirable remains in custody," Quinlan responded uncomfortably. "No charges against him have been dropped, but his trial date will remain in continuance until we have had an opportunity to act on recent developments."

"Can you tell us who your new suspect is?"

Quinlan smiled weakly. "I'm sorry, but that's all I can tell you now. I can't jeopardize the investigation in progress."

"Is it true that police are investigating a link with organized crime?" a female voice persisted. "Specifically the Madalena crime family and a possible tie-in with Carlo Madalena's upcoming racketeering trial?"

Vince stiffened. The voice belonged to Connie.

27

BUDGERIGAR: MELOPSITTACUS UNDULATUS (AUSTRALIA) SCALLOPED BACK. USUALLY GREEN, A SMALL MINORITY MAY BE BLUE, YELLOW OR WHITE. THOUSANDS ARE ESTABLISHED ALONG THE WEST COAST OF FLORIDA AND RANGE NORTH-WARD IN LESSER NUMBERS ALONG THE EASTERN COASTLINE ALMOST TO NEW ENGLAND.

Don Carlo Madalena read the colorfully printed legend and searched inside the meshed enclosure of the aviary. He recognized rose-ringed parakeets and cockatiels among the profusion of birds and wildfowl; plovers and sandpipers and dainty blue-winged warblers trilled softly. He identified their calls in the cacaphony of squawks and screeches reverberating through the cavernous atrium, much like a seasoned conductor attuning his ear to individual instruments in a symphony.

"Can I get you something, Mr. M?" the tall figure standing behind Carlo Madalena's wheelchair asked nervously. "A cold drink maybe?"

The Don brushed him off like an annoying fly. "Leave me be. Go find yourself something to do. But don't go far. I want you here when I need you."

He resumed his search inside the cage for the elusive budgerigar, almost at peace for the first time in weeks. He nestled back into the upholstered chair and inhaled the delicate smells of droppings, and topsoil and damp vegetation hanging in the pregnant air, and felt the iceberg in his chest beginning to melt. He was safe, here inside this sanctuary of birds . . . safe from the incessant pressure of the racketeering trial that was draining his strength and his resolve; safe from the intrigues and artifices of his business, from the ravages of age and illness. If other men found sanctuary inside churches, Don Carlo found it at the Bronx Zoo. Here, amid the pandemonium of noise and restless flight, he found the only inner quiet he had ever known.

Vince entered the aviary from the other end and spotted the Don seated among the scattered visitors circling the enclosure. "Afternoon, Mr. M.," he said, approaching the old man. "I was surprised to hear back from you so soon."

Carlo Madalena extended a bony hand. "You shouldn't be surprised, my friend. Old men like me don't have the luxury of procrastination. Better to get things settled quickly, I think—especially messy situations."

"Everything okay here, Mr. M.?" The tall man had reappeared from the fringes of the crowd.

Madalena nodded. "Get Detective Crowley something to drink," he said curtly. "And bring me a cigar."

"I thought you said they wouldn't let you smoke," Vince joked as the man disappeared.

"This one doesn't have the stones to defy me," Madalena scowled. "He knows I am displeased with him right now, and he's happy just to be walking around."

Vince looked around the aviary. "Jeez, I haven't been to this place in years. Kinda brings me back."

"You came here as a boy?" Madalena asked.

"A couple of times. My older sister brought me."

"Your mother and father?"

Vince shrugged. "Maybe my old man, when I was very young. I really can't remember. He died when I was twelve."

The Don nodded sadly. "I hope he was granted the grace of a peaceful death."

"He was shot," Vince said simply. "He was a cop walking his beat and somebody just shot him. He was gone before he knew what hit him."

"Being a policeman is a risky business. I'm surprised you didn't choose something less hazardous after all that."

"I guess there's risk in anything you do," Vince replied. "I'd rather take my chances in an interesting job than spend my life bored to death."

"Well said. Let's find someplace less crowded to have our talk." Madalena activated a button on the side of his wheelchair, circled slowly, and maneuvered through the crowd to an unoccupied corner of the atrium.

His tall companion returned with Madalena's cigar and

handed Vince a warm can of orange soda. "All they had was panatellas, Mr. M. You want I should unwrap it?"

"This is Johnny Zito," the Don said to Vince. "He has something to tell you about those telephone calls from the Thorpe girl." He fixed Zito with a withering stare. "Don't you?"

"Yeah . . . Well, it wasn't no big deal, if you know what I mean." Zito lit Madalena's cigar with a shaking hand. "What it was, was that this broad had a thing for me, you know? I mean, she couldn't hardly keep her hands offa me—"

"Hold it. Back up a minute, Johnny." Vince eyed the Don and received a cursory nod to continue his questioning. "Why don't you tell me how you came to know Lisa Thorpe in the first place?"

Johnny Zito shrugged. "It was at a party her old man was throwing at *Eros* magazine eight, nine months ago—"

"*Eros* magazine. That one of Ivor Thorpe's publications?" Vince interrupted him.

"Yeah. It's a skin sheet. You know, he puts out a buncha them. Tits, ass, the whole shmear."

"And you met Lisa Thorpe at a party for one of those magazines?"

"Sure. Whadda you think, she was some kind of hothouse flower?" Zito grinned. "Shit, that was one tough babe, if you catch my drift. She was into it all, man."

"Whatta you mean by 'into it all'?"

"Just that. She was a cunt, same as all the rest, only she was used to getting her own way. She didn't like it much when I brushed her off. She kept calling me, trying to get me to take her out. You know, give her a little of the old sizzling tube steak." A sneering laugh.

Vince eyed Zito curiously. "Let me get this straight. You're telling me this girl, this beautiful, rich, world-famous figure skater, was all broke up because she couldn't get a date with some ignorant, greasy Mafia hack?" He turned to Don Carlo. "No offense intended, Mr. M."

Zito surged forward, then stopped abruptly in response to Madalena's baleful stare. "I think what Johnny is trying to tell you is that the matter of the telephone calls was nothing but a romantic interlude," the Don explained. "Nothing as sinister as the news people are trying to make out."

"Yeah. What makes you think a broad like her wouldn't go for a guy like me?" Zito protested. "I ain't exactly ugly, if you know what I mean."

"You ain't exactly smart either," Madalena broke in.

Zito looked wounded. "Hey, Don Carlo, what am I supposed to do when this cunt chases me all over Manhattan, for chrissakes? I'm telling you she was fuckin' nuts—a real Looney-Tune. There wasn't hardly anything or anybody she wouldn't do: men, women . . . animals. She just did whatever her twat told her to do. She even wanted me to use her in one of our productions."

Vince saw Madalena stiffen. He knew that Zito had committed a stupid blunder by calling the old man Don Carlo in front of an outsider, and an unforgivable one by mentioning family business. "Okay, Johnny. Can you tell me the last time you saw Lisa Thorpe?" he asked, unwilling to stretch the Don's patience any further. "That oughta wrap us up here."

"Johnny has assured me he had no further contact with the girl other than over the telephone," Madalena broke in. "And that she initiated any calls there were. I believe you have a record of all of them."

The interview with Johnny Zito was at an end. Don Carlo Madalena dismissed him with a disdainful wave of his hand and looked wearily at Vince. "You see what I have to put up with, Detective Crowley? Pigmies. Vain, shallow *stunads* with big ambition and shit for brains." He closed his eyes and rubbed his temples with the palms of his hands. "I come here for peace and relaxation, and still I can't escape them."

He activated the wheelchair and moved slowly toward the mesh enclosure. "I suppose the birds have their problems too," he went on, stopping next to the guard rail by the cage. "But there seems to be a kind of harmony about them that goes beyond their differences. Just look at them—every size and shape and color." He pointed into the cage with a shaking finger. "See? Goldfinches, lapwings, mynas, macaws. They have no common heritage and still they exist together in peace."

"It *is* peaceful here," Vince concurred.

"Sometimes, sitting here, I wonder whether we are really the superior species with our petty bickering and need to control and dominate. The birds find a way.

They sing their love songs . . ." His voice trailed off
wistfully.

"Maybe they're looking out at us and saying the same
thing," Vince joked.

"I don't think so." Madalena shook his head sadly.
"I'd like to think they're intelligent enough to know
when they're well off. When they look at us they see us
tearing at one another—black, white, yellow. Put us together and all we know how to do is destroy each other. I
see it in my own business. Nobody's satisfied with what
they have, what's rightfully theirs by their birthright.
Everybody wants more. They muscle in where they have
no business being."

Vince listened carefully. He understood that Don Carlo
Madalena was not a man to squander his time on frivo-
lous conversation. Somewhere in all of this was a message.

"Take the Asians," Madalena went on. "Historically,
we've never been able to understand them and they've
never been able to understand us. Our backgrounds and
customs are so different, you see." He turned to Vince to
emphasize his point. "I have never been a man to hate
another person for his beliefs or the color of his skin,
Detective Crowley. Even the Asians, although God knows
they have given me reason to."

Madalena sucked on the unlit stub of his cigar and
field-stripped the burnt ashes. "This is where my problem with them arises." He inserted the butt into his
mouth and began chewing. "Sometimes they fail to see
where their interests leave off and mine begin." He swallowed the cigar, burped loudly, and began to choke.

"Here, Mr. M. Try this." Vince handed him the un-
touched can of orange soda and waited as the old man
drank tentatively.

"It's these goddamn American cigars!" Madalena explained, his eyes watering. "They make the fucking wrap-
pers out of plastic . . . indigestible." He took a deep
breath. "Now where the hell was I?"

"The Asians," Vince reminded him.

"Yeah." Madalena shook his head gravely. "The way I
see it, what's past is past. Sure we had our differences;
Pearl Harbor and all that, but it's a different world today. It don't pay to hold grudges for things that happened then. We should be pulling together for the common
good." He took another sip of the soda and made a sour

face. "What do they put in this shit anyway, mouse piss?"

"You feel your interests are threatened by them?" Vince prodded.

"My interests are threatened by all kinds of greedy bastards." Madalena spat contemptuously on the floor. "But most I can deal with because I understand them for what they are. When they transgress on my interests I know what steps I must take to make them understand the injustice of their actions. Not so the Orientals. They have strange, unfathomable minds, and they are willing to undergo any hardship to achieve their goals. I'm sorry to say this, Detective, but it seems to me that they are much tougher than we are. After I'm gone, my interests will be in the hands of incompetents like that asshole Zito. They leave this world with an army of successors who are just as dedicated and determined as they are. I think their religious beliefs have something to do with that."

The Don dropped his head and rested his chin in his cupped hands. He spoke almost as an afterthought. "Did you know the Buddhists believe that a man can't get to heaven without his head? If they hate someone bad enough, or if they want to send a message to his family and business associates, they cut off his head after they kill him. It's the worst thing you can do to a man after he's dead."

There it was. The old man had taken a long time to make his point, but the point was unmistakable. He'd brushed off the matter of Lisa Thorpe's telephone calls and handed Vince an unexpected bonus to let the matter drop.

Don Carlo had given him Karp's killers.

28

"ONE STILL SMALL VOICE," THE HEADLINE OF IVOR Thorpe's letter to the *New York Times* read. "Again the anguished cries of a murdered child go unheeded in this callous sink of corruption we call the City of New York."

"Get this." Tommy caught Vince's attention across the squad room and read from the newspaper.

> It is as if those responsible for the mechanisms of justice feel they can retreat behind an impenetrable fortress of complacency and self-satisfaction now that the public outcry over the brutal murder of my daughter has subsided. Let them be warned that if mine remains the only cry raised in protest, it will be raised with all of the resources, vigor, and determination at my command, and that this one small, unquenchable voice shall ring throughout the consciences of those responsible for solving this crime until justice is achieved."

Vince looked up from the ledger on Leila Turner's desk. "Still small voice, huh? What chance do you think you and me would have of getting a letter we wrote printed on the op-ed page of the *New York Times*?"

"Some voices are smaller than others," Leila Turner observed wryly, turning the page of the ledger and adjusting the half-lens reading glasses on her nose. "Besides, what're you guys complaining about? If I had half the manpower and resources on my case that they've assigned to yours, it'd be solved by now."

"Maybe it will be anyway," Vince said, stopping halfway down a column of handwritten names and figures. "Check this name against your list."

Turner studied the list of people she had already interviewed in the Karp homicide. "Tranh Van Luc . . . a

Vietnamese refugee. He was one of the boat people back in the late Seventies. Runs an import warehouse with his brother-in-law out on Eastchester Avenue."

Vince checked back through the book. "I got him down for three transactions here. August 26, October 12, and the last one December 8—right before the murder. Small amounts each time, but that doesn't necessarily mean anything. They could be coded."

"What's so special about him?" Turner asked. "There are others who were into Karp for a lot more."

"Who says he was into Karp for anything?" Vince pointed to the entries in the ledger. "Every one for this Luc character are written one space to the right. Check it out."

Turner ran her index finger down the neatly printed columns of numbers. "You're right. In every case the amount is moved over. What do you suppose it means?"

Vince flipped through the pages, making certain that none of the other entries were handled in the same way. "I don't know what it means, but it tells us this guy was different. Karp handled his transactions differently. Also, he's an Asian."

"Why should that have anything to do with it?" There was an edge to Turner's voice. "What're we doing here, targeting minorities?"

"Calm down," Vince reassured her. "We're targeting Asians because Don Carlo Madalena tipped me that Asians did this murder. That good enough for you?"

"I don't get it." Tommy sat on the corner of Turner's desk. "Why would Madalena tip you on anything?"

"I'm not sure, but if I had to guess I'd say that this Tranh Van Luc and his brother-in-law are somehow muscling in on a piece of the Don's action. Carlo Madalena's a smart guy. I wouldn't be surprised if he was setting it up for us to wipe out his competition."

"And in return for the favor we take the heat off his people on the Thorpe investigation," Tommy observed.

Vince looked up from the desk and smiled. "Good work, partner. You're actually starting to think like a detective."

"How about motive?" Leila Turner persisted. "I interviewed Luc and he's a quiet, self-effacing little guy who came over here with nothing and managed to build himself a nice business. He's got enterprise and initiative. This city could use more of that."

"If he's such a hero, what's he doing dealing with a slimeball like Karp in the first place?" Tommy asked.

She checked her notes. "He needed the money for short-term cash flow in his business. Big deal. You telling me you've never been short of cash, Ippollito?"

"Okay, cool it," Vince interrupted them. "The point is, did this enterprising Vietnamese guy's interests and Don Carlo's interests collide, and if so, where? Whatta you think: prostitution, gambling, loan sharking?"

"He's an importer," Turner said. "Oriental dolls, fans, wickerwork, that sort of thing. He took me through the warehouse and it all looked pretty legitimate to me."

"Anything big enough to conceal a couple of pounds of Thai smack?" Tommy suggested.

"A good point," Vince broke in before Leila could answer. "Carlo Madalena wouldn't take kindly to somebody moving in on his Bronx narcotics traffic, and that's just what the B.L.T. is doing."

"B.L.T.? I thought that was a sandwich," Leila Turner said.

"It is. It's also the Burma, Laos, Thailand triangle, the hottest new entry in America's heroin-smuggling sweepstakes." Vince picked up the telephone and dialed Rudy Weichert at Bronx Narcotics.

"Crowley, you old pervert. I thought they woulda kicked you off the force by now," Weichert cracked when he came on the line.

"They keep trying. How's everything going down there, bro?"

Weichert laughed. "Shit, Vince. This is close as I ever came to stealing money legally. You oughta try and get yourself transferred back here. It's not like the old days when you were with us. No more of them Knapp ball busters breathing down our necks the way it used to be."

"Don't remind me," Vince said. "We were afraid to fart because somebody wearing a wire would get it all down on tape."

"History, Vince. This is primo duty now, I shit you not. Why not put in for a transfer, pal? I'd really like working with you again, and this unit could use another standup guy on the roster."

"I'll give it some thought, Rudy. In the meantime, you

think you could run down a name for me? Let me know if you're carrying any paper on a guy I got linked with a homicide up here?"

"If I got it, it's yours."

"Guy's name is Tranh Van Luc. A Vietnamese refugee who runs a local import business."

Silence.

"You still there, Rudy?"

"Yeah. What was that name again?"

"Tranh Van Luc. Want me to spell it for you?"

Another pause. "Negative, pal. Whatta you know about Luc?"

"I asked you first, didn't I?"

"This is not somebody you should be getting involved with, Vince," Weichert told him. "Better let it drop."

Vince shot a sidelong glance at Tommy and nodded knowingly. "This is one of the bad guys, huh, Rudy?"

"Not much I can tell you at this point, Vince," Weichert replied. "Let's just say he's off-limits to you guys up there."

Vince stiffened. "Off-limits, Rudy? I'm conducting a homicide investigation here. I gotta go where this thing takes me. You know that."

"Not when it's liable to fuck up almost six months of careful police work," Weichert said. "A couple of days, no more, and you can line up for a piece of the sonofabitch."

"You guys taking him?" Vince asked.

"Look. Why don't you just tell me what you've got on him," Weichert hedged. "You help me, I help you. You know how it works."

"I got a small-time shylock with his head cut off," Vince said without hesitating. "Luc's my only suspect at this point, and I'm getting ready to move on him. You want me to show restraint, you're gonna have to give me more than you've given me so far."

"Shylock, huh? That makes sense. Luc has a lot of illegal cash to dispose of. He was probably using your guy to push it out on the street for him."

"So he's B.L.T., right?" Vince asked.

Weichert breathed deeply. "Okay. Luc's deep in heroin traffic," he said finally. "We've had his place under surveillance since last spring, and we're just about ready to move in. This is a big bust, Vince. Don't do anything to fuck it up for me."

"I want a piece of the collar," Vince said simply. "I want some of my people going in there with you. Otherwise we go in now and take him for murder."

"You gotta be kidding!" Weichert groaned. "We been on this thing for six months, and you want to walk in off the street and cop the credit? That fucking stinks, Vince."

"That's life, bro," Vince replied. "Look at it from my point of view. My homicide charges supersede your narco charges, so I walk in after you've done all the work and grab the little cocksucker for the three-seven, or we go in there together like this was a well planned-out, coordinated effort and everybody gets a hunk of the glory. One way or the other, I got him. From here on in, it's just a matter of style, know what I mean?"

Again silence. "I think you're blowing smoke, Vince. I don't think you got anything on Luc."

"How long've you known me, Rudy?" Vince asked. "Is that the way I do business?"

"They're gonna fucking kill me down here."

"You'll figure something out," Vince reassured him. "When do I get a timetable?"

"I dunno . . . I'll let you know," Weichert answered resentfully.

"Not too long, huh, Rudy? My people are ready to move on Luc any time now—"

"I said I'll let you know!" Weichert slammed down the receiver.

"So what's up?" Tommy asked when Vince hung up.

"You heard. It all makes sense now," Vince reexamined the ledger on Leila Turner's desk. "My guess is that these figures represent cash Karp received from Luc and the B.L.T. That's why they're in a different column from the amounts he was putting out on the street."

"Got any theories on why Luc would want him dead?" Turner asked.

Vince shrugged. "Who the hell knows? Karp must've screwed him somehow. Maybe he was skimming off the top. Greedy bastard like him was liable to do anything. Whatever it was, it made Luc awful angry, though. One swipe of his machete and he punched Karp's ticket to the promised land, plus sending a warning to anybody else who might've been thinking about double-crossing him.

It appears our self-effacing little friend, Luc, does not fuck around."

"Now what?" Tommy asked.

"Now we wait for Rudy to put us on the team."

"What if he calls your bluff?" Turner asked.

"He won't." Vince closed the ledger and headed back to his desk.

"Crowley, Ippollito, inside on the double!" John Gleason shouted from his open office door. "And bring everything you've got on the Thorpe case."

"Musta gotten another call from the P.C.," Tommy whispered as they crossed the squad room. "He looks like he's about to wet his pants."

"Probably already did," Vince whispered back and shut the door behind them. "You wanted to see us, Lieutenant?"

"You seen this?" Gleason lifted the morning copy of the *New York Times* from his desk and held it aloft.

"You mean Thorpe's letter?" Vince asked.

"I'm not talking about the goddam stock quotations!" Gleason bellowed. "Of course I'm talking about Thorpe's letter!"

"He's pissed," Vince said. "What more can I tell you?"

"You can tell me we're getting somewhere on this investigation, that's what you can tell me!" Gleason fumed. "I'm fed up with all this shit! I'm fed up with calls from the media and the commissioner and from Ivor Thorpe! I'm fed up with reading what a bunch of sorry incompetents we are every time I pick up a newspaper. And I'm fucking fed up that all I get from you two is a lot of double-talk!" He was shaking; the vein in his forehead was an angry slash of purple. "Now, I want to know where we stand, and I want to know where we're going and *exactly* how long it's gonna take us to get there! No more bullshit!"

" 'Exactly' I can't give you, sir," Vince replied. "But I can tell you that we're exploring some promising leads."

"I don't want to hear about promising leads!" Gleason shrieked. "The D.A. is talking about a significant breakthrough, for chrissakes! What breakthrough? Why the hell didn't somebody tell *me* about it? I didn't read anything about a significant breakthrough in your reports. All I ever got from your 'fives' was a lot of gobbledegook."

"Gobbledegook, Lieutenant?"

"You heard right. Gobbledegook! You arrest a suspect, then you talk the D.A. out of prosecuting the sonofabitch. Why? Whose side are you on? I don't see you walking in here with anybody to take his place. As far as I'm concerned we're right back where we started, and that makes me mad. Goddamn mad, if you want to know the truth!"

"We're not back where we started, sir." Vince tried to sound reassuring. "The fact is, we're working on a very solid lead right now, a possible mob connection."

"That's another thing! All of a sudden people from the press are asking about a mob connection. *I* never heard anything about any mob connection. Why the hell am I always the last one to know about these things?"

"They were just speculating, Lieutenant," Vince said. "The fact is, I didn't have a real solid lead until this morning, and I'm following up on it now."

Gleason walked slowly to the watercooler in the corner and took a long, slow drink, trying to compose himself. "Okay," he said finally. "Tell me about this 'solid' lead of yours. Who are we talking about here?"

"Small-time hood named Johnny Zito. From what I understand, he was involved romantically with Lisa Thorpe."

"So? What the hell does that prove?"

"There's more, but I want to have my facts straight before I go into it," Vince said. "I've got a call in to Brooklyn Vice right now. I'll know a lot more once I've talked to somebody over there."

"About what?" Gleason demanded.

"About my suspicions, Lieutenant."

For some reason, that seemed to satisfy him. "You'll get back to me as soon as you know anything, right?"

"Word of honor, Lieutenant. Now that we're down to the short strokes, I wouldn't make a move without checking with you first."

A spastic nod. "All right, then. Was there anything else you wanted to see me about?"

Vince bit his lip. "We're also moving pretty good on the Karp homicide, sir."

"I don't give a shit about Karp." Gleason scowled. "That's Turner's case anyway. You shouldn't have anything to do with it."

"Yes sir. Will that be all?"

"Dismissed." Gleason sat heavily at his desk and popped a Maalox.

Outside, Tommy looked troubled. "You really checking out this Zito guy?" he asked Vince.

"Sure. Why not?"

"I thought you had sort of an agreement with the Don."

"Agreement?"

"You know. He fed you that stuff about Luc."

"I never promised him anything," Vince said, checking his telephone messages. "This is a homicide investigation, you know."

"Yeah. Well, I just figured . . ."

"That I oughta play by the rules?" Vince interrupted him.

"I dunno." Tommy looked confused. "You're always telling me about how things work differently out on the street."

There was a message from a Sergeant Doyle Broderick at Brooklyn Vice. Vince lifted the phone and began to dial. "Look, we're after a murderer here. Better we end up making an enemy out of a scumbag like Johnny Zito than losing a chance to catch him. If we break the rules, we break the rules. Sometimes you just gotta play dirty. You think the killer checked the rulebook before he hacked Lisa Thorpe to death?"

29

NYPD FORM DD-5
COMPLAINT FOLLOW-UP

HOMICIDE/STABBING   JANUARY 26, 1989
LISA THORPE W/F 23   COMPLAINT # 4548
                             Det. V. Crowley

1. At approx. 1330 hours, above date, the undersigned, along with Det. D. Broderick, Bklyn.
   Det. Borough Office, and Det. Ippollito, 37PDU,
   visited the premises at 3706 Coney Island Parkway for the purpose of interviewing subjects con-
   nected with Zebra Films, Inc.

2. Upon arriving at premises we were met by pro-
   prietor, Fredo (The Tomato) DiPasquale, who
   directed us to a section where film-making was in
   progress and where we conducted an on-site interview of all present re the above homicide.

3. Present at the interview were, the above-mentioned
   officers, DiPasquale, Benjamin Shapiro (Film Director), Ian Fuchs (Cameraman), Rodney Lancaster (Actor) "Jersey Bell" Tompkins and "Cinnamon" Shasta Jones (Actresses)?

Nothing is lonelier than Coney Island in the winter.
Vince and Tommy parked their unmarked patrol car in
one of the empty parking spots rimming the boardwalk,
and stepped out into the icy gusts blowing from the
ocean. Detective Doyle Broderick eased his sizable bulk
out of the rear seat and joined them. "Freeze your nuts
off out here!" He cupped his hands and blew into them.

Vince scanned the empty beach. Its snow-swept surface a moonscape of rippling dunes and shallow, seaweed-filled ditches. Desultory clumps of stubborn black grasses struggled against the bitter wind. Sentry files of metal litter cans overflowed, and paper plates and cups pirouetted in the squalls, sailing across the bleak expanse of sand to the water's edge. Caught in the tide, they were buried beneath white froth and churning flotsam.

Farther down the beach he saw the outlines of the amusement park: the parachute jump and the cyclone were metal skeletons silhouetted against the overhang of gray sky. On the steel and wooden facings of padlocked booths were sprayed multicolored layers of graffiti: "SCHOOL SUCKS" . . . "I LOVE JOSÉ" . . . "EAT SHIT!" They mocked the fading inscriptions above the stalls: "BALL-E-O: THREE THROWS FOR A QUARTER" . . . "THE MAGIC CARPET" . . . "MADAME LASORTA: KNOWS ALL, SEES ALL. FORTUNES, NUMEROLOGY, COLD DRINKS."

"Looks like they're working today." Broderick pointed to a scattering of automobiles parked at the edge of the amusement park. "If we're lucky we can have us a little coitus interruptus." He grinned lewdly. "Maybe even 'blow-jobbus interruptus.' "

"You mean, they do it right in the amusement park?" Tommy asked, following Broderick out on the boardwalk.

"Can you think of a better spot?" Broderick asked. "Nobody comes out here in the winter. They got the whole place to themselves."

"Suppose they won't talk to us?" Vince asked. "Can we bust them for anything?"

"Not a chance." Broderick led them toward a low, dilapidated, brown brick structure behind the row of stalls. "They're not doing anything illegal."

"So we could be wasting our time," Tommy said.

"They'll talk." Broderick smiled knowingly. "Technically, this is Johnny Zito's end of the business, but the day-to-day operation is run by a scumbag named Freddy DiPasquale. They call him "The Tomato" because he knows where all the tomatoes in this city are. Freddy can smell pussy in a prayer meeting."

"Sounds like a talented guy," Tommy observed.

"He is, and he's scared shitless of yours truly," Broderick said. "You see, I happen to know that he made some 'snuff' films a coupla years ago back in Paraguay. He knows he'd be in deep shit if I took the time to make the case, so he lets me keep him on a long leash, if you know what I mean."

" 'Snuff' films?" Tommy looked puzzled.

"You know, torture, sado-masochism, shit like that," Broderick explained. "They end up snuffing some cunt, cutting out her heart or butchering her with a chainsaw."

"You're kidding," Tommy said.

"He's not," Vince broke in. "I saw one once, back in '72 or '73 when I was working in Manhattan. A thirteen-year-old girl had been missing for months, and her family had to identify her from the movie." He shuddered. "Christ, it was awful."

"And you're letting this Tomato creep walk around the city?" Tommy gasped.

Broderick eyed Vince wearily. "When your partner's finished crying about all the murdered girls in New York, tell him what the real world's like, okay, Crowley? Freddy DiPasquale will get his sooner or later; if not from me, from somebody else. There's no way he'd gonna spend his old age in some retirement village in Boca Raton. Guys like him end up in garbage cans or gutters—or wearing concrete swim fins at the bottom of the Harlem River. I can wait it out, and in the meantime, he's valuable to me out on the street—what can I tell you?"

Vince squinted, feeling tears freezing on his cheeks. "Don't worry, partner. Maybe he's our killer. Maybe we can nail him for that."

"Speak of the devil." Broderick pointed to a short, stocky figure walking toward them from the brick building. "Looks like Freddy's coming out to see us." They huddled with their backs against the gusting wind until he reached them.

"Broderick." DiPasquale nodded curtly, his arms wrapped tightly around the front of his shiny black suit. "What the fuck are you doing out here?"

"Hey, Freddy, is that any way to greet my friends?" Broderick turned to Vince and Tommy. "This here's Detective Crowley, and this is Detective Ippollito. They want to ask you some questions."

"What're you, fuckin' kidding?" DiPasquale sneered. "You got questions, send me a fuckin' letter." He turned his back on them and began walking.

"Wait a minute!" Broderick caught him by the back of

his suit collar and turned him around. "I don't think you understood, Freddy. These are *friends* of mine. I want you should treat them with a little common courtesy."

"Get your hands offa me, Broderick!" DiPasquale pulled away. "You got no cause to come out here harassing me like this. I run a legitimate business, got licenses and everything. And I'm on good terms with all your vice goons, got the picture?" He shoved his pudgy hands resentfully into his pants pockets.

"Harassing?" Broderick looked quizzically at Vince and Tommy. "I'm not harassing anybody. How about you guys?"

"Come on, willya? I'm fuckin' freezing out here!" Di Pasquale groaned. "Gimme a break, willya? I got a crew working inside."

"Oh, a crew." Broderick winked at Vince. "Why didn't you say so? I know how costly delays can be on these high-budget shoots of yours."

"Why're you busting my chops?" DiPasquale demanded.

"Because they're eminently bustable." Broderick grinned. "Now, you want to take us inside and answer some questions, or you want to stand out here and chew the fat?"

"Nobody goes inside," DiPasquale said resolutely. "I got my orders."

Broderick looked at Vince and Tommy, and shrugged. "I guess that's it, then. The man says we can't go in, we can't go in." He shook his head helplessly. "As long as we're out here, you guys want to take a swim, just so the trip won't be a total loss?"

"Yeah. Maybe The Tomato would like to join us," Tommy suggested.

"Nothing like a brisk swim to get the old body juices flowing," Vince added.

"All right, let's cut the shit!" DiPasquale protested as they took him by the arms and led him toward the water.

"I'll bet he's worried about getting his shiny suit all wet." Broderick ripped Freddy's suit jacket in half at the back seam and wrestled it from his shoulders.

"What the fuck you think you're doing?" DiPasquale was screaming and kicking out in every direction.

"I don't know what you're hollering about." Broderick breathed heavily, removing DiPasquale's pants while Vince and Tommy held him upright at the water's edge. "People come from all over to swim at this beach." He placed his foot at the base of Freddy's spine and kicked him into the freezing water.

"Think he can swim?" Tommy asked as they waited for Freddy to reappear from beneath the rolling surf.

Broderick shrugged. "I never thought to ask him."

"Must really be cold in there," Vince observed, shivering.

"Maybe he's fuckin' dead." Tommy searched the empty ocean.

"Either of you guys want to go in there after him?" Broderick asked casually. "I mean, he *is* just about the world's number one scumbag."

They looked tentatively at one another. "Aw shit!" Vince waded into the icy water with Tommy following. They were almost to their waists when they spotted Freddy farther out, bobbing helplessly on the crest of a breaker.

"Grab the motherfucker!" Tommy yelled at Vince, holding Freddy's leg and pulling him shoreward. Vince inched outward into the numbing surf and somehow managed to wrap his arms around Freddy's shoulders as Tommy tugged him into the shallow water. Together they dragged him onto the beach as the cackle of Broderick's insane laughter rose above the roar of the waves behind them.

"Stop laughing and see if the bastard is still alive." Vince lay on the wet sand and struggled to catch his breath through chattering teeth.

"Shit, he's too mean to die." Broderick nudged Freddy's body with his foot, then turned it over. "Looka that, the dumb shit is still breathing." He dug the heel of his shoe into Freddy's chest and jammed it downward. "All he needs is a little artificial respiration."

The contents of Freddy's lungs and stomach erupted onto his chest with the kick: seawater, chunks of partially digested food, blood, and bile. His eyelids fluttered and his shoulders began to shudder violently. "What's going on?" he asked weakly between spasms of choking.

"Detectives Crowley and Ippollito just saved your life," Broderick answered. "It was one of the bravest things I ever saw. I'm personally gonna recommend them both for commendations. Christ, they oughta get the goddamn Medal of Valor for what they did."

Vince looked up at Broderick. "You're some piece of work, you know that?"

Broderick grinned. "Hey, this is what makes the job worthwhile. It's not all pissing and moaning, right? You know what they say: 'All work and no play makes Doyle a dull fuck.' "

30

THE TOMATO HAD BECOME REASONABLE. HE STOOD SHIV-ering inside the building, poured himself a glassful of whiskey with shaking hands, and drank it in one gulp. "Okay, what is it you want to know?"

"I think it would be better if everybody was here," Vince said. "Didn't you tell us you had a crew working today?"

DiPasquale sank into a wooden chair and refilled his glass to the brim. "Whatta you need to talk to them for? They don't know nothing but performing."

"Why don't you let us decide whether they know anything or not." Vince shifted uncomfortably in his soaking pants and looked at Tommy, who had found a heating vent in the floor and was standing over it. "The thing is, me and my partner need full cooperation at this point, and we really wouldn't be happy if we didn't get it. Know what I mean?"

Freddy drained the glass again and stood submissively. "Everybody's in the back. Watch where you're walking if you don't want to be buried in shit." He led them into a narrow corridor that wound through random heaps of carnival equipment stacked almost to the ceiling. Fading wooden banners and hand-painted signs proclaimed the wonders of the midway: "NATURE'S ODDITIES: BEANO, THE TWO-HEADED BOY, LUCRETIA THE ALLIGATOR GIRL." Broken ceramic pots were heaped among gaily colored chariots and prancing horses and a lone, slumped plaster clown grinning silently at the chasm of the warehouse. "They got shit in here from a hundred years ago," Freddy said, leading them through the labyrinth of stored apparatus. "Probably worth a fuckin' fortune."

He halted at a door marked "NO ADMITTANCE," inserted a key, and opened it inward. "Cool it everybody, we got company!" he warned the people inside. There was a burst of frantic activity in the almost vacant interior as naked bodies scampered for cover behind the room's only adornments: a queen-sized bed, a red velvet sofa, several wood panels inexpertly painted to look like a meadow in summer, a tripod-mounted videocamera, metallic umbrellas to catch the glare from a single skylight in the ceiling. Vince looked around the room and committed it to memory, then followed Freddy, Tommy, and Doyle Broderick inside.

"These guys are detectives who want to ask us some questions. There wasn't nothing I could do to keep them out." DiPasquale held his hands up in apology.

"Don't be shy, people," Broderick chimed in. "Just look at us as six more eyes on the set. You ain't doing nothing we haven't seen before."

"Let's everyone come on out now," Vince added. "I don't feel like interviewing bare walls here."

The first to appear was a fully clothed male Caucasian, roughly forty years old, with no identifying marks or lesions other than an oily, pockmarked face and a profusely sweating upper lip. He was followed by a second, younger male, dressed in purple velvet pants and a leather vest, sporting a haircut that resembled an unmowed crabgrass lawn after a long drought.

"What's going on here?" Velvet pants demanded. "This is a movie set. Nobody's allowed on a movie set!"

"Who're you?" Vince asked.

"I don't have to answer any questions without my lawyer present," he answered stiffly. "I know my rights!"

"Who is this scumbag?" Broderick asked Freddy.

"His name is Benny Shapiro. He's the director," Freddy muttered in response.

"Director?" Broderick eyed him curiously. "What's to direct here? I thought all these people did was fuck and suck?"

"We make films here." Shapiro tugged resentfully at an errant strand of straw-colored hair. "Actors need direction."

"No shit?" Broderick was warming to the possibilities. "Whatta you say to them: 'Lights, camera, *hump*'?"

Shapiro glowered at him, twisted his lock of hair, and pouted.

"And who are you?" Vince asked the sweaty lip.

"Ian Fuchs," he muttered.

"And what to you do here, Ian Fuchs?"

"I'm the cameraman."

"Jeez! You got the best job of all," Broderick said. "All you gotta do is stand there, point the lens, and enjoy the show."

"There's more to it than that," Fuchs whined.

"Oh yeah. You got a lot of technical shit to take care of," Broderick conceded. "Especially them close-ups where everything looks like open-heart surgery. Christ, you can practically smell it—"

"The rest of you get your asses out here now!" Vince broke in. "I got no time to play hide-and-seek here."

"We're not doing anything illegal! What are you trying to do—stifle free expression?" Shapiro shrieked as the others began to appear from hiding. "What do you think this is, anyway, Communist Russia?"

"I think it's a fucking whorehouse, that's what I think it is." Vince stood face-to-face with Shapiro and spoke in a measured tone, "Now, you hear me, shithead, and you hear me real good. Cut the crap now and start cooperating or I will personally see to it that the term 'police brutality' takes on a whole new meaning for you. You give me or my partner any more lip, and we will hound you until the day you die. We will make your life so miserable that a single day without harassment will seem like a day at the beach to you. Am I making myself clear?"

Shapiro nodded uncomfortably.

"And that goes for the rest of you." Vince turned to the others, standing about the room in various stages of undress. "We're not here to bust anybody, just to get a little information. If you got clothes, put them on. We're liable to be at this awhile, and I wouldn't want anyone catching a draft."

Guffaws from Tommy and Broderick.

"Now, who are you?" Vince asked a short, buxom, coffee-colored female who was hurriedly pulling a pair of blue jeans over her ample hips.

"Name's Cinnamon," she muttered.

"Cinnamon what?" Vince opened his notebook.

"Jones."

Vince entered it in the book. "And what's your job here, Cinnamon?"

She eyed Freddy pleadingly. "I work here. I'm an actress."

"I see." Vince wrote it down without smiling. "How about you?" he asked an overweight platinum blonde wearing a black lace teddy with matching nylons and garters.

"I'm called Jersey Bell," she answered nonchalantly.

"Interesting name," Vince noted, writing it in the book.

"I know this one." Broderick smiled. "She got the name from advertising in the yellow pages."

"Oh yeah? What would I look you up under?" Vince asked her.

"Pipe cleaning." She grinned. "You need your pipes cleaned?"

"Not right now." He turned to the only undressed male in the room. "And you are?"

"Rodney Lancaster." The short, bony Hispanic answered, attempting to cover himself with a small hand towel.

"Rodney Lancaster." Vince entered it in the notebook with a flourish. "Now, that's a name that belongs in Hollywood if I ever heard one. Whatta you got under the towel there, Rodney Lancaster?"

Rodney glowered. "I don't have to show you."

"Maybe you didn't hear Detective Crowley real good." Doyle Broderick yanked the hand towel from his grasp.

"Jeez! Look at that, willya?" Tommy gasped.

"What the hell are you wearing on your pecker?" Broderick asked.

"It's a cock ring," Rodney muttered, sliding the circular brass band down the length of his limp penis and cupping it in his hand.

"A cock ring?" Broderick howled. "If that don't beat all! You wear that all the time or just in front of the cameras?"

"Don't knock it if you haven't tried it," Jersey Bell suggested with a smile. "Your old lady would go nuts if you whacked her with one of those babies on."

"Enough of this shit," Vince broke in. "This is a homicide investigation, for chrissakes, not a seminar in fancy fucking. Now, everybody get dressed, get comfortable, and get ready to answer some questions." He stuck the stub of his pencil behind his ear and waited until they were all ready.

"Okay," he said at length. He removed a photograph

of Lisa Thorpe from his jacket pocket and passed it around the room. "I want to know *if* any of you knew her, *when* you last saw her, and what she was doing." He looked at Jersey Bell, who was examining the picture with a faint smile on her lips. "You first."

"It's Lisa, that socialite bitch that got snuffed last month," she said matter-of-factly. "Sure, I knew her. She used to hang out around here all the time."

"With Johnny Zito?" Vince asked.

"I dunno. I don't think I ever saw her with Johnny." She passed the photograph to Rodney Lancaster. "You ever see her with him?"

Lancaster shook his head. "Uh-uh."

"What about it, Freddy?" Vince handed Lisa's picture to DiPasquale. "She ever come around here with your boss?"

Freddy eyed the photo perfunctorily. "Sure, I seen her, lots of times, but mostly she drove out here alone."

"What for?" Broderick asked. "What the hell was she doing out here anyway—acting in the films?"

"Most of the time she just watched," Cinnamon piped up. "She really got it off that way, you know?"

"She never did anything in front of the cameras?" Vince asked.

"She liked to get it on with women," Jersey Bell said. "But it was strictly for enjoyment. No way she'd perform in front of the camera."

"Women? What women are we talking about here?" Vince asked them. "Either of you two involved with her?"

Cinnamon shot a glance at Freddy and shrugged. "Sure. We knew she was Johnny's girlfriend and we figured we could earn some brownie points being nice to her."

"How about you?" Vince asked Rodney Lancaster. "You ever get it on with her."

Rodney scowled. "I don't need tight-assed little snots like her. I got my pride, you know."

Vince let it pass. "Let me get this straight. First you tell me she was Johnny Zito's girlfriend, then you tell me she got her kicks with women." He searched their faces. "So which was it?"

"Look, sometimes it's just that way," Jersey Bell explained. "A lot of people have their real lives and their fantasy lives. They live their real lives one way, and if they get the chance to live out their fantasies they try something different. She got the chance, that was all. It didn't mean nothing."

Vince checked his notes. "You called her a 'bitch,' " he reminded Jersey Bell. "That mean you and her didn't get along?"

"I think we all felt the same way." She looked around the room. "This isn't no game with us, Detective. We do this for a living and it's hard work. When I'm not here, I'm freezing my forty-six-year-old pussy off out on the boulevard, trying to hustle enough money to stay alive one more day. I don't care what you or anybody else thinks. Sex is great when you got your heart in it, but out here it's a job, just like any other job. You may not think we do good work out here, but you better believe we bust our asses trying. You just try convincing an audience you're really hot for something like that—" She eyed Rodney Lancaster contemptuously.

"You think it's easy getting it up over a smelly, fat old whore like you!" Rodney screamed back at her.

"Okay, okay. Fight it out after we're gone." Vince raised his hand for order and motioned for Jersey Bell to continue.

"Like I said, I think we all resented her coming around here like she owned the place. I mean, she had everything. She was young and beautiful and she had all the money in the world. All the stuff none of us ever had. She didn't have to do this, and she made sure everyone knew about it. Drove up here in that expensive BMW of hers like she was out here slumming. And she kept that rich-bitch society nose of hers in the air all the time like she was sniffing shit or something, even in the clinches."

"In the clinches?"

"Getting it on. She was a taker, if you know what I mean. Never gave anything of herself."

"Okay." Vince looked around the room. "When was the last time any of you saw her?"

They exchanged glances. "It had to be a coupla months ago," Freddy answered for them all. "Johnny sent word down that she wasn't welcome anymore, that she wasn't to be admitted on the lot. She just stopped showing up after that."

"I need a date," Vince said, pressing. "When did Johnny tell you Lisa Thorpe wasn't welcome anymore?"

"It was early December . . ." Freddy searched the ceiling. "The eighth, maybe the ninth."

"And that was the last time any of you saw her?"

A mumbled chorus of assent.

"Okay, let's call it a day for now." Vince closed the notebook and stretched uncomfortably in his still-soaking pants. "Don't anybody plan on taking any long trips in the near future. Detective Ippollito here will take your addresses and telephone numbers if you got 'em, and I want you all to stay available, kapish?" He nodded to Tommy and stepped outside.

"Whatta you think?" Broderick asked him while they waited in the crammed hallway for Tommy to finish.

Vince shrugged. "I dunno. The more I find out about Lisa Thorpe, the more I think she was one weird broad. It's kinda crazy, you know? After that garbage about her being a saint and all. Kinda makes you wonder."

Broderick scowled disdainfully. "Man, I stopped wondering about broads a long time ago. If it wasn't for their pussy, nobody'd have anything to do with them."

"Jeez, if I had a pussy I'd be king of the world!" Tommy laughed, joining them.

"You'd be a queen, asshole," Vince corrected him.

"Just a minute . . ." Broderick stepped back into the room for a few seconds and returned with his clenched fist shoved inside his jacket pocket.

"Whatta you got in there?" Tommy asked him. "I'll bet it's that cock-ring thingamajig, right?" He eyed Broderick accusingly. "You took it from Rodney Lancaster, didn't you?"

Broderick grinned sheepishly. "Hey, we live in a changing world, know what I mean? Never let it be said that Doyle Francis Broderick doesn't move with the times."

31

Dog Scarfatti sunk his chopsticks into the container of Chinese take-out and stared uncertainly at the woman seated by Vince Crowley's desk. "You see what she's doing?" He dug an elbow into Walt Cuzak's ribs. "She's talking to her jewelry, that's what she's doing."

Cuzak looked across the room where the woman was engaged in a serious conversation with her crystal necklace. "She's one of those New Age freaks. Says she can tell the future and shit from those stones."

"Shee-it!" Dog removed a lump of unidentifiable meat and soggy vegetables from the container and chewed it lustily. "Everybody's got a gimmick, know what I mean? Guy came in here the other day waving a dead chicken over his head. Said his neighbor conjured up a spell and put bad magic on him. Bad magic? Gimmee a break, willya? I'm telling you the truth, man, I seen more sick motherfuckers since I been up here than I seen in six years downtown."

"So go back downtown," Cuzak replied nonchalantly. "I don't see anyone stopping you."

"What the hell . . . ?" Scarfatti probed the inside of his mouth with a chubby forefinger and extracted a blob of partially eaten food. "Jeezus H. Christ! It's a goddamn bandage!" He held it under Cuzak's nose. "Looka that, willya? Some Chink mixed one of his scabby bandages in with my Mandarin pork!"

"Serves you right for eating that garbage." Cuzak opened his desk drawer and retrieved the brown paper bag containing his lunch. "I pack mine myself, so I *know* what I'm putting in my stomach."

Scarfatti threw the remainder of the container into the wastepaper basket contemptuously. "Don't start with that

204

health-food crap of yours, Cuzak. I seen what you eat. It looks like somebody's lawn.''

Cuzak shrugged. "Go ahead, make jokes. The fact is you don't know dick about what you put in your body. You just keep shoving poison in your mouth, getting fatter and fatter, sicker and sicker. That goddamn bandage was probably the healthiest thing in that whole meal you just ate." Cuzak reached in the bag and extracted a brownish cube wrapped in clear plastic. "See that? Whole grain, dried raisins, bananas, and carob peanuts. Tastes better than a candy bar, loaded with vitamins and minerals, and cleans you right out, sorta like nature's broom.''

"That's your whole idea of having fun—taking a good shit, right? It don't make no difference how rotten the rest of your life is, as long as you got healthy bowels." Scarfatti made a sour face. "I'll bet if I showed up here with two bimbos who had tits like inner tubes, a coupla bottles of guinea red, and a pepperoni pizza, you'd say 'Sorry, Dog, not tonight. Gotta eat some dried shrubs and sit on the crapper. Nature's fuckin' broom, you know!' ''

"Stop that right now!" The woman at Vince Crowley's desk glared at them disapprovingly. "You're setting up unfavorable vibrations in this room that are interfering with my psychic frequencies.''

Cuzak shrugged and went back to his paperwork. Dog Scarfatti retrieved the carton of Chinese food from the wastepaper basket, stirred it tentatively with the chopsticks, and resumed eating. The woman closed her eyes, fondled her beads lovingly, and began mumbling.

Vince entered the squad room and spotted her sitting by his desk: mid-forties with hip-length straight black hair salted into grey. She was beautiful once, he guessed, but now her face was hidden behind layers of chalky make-up, angry slashes of rouge, and too much mascara.

"Something I can do for you, ma'am?"

She opened her eyes. "Are you Detective Crowley?"

"Yes, ma'am."

"Detective Crowley, the spirit of Lisa Thorpe has directed me to you. She has channeled her wishes through me—more specifically, through the energy I absorb from my crystals—and given me information concerning the specifics of her murder.''

Vince shot a pleading glance across the room at Walt

Cuzak and sat heavily. "Yes, ma'am, well, the truth of it is that Lieutenant Gleason is in charge of that case, and any information you have should probably be given to him . . ."

"Lisa Thorpe's spirit directed me to you." Her voice was brittle. "I cannot interfere with the flow of psychic energy she has established."

"Yes, ma'am." Vince opened his notebook. "Can we start with your name?"

She ran a slender hand through her long black hair. "Zircon. My name is Zircon."

"Yes, ma'am." Vince entered it. "And your last name?"

"My name is Zircon, period," she said emphatically. "Last names are an anachronistic tribal method of diminishing the self. My inner self is Zircon."

"Okay, Zircon." Vince settled back in his chair and took a deep breath. "Just what are these spirits telling you about Lisa Thorpe?"

"Lisa Thorpe's spirit," She corrected him.

"Yes ma'am, Lisa Thorpe's spirit. Specifically, just what was it she told you?"

Zircon closed her eyes and fingered her necklace. "It's more a series of images, like a mental tone-poem that burns its message into my subconscious. I see the child before a mirror, brushing her long hair deliberately, stroke after tender stroke. She is humming a melody, a singsong, repetitive air that matches the rhythm of her brush strokes, almost a madrigal. Then the scene darkens and the child recoils in horror as the brush strokes begin to tear her long brown tresses from her head in large clumps. Every stroke of the brush removes more hair until all that is left is a shaggy fringe of gray.

"She stares into the mirror, watching herself suddenly age. The flesh of her face is descending into coarse, dry hollows and gaps. Her sparkling eyes mist into gray. Her sudden tears erupt dead and expressionless, coursing down the furrows of her cheeks . . . falling on the floor." Zircon shuddered involuntarily.

"Yes, ma'am?"

"The floor is covered with her hair," Zircon went on. "Snarls of matted hair floating in a crimson pool. That pool is Lisa Thorpe's blood." She straightened herself up in the chair and blinked as if she were awakening. "The image is intense, Detective. I know it must have something important to do with her murder."

Vince looked at his notes. "Girl brushes hair, girl loses hair . . . blood on floor. Uh-huh. Well, you never can tell. Sometimes these things can tell us a lot." He stood and offered his hand. "I appreciate you coming in like this. If you'll leave your phone number at the desk downstairs, I'll be in touch with you."

She handed him a card. "You are my contact, Detective Crowley. I suggest we not share our information with anyone if we're to keep the creative energies flowing."

"How about my partner, Detective Ippollito?" Vince indicated Tommy who had just entered the squad room. "I can't keep important stuff like this from him."

It was a moment of pure drama; one of those dropdead, nostril-flaring, soap opera moments when the music surges to a crescendo and the actors are frozen before the cameras in heavy, meaningful gazes of desire. This time it was Zircon, devouring the unsuspecting Tommy with her lustful eyes, her trembling lips. "How do you *do* . . ." She extended her hand theatrically, batted her false eyelashes.

"Hi . . ." Tommy shook her hand and shot a nervous glance at Vince.

"I'm getting a powerful energy flow from you," Zircon told Tommy, continuing to hold his hand. "You must have a very strong psychic presence."

"Zircon here has some ideas about how Lisa Thorpe was killed," Vince broke in. "Mostly about hair and blood and stuff like that. She was nice enough to take time out of her busy schedule and come down here to share them with us."

"Great." Tommy squirmed uncomfortably, trying to gently extricate his hand. "We can use all the help we can get on that one."

"Perhaps you and I should get together some time." Zircon looked longingly into Tommy's eyes. "I sense an openness in you, a willingness to experience new things, an untapped reservoir of passion that can only be released by a spiritually kindred soul."

Tommy was beginning to sweat. "Yeah, well, I really gotta get going." He yanked his hand free and shoved it embarrassedly into his pants pocket. "You know, Snuffy put me in charge of Pete Yorio's retirement dinner, and

there's just a whole lotta loose ends I got to wrap up."
He backed away steadily.

"Oh yeah, I forgot about that." Vince stood and headed
for the door with Tommy. "You'll have to excuse us
now, Zircon. This dinner's really a big deal around here,
and if we don't handle it, it won't get done."

"Hey, no big deal." Dog Scarfatti approached them.
"I can see you got important things to talk about here, so
why don't you let me handle the retirement dinner so you
guys can keep this thing going."

Vince's eyes became slits. "No need for that, Dog."
His words were even, hyphenated. "Tommy and I will
handle the retirement dinner. You go back to that important detective work you were doing before we got here."

"Just trying to help." Scarfatti threw his hands in the
air, stifled a grin.

"It would be a shame if we missed out on an opportunity to work together," Zircon said, her unblinking eyes
riveted on Tommy's crotch. "I was hoping we could go
over some of the clues you've uncovered so far and run
them through the psychic mill, as it were. My powers are
best utilized when I'm working with specific information."

"Uh, I'm afraid that information would be classified,"
Vince said, still edging toward the door. "Homicide investigations aren't generally open to the public."

"Please don't think of me as the public." Zircon's
voice had grown silky. "Think of me as a *mon semblable*,
an analogous spirit." She pressed in on Tommy and
searched his face. "I want to make myself very *available*
to you, Detective Ippollito." She stared directly into his
eyes. "Do you understand what that means?"

"I think so." Tommy stretched his neck awkwardly.

"I hope you do." Zircon ran a trembling finger up the
length of Tommy's tie and settled at the top, where
several errant strands of chest hair curled above the open
neck of his shirt. "I believe there is kismet in our meeting, Detective Ippollito." She twisted the chest hair around
a purple fingernail. "We would be tempting fate if we
failed to take advantage of this opportunity, don't you
agree?" A final flutter of her eyelashes and Zircon left
the squad room.

"Holy shit. If that wasn't a bald-faced proposition, I
never saw one," Walt Cuzak observed after she was gone.

"Just what I need, some over-the-hill hippie who talks to her beads." Tommy wiped the perspiration from his upper lip and went to his desk.

"Hey, man, don't knock it until you've tried it," Dog Scarfatti piped up. "Some of the best pieces of ass I ever had were old hippies. Their minds are so blown on acid they'll try anything, and they think every hump'll be their last so they give it all they got."

"Sure, whatta you got to lose?" Walt Cuzak chimed in. "Good-looking young guy like you oughta be getting more ass than a toilet seat, but you're so busy taking courses and writing about shit you probably never get laid. A seasoned old veteran like Zircon's probably got moves you never even dreamed about."

Tommy began sorting through his telephone messages. "Yeah, well, there's just one flaw in the ointment. She's so seasoned she's probably sitting on every communicable disease known to man."

"So let her toot your tube," Scarfatti said. "They don't call old Zircon 'nature's broom' for nothing." He grinned at Walt Cuzak. "You look like your pipes could use cleaning out."

"I don't believe I'm having this conversation with you ignoramuses—" The telephone rang and Tommy answered it. "Thirty-seventh precinct. Detective Ippollito."

"This is George Wiggand, superintendent of the building at 311 Palmer Road in Bronxville." The voice at the other end was clipped, agitated. "I wanta know how much longer you guys are keeping the Thorpe girl's apartment sealed. I have potential buyers for that property and I can't show it."

"Just a minute . . ." Tommy cupped the receiver with his hand. "It's the super from that Bronxville apartment," he said to Vince. "Wants to know how long before he can show Lisa Thorpe's apartment."

Vince shook his head. "Christ, I forgot all about that. You mean the dumb shit still has the place sealed?"

"Looks that way."

Vince lifted the telephone. "This is Detective Crowley. What seems to be the trouble?"

"You told me to keep everybody out of the Thorpe girl's apartment. That was more than a month ago, and I'm losing a fortune every day it sits there empty. Nobody's been here: no cops, no reporters, nobody. So I'd appreciate it if you could give me the go-ahead to show the place."

"Well, sir, you realize this is a homicide investigation."

"I know that, but I'm losing a goddamn fortune!"

"I see. I suppose we could get somebody out there in a couple of days to wrap things up." Vince tried to sound serious. "In the meantime, I'm gonna have to ask you to keep the apartment sealed, okay?"

"A couple of days?"

"As soon as we can shake somebody free."

"Please!" There were tears in the superintendent's voice.

"Why didn't you just tell him to show the place?" Tommy asked after Vince hung up. "We don't need anything more from there."

Vince shrugged. "Whatta you want, we should look like a buncha incompetents?" He tossed Zircon's card into his wastepaper basket. "I don't know whether you got a load of the suit that guy was wearing when we were out there, but I did. Eight hundred simoleans, easy. I can guarantee you that nobody's throwing any benefits for him just because he can't rent Lisa Thorpe's apartment."

"Good point." Tommy strolled to Vince's desk and stood next to the wastepaper basket, retrieving Zircon's card when he was sure nobody was looking.

"Remember what you want is your basic tube tooting," Dog Scarfatti cackled as Tommy sauntered casually toward the door. "Nature's fuckin' broom, y'know."

32

NYPD FORM DD-5
COMPLAINT FOLLOW-UP

HOMICIDE/STABBING
LISA THORPE W/F 23

JANUARY 30, 1989
COMPLAINT # 4548
Det. V. Crowley

1. At approx. 0830 hours, above date, Dets. Ippollito, Turner and the undersigned from 37 sqd. accompanied a specially assembled Bronx Narcotics task force to the warehouse headquarters of Bliss of the East Imports, 311-314 Eastchester Ave., Bronx, N.Y., for the purpose of interdicting a suspected narcotics operation. Present were Lt. Brophy, Dets. Weichert, Broz, Killeen, DiSimone, Matton & Levin, Bronx Narco. ESU personnel: Lt. Briggs, Sgt. McCaffery, and 6 uniformed officers.

2. Upon arrival at premises the street was closed at both ends by patrol cars; vehicular traffic was rerouted and pedestrians restrained from entering the area in question.

3. When the area was considered secure, officers were deployed in strike positions and radio contact was established. Dets. Weichert, DiSimone and the undersigned entered the premises, set up surveillance and waited for opportunistic entry.

4. At approx. 0952 hours, we observed an Asian male, (Ngo Chi Minh, 26), entering premises in a suspicious manner and detained same. Subject

was searched and found to have a 9mm Beretta 42 SW automatic on his person (unlicensed), as well as $62,000.00 in large currency. Subject was read his rights and freely agreed to accompany us inside the warehouse. All units were alerted by radio and a coordinated entry into the premises was begun at 1013 hours.

6. Upon entry we were met by gunfire from the occupants of the premises and returned same. After a firefight lasting approx. 32 seconds, the premises was secured and two additional suspects were apprehended. (Tranh Van Luc, A/M, 34.; Nuyen Van Dai, A/M, 28.) An as yet unnamed Asian female presumed to be Luc's wife was found dead on the premises, apparently a victim of gunshot wounds inflicted during the firefight.

7. Confiscated and inventoried were the following items: Two M-16 rifles; Two Iver-Johnson M1 carbines; one 9mm semi-automatic pistol; one 357 cal. Colt Python pistol; one 44 magnum cal. Smith & Wesson revolver; one machete type knife, 21" long; Approx 90 kilos cut heroin; 13 kilos cocaine; 28 grams marijuana; three marijuana cigarettes; assorted scales, trays, glassine envelopes; Currency in amount of $537,455.00

Rudy Weichert flattened his body against the concrete wall of the warehouse. As he breathed deeply, the moist tissue of his nostrils solidified against the inflowing knife edge of freezing air. He exhaled with difficulty, watching the vaporous cloud of his breath evaporate into the colorless wash of sky, and realized it had been his first breath in a long time, minutes maybe. He'd been choking back the almost irresistible urge to scream, to vomit up the relentlessly tightening fist that seized his gut and twisted it into shreds of immobilizing fear.

Behind Weichert, Vince Crowley edged forward until he hunkered down beside him on the rock-hard earth. The lower portion of his face was sunken into the neckline cavity created by the bulge of his bulletproof vest. Crowley was breathing heavily, too, Weichert knew, trying to melt the icy spasms of terror in his chest. Vince Crowley was as good a cop as Rudy had seen in twenty-three years on the force, but he was no more a superman than the worst of them. They all sweated and shook and prayed to whatever god was convenient when their asses were on the line; then they puked their guts up if they made it out alive. It was just the way things were and nobody talked much about it.

"Over there," Weichert whispered hoarsely, pointing to a rusting, paint-spattered Chevrolet parked near the entrance to the warehouse.

Vince raised his head tentatively above the line of parked autmobiles shielding them from the street and observed the car's driver. An Asian male in his twenties, he sat erect and alert behind the wheel, sweeping the area with anxious eyes. "A bad guy." Vince ducked back behind the safety of a battered fender.

Weichert squinted across the parking lot and spotted Detective Angelo DiSimone huddled against the opposite side of the building. He pointed to the car and DiSimone nodded. "Subject is an Asian male in a late-Fifties Chevy," he said, breathing heavily into the radio linking them with the rest of the task force, four blocks away. "He's just sitting there, sizing up the territory. We're gonna take him if he attempts to enter the warehouse."

"Copy." The radio crackled back.

"Outside of that, there's no activity of any kind. No lights inside, no noise coming from anywhere."

"Just watch your ass," the voice at the other end warned.

Weichert gripped the 12-gauge pump-action shotgun at his side. Running his hand along the oil-rubbed wooden stock, he was comforted by its reassuring bulk. The lead slugs it fired could cut a man off at the waist from fifty feet. He glanced back at Vince and noted with satisfaction that he had unholstered his revolver and was holding it barrel-up behind his right ear. Across the lot, Angelo DiSimone was crouched behind a row of metal garbage cans, his 9mm Smith & Wesson raised in a similar manner. "Everybody stay calm and keep an eye on this sonofabitch," he mumbled into the radio. "I don't wanta give him no reason to bolt."

The subject opened the door of the vintage Chevrolet, hesitated momentarily, and began walking toward the entrance of the warehouse, peering warily through the files of parked automobiles in the lot. He stopped thirty feet from the building, lit a cigarette, and huddled with his back to the wind.

"Come on, motherfucker," Weichert groaned. "Just a dozen more steps. Just move your yellow ass close enough for me to shove the barrel of this gun up it." He shrugged helplessly at Vince.

"Here he comes," Vince rasped as the subject resumed walking. "Take him now if you're gonna take him!"

Weichert was up in an instant, pressed flat against the front of the building, aiming the barrel of the shotgun at a point just below the subject's chin. "Don't you fucking move," he growled in a low, menacing voice. "Don't turn, don't make a motion, don't open your fucking mouth. You say one word and I'll blow your fucking head clear to Canarsie."

The man froze, his eyes wide with fear. "Just walk slowly toward me, motherfucker," Weichert said. "Like you spotted something interesting on the ground. Hands at your sides—real nonchalant like, know what I mean?"

Vince stood as the man approached and caught him around the neck in a vicelike grip. "Up against the wall, scumbag." He cuffed both of the subject's wrists with his free hand, flattened him against the building, and kicked his legs apart as Weichert began patting him down.

"Just look what we got here." Rudy extracted a 9mm automatic from the subject's right boot. "You got a license to carry this here weapon?"

Silence.

Weichert raised the barrel of the pistol and jammed it forcefully into the subject's crotch. "You answer my questions, you slimy motherfucker, or your nuts are gonna be smeared all over this building. I asked you if you had a permit to carry this."

The man grimaced with pain, shook his head no.

Weichert continued his search. "Well, whatta you know about this." He removed a leather money belt from the subject's waist. "There's gotta be all the money in the world in here, partner."

Vince eyed the compartments of the money belt, bulging with wads of neatly rolled bills. "I'll be dipped in shit.

It looks like we got ourselves a real entrepeneur here, partner. Yes sir, a regular John Jacob Astor." He tightened his grip around the subject's throat. "You wanta tell us what you were gonna do with all this money? You going in there to buy some horse—some Thai white, scumbag?"

He strained against Vince's tightening forearm and sputtered unintelligibly as blood trickled from his nose.

"You know what I think we oughta do, partner? I think we oughta take this gook bastard someplace, blow his brains out, and keep this loot for ourselves. That's what I think we oughta do," Weichert said calmly.

Vince nodded. "Not a bad idea, but they probably got a lot more inside."

Weichert turned the subject around, pressed the barrel of the shotgun into his chest, and pumped it once. "What's your name?" he asked through clenched teeth.

"Minh . . ." he answered weakly.

"Now, you listen to me, Minnie. What you're gonna do is go up to that door and knock on it, or do whatever it is you do when we're not here. If I think you're jerking us around, I'll take your legs off and let you flop on the ground for a while before I put you out of your fucking misery, you got that?" Weichert pumped the shotgun again for emphasis.

"I get killed," Minh whined.

"You're gonna get killed anyway, slimeball. You were a fucking dead man the minute you set those slanty little eyes of yours on my partner and me. What you're bargaining for now is time." Weichert lifted the barrel of the shotgun from Minh's chest and pointed it toward the door of the warehouse. "What's it gonna be, Minnie?"

Minh shook his head in resignation.

"Okay, we're doing it," Weichert rasped hoarsely into the radio as Vince unlocked the handcuffs. "We're going inside as soon as everybody's in position." He dropped the radio to his side, took a deep breath, and expelled it into the chill morning mist.

Vince could see detectives moving stealthily forward in the street beyond the parking lot. Armed with shotguns and M-16 automatic rifles, they were taking up positions behind bushes, trees, and parked automobiles. He could feel his heartbeat begin to quicken, hear his labored breathing as he struggled to suppress the waves of nausea building in his abdomen. His ears became blocked, his vision blurred, his senses deadened as the drama unfolded before him.

Weichert steadily prodded Minh toward the door of the warehouse. It was a silent, slow-motion pantomime, like the hauntingly beautiful images of stately Kabuki dancers he remembered seeing in travelogues on TV. The deliberate, almost ritualistic knock on the door—one tap, then three, then one again . . .

"It's going down! It's going down!" Weichert barked shrilly into the radio. Vince was shocked back to reality and began running. "Move in! Everybody move in!" Rudy knocked Minh to the ground and hurdled his limp body like a track star, rushing headlong into the building past the startled young woman who had opened the door. DiSimone followed, jerking left to right behind his waist-slung M-16 automatic rifle, screaming at the top of his lungs: "Out in the open, all you motherfuckers! This is a raid!"

Vince dove to the floor as they were met by an answering fusillade of gunshots from inside, and rolled away from the door to avoid being caught in a crossfire from backup units storming the building in response. Angry bursts of automatic-weapons fire were punctuated by jarring, ear-splitting explosions from the pump-action shotguns. Their lead slug charges tore apart walls and furniture in an indiscriminate gale of destruction. He heard the screams of men so filled with panic they could only stand their ground and shoot—hollow screams, gutteral screams, screams of pain and anger and sheer terror.

He had rolled behind a table or a desk, trying to focus across his wavering gunsight on flashes of muzzle fire diffused through billowing clouds of smoke and dust. He squeezed the trigger, once, twice. The recoil sent shock waves up his spine; the shots exploded in his ear. He winced at the pain and allowed the pistol to fall limply to his side as the barrage subsided to an occasional crackling salvo, then died altogether.

"No shoot. I give up." A skinny Oriental emerged from behind an overturned metal filing cabinet, followed by a second. "No shoot!"

Weichert leveled the shotgun at them and pumped it vigorously as several of the detectives approached them with caution. "Where are the rest of you motherfuckers?" he demanded.

"Just us," the first answered. "No more us fellas here." He shrugged his shoulders submissively.

Weichert stepped forward and caught him flush on the jaw with the butt of his shotgun, driving him to the floor in a sickening crunch of torn flesh and shattered bone. "You little prick! I said, where are the rest of you? There were more than two of you shooting at us!"

"Two . . . two . . ." he stammered through bloodied, broken teeth. "Only two, mista cop, I swear . . ." He groveled on the floor, holding up two bony fingers.

"He telling the truth?" Weichert menacingly asked the second Asian as other detectives searched him roughly for concealed weapons.

"Only two, boss. Swear to God."

"Shee-it." Weichert lowered the shotgun and walked slowly to the wall where Vince was sitting. "I coulda swore there was a dozen of the motherfuckers."

"They had plenty of firepower, Rudy." DiSimone held up two M-16 automatic carbines. "Sonsabitches were prepared to fight a war."

"Well, they better goddamn be prepared to *die!*" Weichert glowered at the two. "You little bastards better tell us what we want to know, or you're going down on the record as battle casualties, you dig? I'm gonna personally make you responsible for all our boys who went down in your fucking rice paddies or starved to death in your fucking prison camps." He raised the shotgun and pointed it at them. "One bully-bully for every MIA back in that shithole you call a country, how's that for justice, motherfuckers?"

"What about him?" Vince pointed to Minh, who was sitting cross-legged just outside the door, giggling uncontrollably.

"What the fuck's so funny?" Weichert kicked him in the ribs, knocking him over.

Minh bounced back up like a rubber toy. "I don't know . . ." He inspected his intact hands and arms as if he was seeing them for the first time. "I don't know . . ."

"This one wasn't so lucky, Sarge." A detective lifted the limp torso of the woman who had opened the door; her head had been blown away by a dum-dum shotgun charge. "Shit, she wasn't even shooting at us."

"Do your crying to somebody else." Weichert stepped over the woman's lifeless form, walked outside onto the concrete entranceway, and stood silhouetted against the overcast sky. "I been crying ever since I got into his job. I got no tears left."

33

JOHN GLEASON STOOD STIFFLY IN HIS DOORWAY AS THE
room swelled with unfamiliar faces, and immediately calculated that something he was not even remotely aware
of was going down. "Inside. Now!" he hissed as Vince
Crowley passed him in the parade filing past his office.
"Bring Ippollito with you." He wheeled and went inside.

"Yes sir, Lieutenant." Vince entered Gleason's office
with Tommy following. "You wanted to see us?"

"What the hell is all this?" Gleason's lips were nar-
rowed against his clenched teeth. "Who are all these
people anyway?"

"Bronx Narcotics, Lieutenant. Detectives Ippollito,
Turner, and myself just went on a raid with them. We
busted a big B.L.T. distribution house out on Eastchester
Avenue; Bliss of the East Importers. About the only
thing they were importing was Thai white."

"Heroin? You went on a drug raid?"

"Yes sir. We had information that these were the same
guys that snuffed Karp, so we asked in on the collar."

Gleason turned and walked slowly to his office window, trying to sort it all out in his mind. "How many
from this squad did you say were involved?" he asked
finally, trying to mask the bewilderment in his voice.

"Just me and Tommy and Leila Turner, Lieutenant."

"Anybody else know about it?"

Vince looked at Tommy and shrugged. "I suppose
anyone who was in the office the other day coulda picked
up on it."

"I was in the office the other day!" Gleason turned
and glared at them. "Did anyone bother to check with me?"

Vince and Tommy eyed each other nervously.

"You include a *female rookie* and you don't even bother
to inform your commanding officer that an operation like
this is in progress?"

"Begging the lieutenant's pardon, but Turner was there because the Karp homicide was her case," Tommy broke in. "The drug raid was just a part of that investigation."

"And nobody here felt it was important enough to tell me about it?" Gleason's voice was reaching the hysterical point.

"You made it clear to all of us that you weren't interested in the details of that case, sir," Vince said evenly. "We tried to keep you informed as best we could, but things started happening pretty fast out there."

Gleason sat heavily and fumbled in his desk drawer for an aspirin. "*Turner* was there?" he asked incredulously.

"Yes sir. She's sharing in the collar," Vince said. "Judging from what we observed at the scene, it oughta be a pretty good one for her, too. My best guess would be that we confiscated twenty or thirty million bucks worth of street-value horse and another half a million in cash. Those kind of numbers'll give anybody's career a goose."

Gleason's eyes lit up. "The press been notified about this yet?"

Vince shrugged. "I dunno, sir, but you know how they are. It won't be long before they're here looking for a statement." He cast a sidelong glance at Tommy. "I guess the P.C. and the Chief of D. would feel pretty good about it if they were invited up here for the show."

"Thirty million dollars worth of heroin, you say?"

"Street-value, Lieutenant. They're inventorying it downstairs right now, along with some coke and a lot of weapons."

"Makes a pretty good spread, does it?" Gleason asked.

"When they stack it up, it'll look like all the dope in China," Vince assured him. "And there's enough money and weapons down there to keep a banana republic at war for a year."

"Plus we got the Karp killing wrapped up," Tommy added.

"Good." Gleason nodded perfunctorily. "I'm sure you both have things to do at this point. Send Turner in here as soon as she's free. I want to congratulate her." He pretended to become interested in some paperwork on his desk.

"How do you like that?" Tommy asked when they were back in the squad room. "The sonofabitch wasn't even interested that these guys iced Karp."

"Maybe," Vince corrected him. "We won't know for sure until we get the lab results on that machete we found."

"Or one of them confesses," Tommy said. "My guess is that once their P.D.s tell them they're facing major felony/life, they'll bust their asses turning over on each other."

"Could be you're right—" Vince's telephone rang and he answered it. "Crowley here."

"Alex Guzman, Detective Crowley. I'm just calling because I thought you might be interested in what's going on with Ricardo Mirable down at the rehabilitation center."

"Ricky? Yeah . . ." Vince readjusted his thoughts. "How's the kid doing?"

"A lot better than I thought he would," Guzman said. "I don't know how these things work, but every now and then it just seems to go the way it's supposed to go. All the reports I'm getting about Ricky are positive, even glowing. I guess maybe he still has enough mind left to know when he's had enough."

Vince felt a surge of elation. "Jeez, that's great. You think I could go out there and visit him? Maybe bring him some food or something?"

"I'm afraid not. They don't allow visitors for the first month," Guzman told him.

"How about if I call, give him a little encouragement?"

"Sorry to say that's out, too. They're pretty strict about keeping their patients isolated in the beginning. It's nice to know you care, though. I'll see to it that Ricky knows you asked about him."

"I'd appreciate that. And let me know if there's anything I can do."

"Well, if you really mean that, you can give some thought to what happens to him after he's released from the program. He's going to need a place to stay."

"Don't they have halfway houses . . . places like that?"

"Sure, but I doubt Ricky would stay in one of them. He's a free spirit, you know, and I doubt he'd take well to the discipline once he's feeling better. I'm hoping we can find something with a clean, positive environment and a lot less regimentation."

"Yeah, I can understand that . . ." Vince caught Rudy Weichert signaling him from the open door of the squad room. "I gotta go now. I'll call you if I think of anything, okay?"

"I can't ask for more than that."

"Tell Ricky I wish him the best." Vince hung up and crossed the room.

"We're starting to interrogate the gooks," Weichert informed him. "I thought you'd want a piece of them before there's nothing worthwhile left."

"Anything good so far?" Vince asked, accompanying him into the hallway.

"Not a lot. We're waiting for some paper to come up from B.C.I., and we're running a check through Immigration. If we find out that any of these guys are illegal, we got 'em where the short hairs grow."

"Who're you questioning first?"

"That skinny prick, Luc. He seems to be the head of the whole shmear."

"I think that's a mistake," Vince said as they walked through the downstairs corridor toward the interrogation rooms. "Me, I'd start with Minh. He was there buying, not selling. That means he's not as tight with the other two as they are with each other. Besides, he seemed a little off balance back there at the warehouse. Let's give him a rattle and see if he holds together."

"Be my guest." Weichert held open the door to one of the rooms off the corridor and allowed Vince to enter. Inside, Minh was sitting forlornly, handcuffed to a straight-backed wooden chair, guarded by a single uniformed officer.

"How's it going, Minh?" Vince signaled the guard to unlock the handcuffs and offered him a cigarette. "They treating you okay down here?"

"I want public defender," Minh said sullenly. "I know my rights."

"Sure, you do," Weichert said. "All you slope-headed sons of bitches know your rights, don't you?"

"Okay, okay, let's all calm down now," Vince placed a reassuring hand on Minh's shoulder. "Name-calling isn't gonna get us anywhere, so why don't the three of us just get down to why we're here in the first place."

"I no doing nothing," Minh muttered. "You don't have no reason hold me here."

"How about carrying an illegal firearm, scumbag?" Weichert howled. "How about the sixty-odd grand we

found in that money belt of yours, you little turd? What
the hell were you gonna do with that, play fuckin'
mah-jongg?"

"Wait a minute . . ." Vince motioned for calm. "Maybe
we oughta approach this from a different way." He winked
imperceptibly at Weichert. "Our friend Minh here's got a
good point when he says we got no real reason to hold
him. I mean, how do we actually *know* he planned to
spend that money on heroin? Maybe has going in there
to strike up a deal for chopsticks or something. As far as
the gun is concerned, he coulda borrowed it. That's a
dangerous neighborhood, if you know what I mean. I
wouldn't want to be caught there without a firearm."

He paused, lit an unfiltered Camel, and inhaled deeply.
"We may just have to let our friend here go once we get
the immigration stuff cleared up."

The muscles of Minh's jaw tightened reflexively.

"Yeah, that immigration thing's the only real case we
can probably make against this little shit," Weichert said.
"And then all we can do is have him deported back
where he came from."

"I'm sure it's all a bureaucratic screwup," Vince said
to Minh. "There's no way an upstanding citizen like you
could be in this country illegally, is there?"

Minh stared straight ahead, beads of sweat beginning
to trickle down his forehead into the narrow slits his eyes
had become.

"Shee-it, that'd be fuckin' terrible!" Weichert groaned.
"What're we talking here, Vietnam? I'll bet those Viet
Congs would just fuckin' love to get their hands on
somebody who sneaked outa their country so he could
make an illegal buck in the good ol' U.S.A. Whatta you
think? Are we talking tiger cage here? Maybe one of those
work brigades where everybody gets their asses reedu-
cated by shoveling buffalo shit under the hot sun all day.
Sounds good to me." He guffawed loudly. "How about
fuckin' Cambodia? I'll bet old Pol Pot would give his left
nut to get a jewel like you back in the country. Eight or
ten months of living on two hundred calories a day oughta
get you down to your fighting weight—make you lean
and mean like the rest of those little yellow bastards—"

"This isn't getting us anywhere," Vince interrupted him.
"I'm sure Minh'll have a real good explanation if his
papers aren't kosher."

"Don't give me that 'good cop' routine," Minh snarled. "I don't mind being fucked over, but I won't be patronized."

"Jeezus! What happened to his coolie accent?" Weichert gasped. "You think he talks like that all the time, or just when it starts to look like he's gonna get his ass impaled on the village stake?"

"I'm not interested at your pitiful attempts at humor," Minh said dryly. "Get me a P.D. who knows what he's doing, and maybe we can work something out."

"Like what?" Vince asked.

"Like maybe where Luc and Dai are getting the stuff."

"You know their overseas supplier?"

"When my lawyer gets here." Minh stretched out in the chair for the first time. "Got another cigarette, good cop?"

Vince handed him a Camel and lit it. "What else can you tell us about these guys? Like, how about murders? Did you ever hear about a guy named Karp?"

Minh took a deep drag of the cigarette and exhaled it, watching the thin cloud of smoke float lazily to the ceiling. "You know, that's what I love about this country. Everything has a price and nobody gets nothing for nothing."

34

"A MAJOR DRUG BUST IN NEW YORK . . ." VINCE watched the TV screen as the fashionable young anchorwoman on the eleven o'clock news read the day's lead story from the teleprompter. ". . . One person was killed this morning as an organized police task force raided an alleged drug-distribution center in The Bronx, seizing an estimated forty million dollars worth of heroin and cocaine."

Forty million. The amounts were always multiplied for public consumption.

"Units of the Bronx Narcotics Division accompanied by local law-enforcement officers swept in during the early hours on a Bronx warehouse occupied by Bliss of the East Import Company of 311-314 Eastchester Avenue, operated by Vietnamese immigrants Tranh Van Luc and Nuyen Van Dai, and confiscated drugs, weapons, and close to one million dollars in cash after a furious gun battle in which one Vietnamese woman lost her life."

"It was like a battle zone in there. From the firepower they had, it looked like they were getting ready for World War Three," the Chief of Detectives said somberly into the camera. He was replaced on the screen by a sweeping display of the confiscated drugs, weapons, and cash.

Another guy who wasn't there and knows all about it.

"What made this raid particularly significant was the presence of a woman on the task force." The camera panned in on Leila Turner, standing uncomfortably between the Police Commissioner and Lieutenant John Gleason. "Detective Third Grade Leila Turner assumed a significant part of the investigative work leading up to what is being described as one of the largest drug busts in the history of the city, and is credited with a major role in the capture of the two alleged heroin kingpins."

225

"We are proud of all the women on the police force of the city of New York," the Police Commissioner said, beaming into the camera. "And particularly proud of Detective Turner, a black woman, whose courageous performance today in the face of extreme danger should put to rest any lingering doubts about a female police officer's ability to perform at the same level as her male counterpart. Detective Turner has acquitted herself with valor in the highest tradition of the department, and we are just proud as punch of this little lady—"

Vince pressed the off button on the remote control and the screen went black. "I'm glad he explained she's a black woman. I mean, nobody could really tell by looking at her. Know what I mean?"

Connie frowned. "Why didn't you leave it on and hear what *she* had to say?"

"You kidding?" Vince moved closer to her on the king-sized bed and nuzzled her ear with his nose. "They're not going to let her say a word. Leila's still got some integrity left. She's liable to tell it like it was."

"You saying she wasn't really there?"

"She was there, all right. Out in the street someplace where she was supposed to be." He pulled her down next to him on the mattress and kissed her. "What the hell difference does it make anyway?"

Connie pulled away from him and sat, dangling her feet over the side of the bed. "Don't you ever get enough?" she asked irritably.

"Lighten up. That was the P.C. talking there, not me. Besides, I'm a growing boy with needs and wants." he stretched luxuriously on the satin sheets.

"Pervert . . ." She stood and wrapped herself in a thigh-length cotton robe. "You're all a bunch of perverts."

"Hey, I'm the one who's supposed to be ticked off here, after you let the cat out of the bag at the P.C.'s press conference," Vince protested. "That question you asked him about a mob connection almost blew the whole Thorpe investigation."

Connie eyed him skeptically. "Why is it I get the feeling you'd be a lot angrier than you are if that was the case?"

He grinned. "Because it really isn't—not entirely anyway. I was really burned in the beginning, but it actually worked out pretty well. As it turned out, it put pressure on the mob. They felt they had to give me something so I'd back off."

"And that was . . . ?"

Vince paused, watched her standing in the clinging robe. "Did anyone ever tell you you got a great body for an old broad?"

Connie scowled and headed for the kitchen. "I'm making some eggs whether you want them or not."

"I want them." Vince slipped into his undershorts and joined her. "Scrambled, with some cheese and hot sauce, okay?"

She began rummaging through her refrigerator for the ingredients. "Are you feeling better now?"

Vince checked his vital signs. "Uh-huh. Just a little tired I guess . . ." His voice seemed a hollow echo in his ears, still ringing from the explosions of gunfire earlier that morning. "It's been a rough day. A rough couple of days."

"I don't suppose it helps when someone else gets the credit," Connie said.

Vince shrugged. "Hey, that's life. If I'd let it get to me, I would've quit the department a long time ago. Once you get past grunts like me it's all bells and whistles. Not much different from what you do."

Connie stirred the eggs absently. "At least we don't make any bones about it. We *say* we're entertainment. The police department isn't supposed to be entertainment."

"Sure it is!" Vince grinned. "What would you news people do if we didn't supply you with entertainment you could put on the air? Just look at the eleven o'clock news—murders, robberies, arson. If that isn't entertainment for the folks sitting at home, I'd like to know what is."

"Then, it's the criminals who are the entertainment," she corrected him. "The police are supposed to be believable, and they're not when they pull stunts like that piece of business tonight. That senile old fool you call a police commissioner condescending to blacks and women isn't going to improve the department's image. It just makes them look clumsier and more insensitive than they really are."

"Hey, what can I tell you?" He raised his hands helplessly. "It's a Barnum and Bailey world out there. Nothing's real anymore. It's all mirrors and tap dancing these days. I had a woman in the house yesterday who talked to her jewelry. She had a necklace that told her all about the Lisa Thorpe murder. How's that for home entertainment?"

"No kidding?" Connie dished the eggs onto plates and brought them to the kitchen table. "And just who did this necklace tell her was the murderer?"

"I guess it never really said. Mostly it was a lot of stuff about Lisa brushing her hair and pulling it out by the roots. Just a lotta mumbo-jumbo." He dug his fork into the eggs.

"I wouldn't be so quick to dismiss that sort of thing if I were you. We both know about psychics who've made real contributions in criminal investigations," Connie reminded him. "Why not give her a try? I don't see you making a lot of headway on your own."

"Not this one," Vince replied. "All she was interested in was getting into Tommy's Jockey shorts. Besides, she had the facts all wrong. She had Lisa Thorpe brushing her hair, and the fact is, she used a comb."

"How would you know a thing like that?"

"We found it at the scene—one of those pointy-handled jobs."

Connie thought about it. "Lisa Thorpe had long hair didn't she?"

"Yeah. Practically to her waist."

"Then she wouldn't have used a comb," she said emphatically. "No woman with hair like that who cared as much about her appearance as Lisa Thorpe did would ever use a comb. Hair like that has to be brushed over and over, hundreds of strokes a day."

"That's really weird . . ." Vince shook his head. "The necklace lady had her brushing it over and over, just like that."

"And you didn't find a hairbrush in the room?"

He reconstructed the murder scene in his mind. "There was a brush, but it was in her purse."

"So that was hers!" Connie said triumphantly. "See? The comb must have belonged to whoever was in the room with her."

"Could be." Vince finished his eggs and lit a cigarette.

"And whoever was in that room with her had to be a woman," she continued.

Vince smiled. "You're a regular Sherlock Holmes, you know that? I think I oughta move in here permanently so I can have you solve all my cases for me."

"You're just not going to give me any credit, are you?" Connie cleared the dishes from the table angrily. "You're just as much of a Neanderthal as that boob of a Police Commissioner of yours. You're such a chauvinist you won't even admit the killer might have been a woman."

"Hey, that's not fair." Vince protested. "I really do value your opinion."

"Sure you do, Detective Crowley. You're just proud as punch of me, aren't you?"

He shook his head hopelessly. "Okay, how do I get myself out of this?"

Connie thought about it. "Were you serious about moving in here permanently?"

"Well, you know. I guess I was just being a smart-ass." Vince hedged.

"Serious or just blowing smoke, detective?" Connie sat across from Vince and stared directly into his eyes. "Are we going to set up housekeeping and stop all this shilly-shallying once and for all?"

"Shilly-shallying? Is that what we've been doing?" he asked weakly.

"Serious or blowing smoke, Crowley?" Connie demanded.

"Jeez, serious I guess."

"When?"

Vince felt his stomach tighten. "How's about as soon as I wrap up this Thorpe homicide?"

Connie grinned. "Then start looking for a woman. I don't want to wait any longer than I have to."

35

"DON'T ANYBODY SAY A WORD!" LEILA TURNER glared at the others as she entered the squad room. "The first person who opens his mouth gets a fat lip!" She sat down and sorted through her paperwork angrily.

"Jeez, if that's the way heroes act, I'm glad I don't know too many," Snuffy Quade muttered.

"That's it!" She slammed her fist on the desk. "I've had it with this whole damn department, from the bunch of you right up to that slobbering idiot of a P.C.! I never asked for special treatment. I didn't ask to be dumped in this drainage ditch with a bunch of over-the-hill losers like you all." She stood and faced them. "Just look at yourselves. You call yourself policemen? You good old boys couldn't find a nigger in Harlem if your lives depended on it. You sit there, smug and self-satisfied, putting in the time until you can take your pensions and run—hoping nothing much changes until you're out of here. Well, to hell with the bunch of you. They offered me a new assignment downtown, how about that? I guess they want their showcase out in the open where people can see her instead of buried up here in this Keystone Cops comedy you call a police precinct."

No one said a word as she sat. Nobody moved a muscle.

"I told them to stick it," Leila said softly.

The room erupted in applause.

"Jeez, I'm glad that's over . . ." Walt Cuzak breathed a sigh of relief.

"Yeah. Now we can get back to putting in the time until we can split on those fat pensions," Vince agreed.

"Lap of fucking luxury, man." Walt shook his head. "Me, I'm getting myself one of those big mother yachts and parking it out in the harbor at Monte Carlo like Aristotle fucking Onassis, know what I mean? Row ashore

in my dinghy every night and squander them big bucks
I'll be getting on roulette and baccarat."

Leila went back to her paperwork, trying to stifle a
smile.

"A Palm Beach villa for me," Snuffy chimed in.

It would go on for a while, she knew. When they were
their own audience, the men of the Thirty-seventh did
not have a delicate sense of comic timing.

Tommy walked into the room and pulled his chair next
to Vince's desk. "Here's the lab reports on everything in
the room at the Shangri-la. As far as that comb was
concerned, there's not a helluva lot to go on outside of
Lisa Thorpe's blood on the handle. A couple of partial
prints, too smeared to read . . . that's about all."

"How about hair samples?"

Tommy checked the report. "There were various unidentifiable quantities of hair found throughout the room,
but that doesn't mean anything. That place probably
hadn't been vacuumed in a month."

"No hair in the teeth of the comb itself?"

"Uh-uh. What're you getting at, anyway?" Tommy
asked.

"I'm not really sure. I got this feeling that Lisa Thorpe's
hair could hold the answer to this killing for us."

"Her hair?"

"Yeah. It's been eating at me ever since that Zircon
bimbo was in here."

"Zircon? She's a fruitcake, Vince."

"Maybe so, but she could just be right on the money for
this one, whether she knows what she's talking about or
not." Vince thumbed through his Rolodex and found the
number for Mr. Julian. "It might just be that we've been
on the wrong track all along, partner."

"How's that?"

"Let you know once I've got my facts straight . . ." He
dialed the number.

"Vincent, how perfectly delightful to hear from you,"
Mr. Julian gushed into the telephone. "Don't tell me. I'll
bet you called to ask me to the tea dance at the Pink
Flamingo this afternoon."

Vince smiled. "Not this time, Julian. I'm afraid this is
a business call."

"A business call, oh God," Julian moaned. "That butch

bastard of a P.O. called you and told you I moved into my friend's apartment without notifying him, didn't he?"

"Nothing like that, Julian."

"Well, what, then? It can't be anything I've done. I haven't sold any dope in eons. Not even one little joint."

"You're in the clear, Julian, honest," Vince reassured him. "This time I need your expert opinion on something."

"You've finally decided to do something about that dreadful hairdo of yours. God, it's about time. I can take ten years off, darling."

"Wrong again, Julian. What I want is information about combs, specifically the kind with those long, pointy handles."

"Rattail combs," Julian volunteered. "What about them?"

"Would a woman with long, straight hair use a comb like that?"

"Not unless she wanted to look like a complete frump," Julian huffed. "Those are strictly for short, short hair. The rattail is used to tease it up. I'm surprised you didn't know that, Vincent."

"That's what I got friends like you for, Julian. Now, I got one more question for you." Vince shot a quick, expectant glance at Tommy. "Would a man ever use a comb like that?"

Julian chuckled. "That depends on what you mean by 'man,' darling. If you're talking about those hairy-chested macho types you grow up there at the Thirty-seventh, I doubt it very much."

Vince rolled his eyes. "Can we get real here for a minute, Julian?"

"Actually, it wouldn't make any sense for a man to use a comb like that, no."

"Thanks a million, Julian. You've been a big help."

"Anytime, Vincent. And let me know when you're ready to do something about that thatch you call hair. Come in anytime. I'll give you a wash and set on the house."

"I just may take you up on that one of these days. Thanks again." Vince hung up.

"So?" Tommy asked.

"So I dunno. It's starting to look like we might've been on the wrong track all along, partner. If that comb is a woman's comb, it follows that whoever was with Lisa

Thorpe that night was probably a woman. That make sense to you?"

Tommy shook his head disbelievingly. "A woman?"

"Why not? Lisa Thorpe liked women. Our friend Jersey Bell told us that."

"Then again, that comb coulda belonged to somebody who was in that room before Lisa Thorpe ever got there," Tommy speculated. "The Shangri-la's a real scummy place, Vince. There's probably all kinds of shit lying around that they never clean up."

"True," Vince conceded.

"Plus, it woulda had to be some strong woman to hold her down the way the killer did."

"Also true, but we might be talking about a dike here, and some of them are as strong as men."

"Stronger," Snuffy volunteered. "I spent three days in the hospital when I was a rookie because I was dumb enough to try to break up a fight between two dike motorcyclists who ran into each other on Kissena Boulevard. I was lucky to end up with my nuts intact."

"The point is, we gotta run with this until we come to a dead end," Vince said to Tommy. "And the best place I can think to start is back with our friend Zircon. You still have her card?"

He was interrupted by the phone ringing. "Detective Crowley."

Guzman was jarring and direct: "Ricky split."

"What the hell?"

"He left, that's all," Guzman answered simply.

"You mean he can just walk outta there any time he wants? What kind of a place are they running anyway?"

"Hey, nobody's at fault here. Liberation House isn't a prison. It's an alcohol and drug rehabilitation program," Guzman reminded him.

"But I thought he was doing so well."

"Me too," Guzman concurred.

"So what coulda happened?"

"I don't know. It's hard to tell what goes on in some of these kids' heads. One minute you think you got them and the next minute they're gone. Maybe Ricardo had it for a while and lost it. Maybe he was conning everyone from the beginning. How can you figure it? The call of the street is pretty strong, Detective Crowley. I warned you not to expect too much."

Vince felt his gut churning. "Any idea where he might've gone?"

"Not a clue. This is his city. He knows every alleyway, every abandoned building." Guzman breathed heavily into the phone. "Do yourself a favor, Detective Crowley; let it go while you still have some objectivity left."

"Well, maybe I'm not ready to quit on him yet," Vince said.

"I can't say much for your grasp of reality, but I admire your spirit. Good luck, Detective." Guzman hung up.

Vince thumbed absently through the rest of his messages, discarded them all, and drove across town to Tom Quinlan's office. "I figured I oughta be the one to tell you that Ricky Miracle bolted from the drug program." He told the Bronx D.A.

"That's great, just fucking great," Quinlan groaned. "I don't suppose you know where the little bastard went to."

"Not yet, but we're working on it."

"Well, don't work on it too hard," Quinlan said. "Maybe he'll shoot an overdose and die in some doorway for us—save us the embarrassment of having to kick him loose."

"You're all heart, Tom. You know that?"

"Heart don't get you shit," Quinlan replied dryly. "Anything else?"

"While I got you on the phone, what's happening with our friend Minh?"

Quinlan laughed. "Now, there's a guy you don't want for a friend. He's turning over on everybody but his old lady to save his ass, and he'll probably give her up if he thinks it'll help keep him out of stir."

"How about the other two?"

"Luc and Dai? They're still clammed up on their lawyers' advice, but Minh is giving us all we'll ever need. He's a regular gold mine of information."

"He fill you in on Karp?" Vince asked.

"Did he ever. Naturally he says he wasn't involved, but it went down pretty much the way you figured it. Karp was putting their money out on the street for a commission, which he apparently thought was too small since he started skimming off the top. They found out about it, punched his ticket, and left a warning to anyone else who might get ideas about messing with their property."

"So you're charging them with murder one?"

"Looks that way. Along with a whole shitload of drug specifications."

"And Minh?"

"He walks. Once the trial's over he disappears inside the witness-protection program."

"Scum like that . . ." Vince shook his head.

"Hey, sometimes the scum rises to the top, know what I mean?"

"While a kid like Ricky Miracle sinks to the bottom."

Vince returned to the squad room and was greeted with a flurry of excited activity. "What's up?" he asked.

"Oh man." Tommy rolled his eyes. "The shit really hit the fan after you left. Gleason flipped out and tried to move on Leila."

"He *what*?"

"Tried to make the moves on her." Tommy pointed to Turner's desk, where she was speaking animatedly between spasms of hysterical crying. "He called her in his office and musta grabbed for her. Next thing we all knew, she was screaming at him inside, and he ran out of the squad room with blood all over his face."

"I'll be dipped . . ." Vince walked to Leila Turner's desk. "You okay?" he asked.

"That *pig*!" She spat on the floor. "He put his filthy hands on me . . . tried to open my blouse!"

"She damn near killed the son of a bitch." Street Crime grinned up at Vince. "She cold-conked him with that bowling trophy he keeps on his desk."

Vince tried not to smile. "Maybe you better go home, Leila. Let me get somebody to drive you—"

". . . Tried to open his fly, but I got him solid with my knee."

"So much for the rest of his sex life." Street Crime winced.

Leila smiled for the first time. "Now, that's what I call real affirmative action, know what I mean?"

36

SUDDENLY THEY WERE RUDDERLESS. IT TOOK LESS THAN A day for their initial reaction of hilarity and exultation over John Gleason's embarrassment to turn solemn. Passing his empty office, all of them began to understand in some small way that his humiliation was their humiliation, that his disgrace was a defeat for them all. Suddenly the issues of his personal style and competence seemed less important than the shame his failure brought upon the house. For all his pettiness and vanity, John Gleason had been a member of the family and the family owed him mourning. A cop was down.

Vince and Tommy abandoned the oppressive atmosphere of the squad room and drove north on the Hutchinson River Parkway. Beyond the soot and slush of the Bronx, the rolling hills of Westchester County were still blanketed with layers of undisturbed snow. "Ever think you wanted to live out here in the country?" Tommy asked as they crossed the Connecticut border.

"Sometimes," Vince conceded, his thoughts still back at the precinct. "And you?"

"I dunno. I don't think so," Tommy said. "The place is fulla Yuppies. They're real colorless, know what I mean? They got no *kishkes* like the people in The Bronx."

Vince smiled. "You mean like Zircon."

"Forget Zircon!" Tommy made a sour face. "The less I hear about that broad, the better my life is gonna be from now on." He stared morosely out the window. "I'm sorry you ever sent me out there to interview her again. She kept jumping up from the bed every thirty seconds or so to talk to her crystals and confirm the visions she was getting."

I see the child at prayer . . . Vince rolled Zircon's latest images around in his mind. *She is being slowly consumed by a fiery cross.*

"So if it's all right with you, I'd appreciate it if we could get onto something else, okay?" Tommy said.

"Hey, I'm willing to let it drop if you are," Vince said, needling him. "All I wanted you to do was take her statement. While you were out there dipping your wick, I was back at the house doing serious police work."

"Like what?"

"Like finding out that Ivor Thorpe was close to going bankrupt a year or so ago. That he had to sell off a chunk of his publishing empire to a guy named Roscoe Sturtz to raise enough cash to stay in business. That name ring any bells with you?"

"Not off the top of my head," Tommy admitted.

"Well, he's a big-shot Wall Street lawyer who just happens to be a front for the Carlo Madalena crime family. That would explain those phone calls Thorpe made from his office to the Downtown Athletic Club."

"How'd you find that out?" Tommy asked.

"Put in a call to Dennis Sloan at his brokerage house."

"Your ex-wife's old man?" Tommy eyed him in amazement. "I thought you hated the sonofabitch."

Vince shrugged. "You don't have to love somebody to get information from them, partner." He pulled off the parkway at the Greenwich exit and headed toward the convent of the Little Sisters of Charity.

"So whatta you think? You agree with me now that Thorpe is somehow involved in his daughter's death?" Tommy asked.

"Not necessarily, but it helps explain why he was so set on getting Ricky Miracle convicted," Vince said. "It wouldn't have looked real good for him if it got out that he was doing business with the mob."

"What you're saying is he was more interested in saving his reputation than catching his daughter's real killer."

"It's sure starting to look that way." Vince pulled into the driveway of the convent, parked the car, and led Tommy to the offices of the mother superior.

"I hope we're not coming at a bad time," he said, apologizing to Sister Michael as she ushered them inside. "We've uncovered a couple of loose ends that we want to tie up."

She asked them to sit and went behind her desk. "As I told you before, Detective Crowley, I want to offer all the help I can, but there's not much more I can add to what I told you before."

Vince shifted uneasily in his seat. "Well, Sister, it seems some new information about Lisa Thorpe has surfaced since the last time we talked, and I was hoping you might be able to shed some light on it."

"If I can." She smiled thinly.

"It seems a number of Lisa's romantic involvements were with women . . ." Vince gulped hard. "I was wondering whether you noticed any of those . . . tendencies when she was here."

Sister Michael stiffened. "I'm quite sure I have no idea what you're talking about."

"Begging your pardon, Sister, but I think you have a very good idea what I'm talking about," Vince said. "I think you knew all about that part of her, or if you didn't know, you had good reason to suspect."

"Are you saying I've lied to you?" Her voice had grown suddenly hard.

"Nothing like that, Sister," Vince assured her. "I just think you might be protecting Lisa—protecting her memory maybe—for the good of your order. I can understand that, but I also have a homicide to solve and I have to get at the truth, no matter whom it hurts."

She bowed her head, suddenly shrunken behind her desk. "I don't see how that can help you find Lisa's killer."

"I'm afraid I can't get into the specifics with you, Sister. All I can say is I need that information from you, and I'm willing to subpoena those records you told me about to get it. I hope it won't come to that."

She paused, measuring her words. "Please understand, Detective Crowley. My first loyalty and concern must be to this community. That is my job. That is my sworn responsibility. We are a community of women, hopefully women of virtue and character, but women nonetheless. We have our differences and our shortcomings like women everywhere, but most of all we share a common love for God and for one another. In all candor I have to tell you that there are infrequent occasions where the boundaries of that love become blurred, Detective. That shouldn't surprise a worldly man like yourself."

"And Lisa Thorpe?"

"Lost sight of those boundaries." There was a catch in her voice.

"And that was the reason she left?"

"Was asked to leave," Sister Michael corrected him. "For the good of the order."

"I see." Vince nodded and shot a nervous glance at Tommy. "Now, I have to ask this question, Sister, and I hope you won't take offense. Lisa couldn't do this alone. She needed a partner . . . *more* than one maybe?"

Sister Michael inhaled deeply and gripped the armrests of her chair until her knuckles whitened. "In good conscience, I've said all I can. To go beyond what I've told you already would be a dereliction of my duty as head of this community. I am sworn to uphold the dignity of this order and of its individual members, and so I must refuse you that information. You are, of course, free to subpoena our records as you say. That must be your decision." She stood, ending the discussion.

"I *will* find out, Sister," Vince said, following Tommy through her office door.

"I know you will." Her voice seemed faraway. "It's in God's hands now."

"Jeez!" Tommy moaned as Vince pulled the car out of the driveway and steered toward the parkway. "This really stinks, you know that? I went to Catholic school, for chrissakes."

"Me too," Vince said. "But we gotta go where we gotta go. Did you notice that wooden cross that she had hanging around her neck?"

"Yeah, what about it?"

"I'm not sure . . ."

"All nuns wear crosses."

"There's something different about this one—the leather thong, I dunno." He pulled onto the Merritt Parkway and headed back to The Bronx.

"You're not gonna believe this." Pete Yorio met them on the stairs outside the squad room. "They sent up a replacement for Gleason, and he's right out of central casting."

"Like what?" Tommy asked. "A real hard-nose or something?"

"I'll let you find out for yourselves. He asked to see you both when you came in." Yorio smiled broadly and bolted down the steps.

"Now what?" Vince groaned and knocked tentatively on the CO's door.

"You must be detectives Crowley and Ippollito." They were met at the door by a vision out of a Charles Dickens novel: a short, balding man in his mid-sixties wearing a three-piece English tweed suit, a black bowler hat, and a puckish grin. "I was just on my way downstairs to get some pastries to go with our coffee. Do you have any particular preference?"

"Sir? I understood that you wanted to see us," Vince stammered.

"Yes, of course. Yes, of course." He retreated into the office and removed the black bowler. "My name is Timothy McLarnen—Captain McLarnen—and I've been assigned as a temporary replacement for your commander, John Gleason." He shook his head sadly. "Terrible about the poor man, simply terrible. He will be in my prayers at daily mass as I'm sure he is in yours." He walked to the desk and rummaged through a pile of manila file folders. "I've been going over your caseloads during the short time I've been here, and I must say I'm impressed with your thoroughness and dedication. I've been a police officer for thirty-one years now. I started out on the streets, learned police work from the bottom up, as it were, and I have to say I consider myself fortunate indeed to have been sent up here with a group of such thorough professionals."

Vince shot a nervous sidelong glance at Tommy. "Well, sir, we give it our best." He felt himself beginning to sweat profusely.

"And it's more than good enough." McLarnen beamed. "Naturally, I have no intention of instituting any new rules or procedures during my stay here. I'm confident that you'll perform at the same top-notch level for me as you did for my unfortunate predecessor, God be with him. And now, if there's no more business, I'll be off for those pastries. Prune okay with you?"

They both nodded dumbly as they stood in the open doorway and watched him start down the stairs.

"You hear what I just heard?" Tommy whispered.

"I think so." Vince turned to Walt Cuzak. "What's with Mr. Micawber here, Walt? This some kind of scam from downtown or something?"

Cuzak shrugged. "Gotta be something scuzzy. They just don't make cops like him anymore."

"And one more thing," McLarnen yelled back into the squad room from the foot of the stairs. "I took the liberty of sending those two from the Major Case squad back downtown where they came from. I don't think it's in the best interest of the police department for professional detectives to be watched over like a bunch of children."

There was a God after all.

37

5:47 A.M., THE TURNAROUND TOUR. STREET CRIME HAD the duty and Vince was making a halfhearted attempt to catch up on his DD-5s. Tommy was back to writing the great American novel and Walt Cuzak was at the water-cooler, gargling with an unknown substance that smelled like crankcase oil. Everything was almost back to normal after their initial jolt of disbelief over Captain Timothy McLarnen. Cops are not notoriously resilient and change is often seen as their enemy, but even the most cynical of them had to admit that the new C.O. was a breath of fresh air. They were pinching themselves, hardly believing their good luck.

It had been a slow night at the three-seven; a night to hit the paperwork, balance the checkbook, shoot the shit . . . Vince found himself drowsing off, lulled into a sense of peace and well-being by the familiar sights and sounds of the station house. He could feel himself slipping, his mind and body caught in the warm, sensuous embrace of memory . . . recurrent pinpricks of time soothing him; jarring him back to consciousness; soothing him again . . .

The harsh ring of the telephone snapped him out of it. "Got a report here from a radio unit in Sector Dog." Street Crime relayed the information as he took it down in his notebook. "A fire out at Baychester Avenue and Boston Road. One DOA so far."

Baychester Avenue and Boston Road. That was the Shangri-la Motel. Vince went to Street Crime's desk and double-checked the report. "What was it, the motel or the diner?" he asked.

Street Crime shrugged.

"Okay, partner." Vince jostled Tommy as he passed

his desk. "Put the great American novel on hold and let's see what's going on out there." He grabbed his coat and headed downstairs.

They drove in silence, listening to the rhythmic sweep of windshield wiper blades, tires sloshing through the remnants of sooty snow, the sibilant wheeze of the defroster, the discordant crackle of the short-wave radio puncturing their reveries. For Vince, this was the best time to be a cop, the time between eruptions of good and bad when the job took care of itself and all that seemed to matter was being there, answering a call, he and Tommy on parade . . . posturing, preening, moving through the avenues and alleyways of The Bronx like knights on horseback. Even in these empty, sleeping streets both of them felt it, exalted in it . . . understood that beyond the anger and frustration there was pride; beyond the grinding boredom and low pay there was energizing passion. It was about dreams and dreams fulfilled. It was about being a kid again.

"Guess again, partner." Tommy maneuvered the car through a crowd of emergency fire and ESU vehicles. "Looks like it isn't the motel or the diner. From here it looks like that empty shack on Shapiro's Christmas-tree lot."

Vince felt sick. He followed Tommy, step after plodding step, toward the pile of smoking debris that had once been the shack, knowing what he would find when he got there.

"What's up?" Tommy asked M.E. Shem Weisen, who was leaning against the side of a pumper, smoking a cigarette.

"Coupla neighborhood kids torched the wooden shack that used to be there." He motioned to three youths in their early teens, standing handcuffed at the periphery of the lot. "I dunno whether they knew it or not, but there was a vagrant sleeping inside when they did it."

"Any idea who it was?" Vince tried to mask the tremor in his voice.

Weisen shook his head. "I just pronounce 'em. I leave the ID up to somebody else."

"Mind if I have a look?" Vince asked.

"Be my guest." Weisen pointed to the black coroner's

van standing at the curb. "You won't be able to tell much from what's left, though."

Vince accompanied Weisen to the van and stepped inside. The M.E. unzipped a black plastic body bag, shuddered involuntarily, and stepped aside. "The poor sonofabitch must've really been juiced. It looks like he never even tried to get out when the fire started. You gotta figure he was dead from asphyxiation before the flames ever got to him."

"Christ, I hope so." Vince stood transfixed before the mound of charred flesh that had been Ricky Miracle. "I hope there was no pain."

"You knew him?" Weisen asked.

"Yeah. He was a kid—just a kid I knew. I thought he might have a chance to get off the streets."

Weisen zipped up the body bag. "Nobody close to you, was he?"

"No. Nobody close." Vince felt tears welling in his eyes. "This job fucking stinks, you know that?"

"Times like this, it sure does."

Tommy was waiting in the squad car when Vince returned. "Sorry about that, partner. I know you took an interest in the kid."

Vince shrugged. "What the hell. It doesn't pay to get too close to somebody like that. I shoulda known better."

"For what it's worth, he's probably better off," Tommy said. "Remember you told me that when that woman jumped with her baby."

"Sure." Vince shook his head absently.

"I did some reading after that and found something in a Hindu book, the *Bhagavad-Gita*, that kind of puts it all into perspective for me:

> The sun is come to parch the fields.
> The hot wind blows them to powder,
> carries them to the heavens where they
> blot the sun and fall again as rain.

"I think it means that good and bad are all cut from the same cloth. We get a little bit of each, but it all evens out in the long run."

"Makes sense." Vince nodded.

"Want me to run off a copy for you?"

"Uh-uh. I think I can remember that. 'Win some, lose some,' right?"

"Yeah, maybe so," Tommy said. "Where to now, partner, back to the house?"

"Not yet. How about we head out to Bronxville? I want another look at Lisa Thorpe's apartment."

Tommy checked his wristwatch. "Sure. It's after seven. Somebody should be stirring out there by now."

The drive took less than fifteen minutes on the almost deserted parkway. Tommy circled the apartment parking lot several times before finally stopping in a tow-away zone, affixed a POLICE ON DUTY card to the windshield, and followed Vince into the condominium complex.

"You know what time it is?" the superintendent asked, answering Vince's call on the lobby telephone.

"0721 hours."

"So come back later," the super growled.

Vince took a deep breath. "Listen, pal. I've had a rough day so far and I'm not in any mood for your bullshit. You get your ass up here to this lobby in the next five minutes, or I'll personally make sure that apartment stays sealed until the twenty-first century, kapish?" He slammed down the receiver.

The super appeared in an instant, rubbing his eyes groggily as he emerged from the lobby stairwell. "You ain't gonna make any noise up there, are you?" he asked, leading them into the elevator. "Most of my people are still asleep."

Vince shrugged. "This is a homicide investigation, pal. We gotta do what we gotta do."

"Yeah, I just might have to flush the toilet," Tommy said. "Sometimes we have to do that when we're on homicide investigations."

"You busting my chops?" The super eyed him warily. "Whatta you got to flush the toilet for?"

"You want me pissing all over the rug up there?" Tommy tried hard not to smile.

"Wise guys," the super muttered as he opened the door to Lisa Thorpe's apartment with a passkey. "World's fulla wise guys."

Inside, they surveyed the residue of Lisa Thorpe's last

day alive, the undisturbed clutter left by someone not yet old enough to be a disciplined housekeeper. Some of the original debris was gone. The leftover sandwich, cigarette butts, and ceramic mug half filled with coffee had all been taken by CSU personnel for forensic examination. The bed was still unmade, the nightgown still lying carelessly across the pillows. Dresser drawers stood open and empty, their contents carted away to be analyzed over and over again for possible leads. The only difference was the air; leaden now, moldering. The soft, lingering smells of Lisa's body lost forever in pinpoint shafts of circling dust.

"You want I should stay?" the superintendent asked.

"You can go back to bed," Vince told him. "We'll only be a couple of minutes here."

"Then I can clean the place up and show it, right?"

"Soon as we're gone." Vince escorted him to the door and closed it behind him.

"Now what?" Tommy asked.

"Piss call—in order of seniority." Vince said. "Call the house while I'm in there and tell them where we are." He went to the bathroom and shut the door.

Inside, he stood at the john and stared idly at the rear wall. Suddenly his gaze was riveted to the framed photograph of Lisa and the nuns. "Tommy," he yelled through the closed door, "wasn't that a metal cross we found on the dashboard of Lisa Thorpe's car?"

"Yeah, with a long chain," Tommy yelled back.

Vince examined the photograph carefully: Lisa Thorpe stood in the plain blue cotton smock of a novice, a simple hand-hewn wooden cross dangling from her neck. Behind her, older sisters of the order smiled sweetly for the camera. All of them wore traditional black habits, and all wore ornate silver crosses. He searched the faces in the picture, overlaying their physical characteristics on the montage of faces imprinted in his trained investigator's mind. Instinctively his eye tracked their cheekbones, eyebrows, noses . . . Suddenly he froze.

Her face seemed younger, unlined and serene like the faces of nuns everywhere. Her eyebrows were heavier, darker, but unmistakably similar. Vince tried to envision her head not shrouded by a black veil, and calculated the shape of her face with its cheeks unbillowed by the tight-fitting wimple. It was the same face now. The overlapping images blended, the dancing eyes her final, unwitting betrayal. It was one of those rare times in the life of a policeman when everything comes together in one flaring moment of awareness . . . when all the threads are suddenly woven into a coherent pattern with the addition of a single, meaningless stitch.

Vince had his killer.

38

V INCE STOOD AT THE FRONT DESK OF THE EMERGENCY room in Mercy Hospital while the duty nurse calmly administered to a large, sweating black man who had lost the business part of his left hand to a factory drill press. The man sat silently as she unwrapped blood-soaked layers of homemade bandages from his hand. He winced only occasionally, masking his tears and fear from his fellow workers, who were standing nearby.

"There are several fingers missing here," she said, almost routinely. "Did anyone think to bring them?"

Embarrassed shrugs. "They were mashed up pretty bad," one of the men answered.

With clean gauze she pressed the pumping apertures where the fingers had been and halted the flow of blood. "See what I'm doing here?" she said, addressing one of his wide-eyed companions as one might instruct a confused child. "Hold him where I'm holding him and apply pressure until the doctor gets here." She stepped back behind the desk, leaving them standing bewildered in the emergency-room aisle.

"Gets pretty rough in here, doesn't it?" Vince caught her attention as she wiped blood from her hands with a paper towel. "Looks like you could use some more help."

She remained expressionless. "Can I help you?"

"I'm Detective Crowley, Thirty-seventh precinct." He displayed his badge. "I was told I could find Mary Boyle down here."

"I think she's assisting in surgery. Do you want to wait or do you want me to page her?"

Vince shrugged. "I'd like to talk to her, but I don't want to mess up an operation or anything like that."

"Well?

"If It's not risking anybody's life, I guess so."

Mary Boyle, Mary Boyle. Call the desk," she droned

into the telephone receiver, then replaced it irritably as the message resounded throughout the hospital corridors.

Vince turned his attention back to the man with the injured hand. He seemed more at ease now, attempting a few brave smiles in response to the encouragment of his coworkers. Across the aisle he could see the waiting room and its rows of plastic chairs filled with the sick and injured awaiting treatment. They were mostly black and Hispanic, dumped into the molded configuration of the chairs. Limbs and joints were strangely out of place. Bandaged heads drooped in restless sleep. Broken bodies sprawled ingloriously in wheelchairs or slumped across aluminum walkers. Most were resigned and stoic.

They were the poorest of the poor of The Bronx, he knew, the castaways of the street. Those who could afford better would be visiting family doctors or resting in hospital beds upstairs, voices raised in complaint because they knew they would be listened to. Here the sick and dying sat quietly, waiting to move up a notch in the waiting order.

A bleary-eyed Asian doctor arrived. Examining the black man's mutilated hand, he instructed an orderly to place him in a wheelchair and take him to the Primary Care Unit on another floor. After he was gone, his coworkers whispered awkwardly in the aisle, unsure if their hasty departure would seem disrespectful or uncaring. They eyed the clock on the wall, calculating their lost wages, then slowly left the hospital, knowing they would get no word of their friend's condition. Nobody would come to tell them that their sacrifice had been worthwhile.

Vince watched the clock too. The steady tick of the second hand beat a muted tattoo in the silent waiting room, inching mercilessly forward. He was finally poised at the edge of success. The countless hours of following leads that led nowhere, chasing that elusive fragment that would fit into the scheme and finally form a pattern, was coming to an end.

Every cop knows in his heart of hearts that the job is at the very core a game. Kids don't play cops and robbers for nothing. They understand in the purest sense that the chase is what makes the game fun, and winning in the end is the payoff. All the posturing and preening, the swagger and the glitz; uniforms and sidearms and two-fisted, virile camaraderie are nothing if they cannot win.

Winning gives them meaning, it gives them substance and validity. To win means to be a successful hunter . . . to feel a quickening heartbeat as the quarry becomes revealed . . . the pulsating rush of adrenalin as he dances in your gun sights . . . the thrill of final capture. *Nobody would even play the game if they couldn't catch the bad guys.*

Now if there was to be a victory, it would be a shallow one, he knew. In the end, the questions about Lisa Thorpe's death would be answered, and there would be no real satisfaction in it for him. The celebrity case that had attracted so much publicity, created so much politicking and spying and backbiting and so many photo opportunities had reached the bottom line. Everything that had happened up to now was bleeding slowly away, like the last feeble puffs of air escaping from a spent balloon.

"Can you tell me what it is you want to see the sister about?" The nurse at the desk cupped the telephone receiver in her hands.

"Tell her it's police business."

The nurse relayed the message and hung up the phone. "She's upstairs in room twenty-two. Take the elevator one flight up and turn to your left." She returned to reading the charts on her desk.

Vince followed her directions and found himself in a section of the hospital marked "DIAGNOSTICS." He passed unadorned cubicles smelling of soap and anesthetic, stainless steel and vinyl tables covered with paper, white metal medicine cabinets and oversize scales. He paused before room twenty-two and knocked.

"Come in, Detective Crowley." There was a slight trembling in her voice.

"Sister . . ." He shut the door behind him.

"I told you to call me Mary." She was seated in a straight-back chair in the corner of the room, her hands were folded in front of her on her lap. "I don't see any reason for us to stand on ceremony at a time like this."

He reddened. "Well, I guess old habits die hard."

"You're a Catholic, then?" There was a hint of a smile at the corners of her mouth.

"I was." He felt strangely foolish. "I had nuns—"

The smile erupted. "Didn't everyone?"

"I guess." Vince shuffled uncomfortably. "But that's not the reason I'm here—"

"Why not let me make this easier for you?" Mary Boyle interrupted him. "Sister Michael called me yesterday and told me to expect you. She told me it would only be a matter of time before you found out that we belonged to the same order, that I'd been at the mother house with Lisa."

Vince reached into his jacket pocket and removed the silver cross and chain. "I think this belongs to you, Mary."

She reached for it and cradled it in her lap as if it were a wounded bird. "I removed it in the car," she said softly. "It would have been a desecration to bring it into a place like that."

"Lisa's cross would have been a wooden one." Vince said, more as a reaffirmation of the facts than a boast.

Mary Boyle fondled the cross absently. "Lisa wore hers even after she left the order. I burned it in the hospital incinerator."

I see the child at prayer. She is being slowly consumed by a fiery cross . . .

"You weren't wearing a cross when I interviewed you, or anything else that told me you were a nun," Vince said. "I didn't put it all together until I saw that group picture you had taken at the novitiate."

"Those were good days," she said wistfully. "It was foolish of me to think I could bring them back. Lisa was so cold that night she drove us to the motel—so bitter. I should have known then that she was beyond redemption."

"I think I'd better inform you of your rights before you say anything more." Vince moved toward her.

"Don't come any farther." Mary Boyle unfolded her hands, revealing a hypodermic syringe poised in her fingers. "This is filled with a particularly fast-acting nerve toxin. All I need do is scratch the surface of my skin and I'll be dead in seconds."

He froze. "You don't want to do that, Sister."

"Mary," she reminded him. "I gave up the right to be called 'Sister' a long time ago."

"Suicide is a sin."

She nodded. "I see you have a highly developed sense of sin. The nuns taught you well. Did they tell you about the seven deadly sins—about anger and pride and covetousness and lust? Of course they did. Everyone who ever went to parochial school knew all about those sins." She smiled a sad smile. "We seem to be about the same age, Detective Crowley. For all we know, we went to the same schools, learned all about sin from the same nuns. I was a child of Mary then. We all were."

Vince began inching forward and she raised the syringe menacingly. "Not yet, Detective. Not until you've indulged me a bit more."

He stepped cautiously back.

"You know what a child of Mary is, don't you?" she went on. "It's that part of being a young Catholic girl that tells me I must bury my feelings. The things I want in my innermost self are vain and sinful, and I can overcome them only through prayer and vigilance. I must pray every day that Our Lord will forgive my base, uncontrollable thoughts, and that He give me the strength never to act on them." There were tears welling in the corners of her eyes.

"I loved Lisa." She choked on the words. "I loved her more than I ever thought it was possible to love. To me she was light and truth and bliss, and for the first time in my life I was delivered from the pain of the sin inside of me. I believed for the first time in my life that what I felt was far too spiritual to be a sin. I believed that when I was with Lisa I was speaking with the language of my soul."

The tears were streaming down her cheeks now, and her voice was no longer clear and controlled. "When I was very young, I was made a bride of Christ, Detective Crowley. I still believed I could overcome what I was inside by prayer alone. I was told that He would strengthen me and comfort me. Knowing Him I would know perfect love and that would be all I would ever need. But I needed more. I needed so much more—"

"Loving someone is no reason to kill them," Vince broke in.

"Do you think I killed Lisa because I loved her?" She stared at him through the film of her tears. "No, never because of that."

"Why, then?"

"Because of what she had become and what she made me become. Because I couldn't stand her cruelty any longer. I watched her turn inside out, Detective. I watched her soul rot. Some hideous inner force twisted her into an instrument of evil, caused her to grovel in slime and filth. She tore away parts of her own precious body because they had become inconvenient to her. I saw in her the worst of what I had feared in myself—the demons I had been running away from all of my life. When I looked in the mirror I saw *her* face. When I tried to pray, I felt *her* pain. I knew that deep inside she was suffering terribly—as I was." She caught herself, sat upright in the chair. She rearranged the folds of her skirt with an open palm. "I asked her to meet me that night after her shift was over—"

"You don't have to tell me this, Mary," Vince said. "Your lawyer would advise you not to. Anything you say can and will be used against you in a court of law."

". . . I needed to speak to her one more time, to try to reason with her, show her just how sick she had become. I realize now she picked that place to mock me, to hold her depraved world under my nose and laugh at my discomfort, but I refused to give in to her. I asked her to kneel and pray with me. I told her it wasn't too late for either of us. That God was infinitely kind and forgiving, and that he loved us both as we had once loved each other." The tears had started again. "She was too far gone, Detective Crowley. She sat there on the corner of the bed and ridiculed me. She told me about men she had done unspeakable things with—and women. When I pleaded with her to stop she laughed at me, a thick, gutteral laugh that came from whatever serpents inhabited her body—gurgling, growling, sucking evil incarnate. I will never forget that laugh, Detective Crowley. I hear it all the time, awake or asleep, it makes no difference. I hear it now . . ." Her voice trailed off. Her hands fell limply to her sides.

Vince rushed forward and kicked the hypodermic away as it clattered noisily on the floor. Without thinking, he put his arms around her and held her while she sobbed softly into the folds of his overcoat.

He was crying, too.

39

VINCE SAT IN THE BACK ROOM OF FLYNN'S SHANTY IN THE Castle Hill section of The Bronx trying to remain attentive to the hubbub of overlapped conversations at the table . . . the coarse, undemanding banter of men who felt at ease with one another; who had let down their guard. The occasion was Pete Yorio's retirement dinner . . . Flynn's best: Roast pork, sweet and tender, with mashed potatoes swimming in rich brown gravy; sauerkraut steeped in pork fat; shared, uncertain memories, good-natured insults, bad jokes—the reassuring blend of old friends brought together with plenty of booze to lubricate their dialogue.

The old-timers were there, Walt and Steve and Snuffy; along with a smattering of veterans from other areas of the city who'd known Pete before he came to the three-seven. All in all, there were four circular, wooden tables of ten men each; forty men who had known the cop who'd handed in his badge that day and cared enough to come and send him off.

They spoke about men who had come and gone before them, guys who knew what being a cop was really all about: pride and dedication and brotherhood. And then they drank some more and spoke about what it had become, about gay cops and female cops and cops with purple hair, and they wondered among themselves what made them stick it out. And one by one they stood and toasted Pete again and told him how they envied him and how they would be following soon. They too would hand in their shields and ID cards at the desk and walk away with no regrets, no looking back.

Captain Timothy McLarnen stood and waited patiently for their attention. "I want to thank you all for asking me to come this evening. This is a special time for you all, and I appreciate being asked to participate." The noise in the room died down. "I've just met most of you, and perhaps it is presumptuous of me to stand and make a speech, but I am, alas, an Irishman and you know what they say about Irishmen. We're at our best at wakes and weddings, since there's a little bit of laughing and a little bit of crying and a whole lot of bullshit at both."

A scattering of polite laughter.

". . . And so it is at a policeman's retirement. A time for us to toast our departing comrade, to share a glass or two with old companions; to look back and to laugh and cry a little bit; and speak among ourselves about the way things were . . . about men we knew and loved who left their mark upon us, then left us. About how sad we felt . . ."

Timothy McLarnen paused, looked out over the tables in the room. "I think there comes a time in the life of every policeman when all his reasons for joining the force are finally justified . . . a time when he senses that he is standing at the pinnacle, resting among the angels. He's past the point of fearing he will come up wanting, and the sadness of the job has yet to reach him. His friendships and surroundings fill him with delight and he knows at last that being a policeman is the proudest, grandest thing a man can be on this green earth of ours.

"And when the feeling's just sunk in, he walks into another time not far beyond and everything is different. He sees his old friends gone; his time, his essence, mocked by younger men and wonders how it happened. How is it he could look away for just a moment and it all changed? But he does the job, because the job is what he is. Because everything he does when he is not doing the job is waiting. He does it, then, not with the infatuation of youth, but with the hope that if he can no longer stand beside angels, he can at least be on their side. And maybe, he thinks, if he hangs on long enough, a flicker of that proud, grand moment will come again to remind him why he took the oath so many years ago.

"I have been blessed to know a few good men in my years on the force, and a few bastards as well. And the good men were giants and the bastards were better than most. I salute them all, as I salute you men of the thirty-seventh precinct in The Bronx." He raised his glass before them. "And if I may—and the souls of Irish poets do not smite me where I stand—I salute you all with the words of an honored Englishman, A. E. Housman.

"Goodnight my lads, for naught's eternal;
No league of ours for sure.
Tomorrow I shall miss you less,
and ache of heart and heaviness
Are things that time should cure.

Over the hill the highway marches
And what's beyond is wide:
Oh, soon enough will pine to naught
Remembrance and the faithful thought
That sits the grave beside.

The skies they are not always raining
Nor gray the twelvemonth through;
And I shall meet good days and mirth,
And range the lovely lands of earth
With friends no worse than you."